ESCAPE: EXODUS BOOK THREE

Praise for Gun Brooke's Fiction

Fierce Overture

"Gun Brooke creates memorable characters, and Noelle and Helena are no exception. Each woman is 'more than meets the eye' as each exhibits depth, fears, and longings. And the sexual tension between them is real, hot, and raw."—*Just About Write*

Coffee Sonata

"In *Coffee Sonata*, the lives of these four women become intertwined. In forming friendships and love, closets and disabilities are discussed, along with differences in age and backgrounds. Love and friendship are areas filled with complexity and nuances. Brooke takes her time to savor the complexities while her main characters savor their excellent cups of coffee. If you enjoy a good love story, a great setting, and wonderful characters, look for Coffee Sonata at your favorite gay and lesbian bookstore."—*Family & Friends Magazine*

Sheridan's Fate

"Sheridan's fire and Lark's warm embers are enough to make this book sizzle. Brooke, however, has gone beyond the wonderful emotional explorations of these characters to tell the story of those who, for various reasons, become differently-abled. Whether it is a bullet, an illness, or a problem at birth, many women and men find themselves in Sheridan's situation. Her courage and Lark's gentleness and determination send this romance into a 'must read.'"—*Just About Write*

Course of Action

"Brooke's words capture the intensity of their growing relationship. Her prose throughout the book is breathtaking and heart-stopping. Where have you been hiding, Gun Brooke? I, for one, would like to see more romances from this author."—*Independent Gay Writer*

September Canvas

"In this character-driven story, trust is earned and secrets are uncovered. Deanna and Faythe are fully fleshed out and prove to the reader each has much depth, talent, wit and problem-solving abilities. *September Canvas* is a good read with a thoroughly satisfying conclusion."—*Just About Write*

The Supreme Constellations Series

"*Protector of the Realm* has it all; sabotage, corruption, erotic love and exhilarating space fights. Gun Brooke's second novel is forceful with a winning combination of solid characters and a brilliant plot. The book exemplifies her growth as inventive storyteller and is sure to garner multiple awards in the coming year."—*Just About Write*

"Brooke is an amazing author, and has written in other genres. Never have I read a book where I started at the top of the page and don't know what will happen two paragraphs later. She keeps the excitement going, and the pages turning."—*MegaScene*

Visit us at www.boldstrokesbooks.com

By the Author

Romances:
Course of Action
Coffee Sonata
Sheridan's Fate
September Canvas
Fierce Overture
Speed Demons
The Blush Factor
Soul Unique
A Reluctant Enterprise
Piece of Cake (novella)

Supreme Constellations series:
Protector of the Realm
Rebel's Quest
Warrior's Valor
Pirate's Fortune

Exodus series:
Advance
Pathfinder
Escape

Novella Anthology:
Change Horizons

ESCAPE: EXODUS BOOK THREE

by

Gun Brooke

2017

ESCAPE: EXODUS BOOK THREE

ISBN 13: 978-1-62639-635-7

This Trade Paperback Original Is Published By
Bold Strokes Books, Inc.
P.O. Box 249
Valley Falls, NY 12185

First Edition: January 2017

CREDITS
Editor: Shelley Thrasher
Production Design: Susan Ramundo
Cover Design By Sheri (graphicartist2020@hotmail.com)
Cover Art By Gun Brooke

Acknowledgments

My love for science fiction is still strong, and I am so glad that my readers still find my sci-fi stories to be to their liking! Thank you, dear readers, for emails, notes, Facebook greetings, and general encouragement. Building worlds is difficult, but so very rewarding. For my readers to enjoy entering my worlds and the space where my characters live their lives is quite magical.

My editor, Dr. Shelley Thrasher, is the person who makes sure my books are the best they can be. We have worked together on eighteen books now, and quite a few short stories, and I can't imagine my writing experience without her. Always supportive, always frank in the kindest of ways, and great to work with, I just love you, Doc.

I want to acknowledge Len Barot—aka Radclyffe—my publisher who has created such a nice home for her authors. Also, my heartfelt thank you to Sandy, Connie, Stacia, Cindy, Lori, proofers, etc. Your efforts don't go unnoticed and are very much appreciated.

My first readers who help me through the earliest draft by spotting mistakes and other issues—and generally giving their opinion: Laura, Eden, Maggie and Sam—you are all such troopers!

On a personal note…nobody writes in a vacuum. My family, both biological and chosen, mean the world to me, and without their encouragement and appreciation, I would not be able to push through those moments when health and lack of stamina throws a wrench or two in the wheels.

Lastly, but no less importantly, as a dog lover I know that my life will keep being blessed with my canine family members. We just welcomed a Russian girl, a white mixed breed we call Esti, and together with our retriever mix Hoshi, she will be much loved and cared for.

Dedication

To Malin
My daughter—my firstborn

To Henrik
My son—my "baby"

To Elon
My soulmate, who gives me everything that truly matters

PROLOGUE

D id you find out more about where exactly they keep the Seer, Caya Lindemay?" the tall woman the participants in the meeting referred to as Number One asked.

"In luxury." A baldheaded man, Number Five, spat the words. "At the presidential level on cube one. All her meals are carried to her from a caterer on cube six."

"Luxury? A prison is still a prison," a woman, Number Eleven, stated dryly.

"In protective *custody*," the bald man said and flicked his chubby hand in the air. "The president is quite taken with her, or so the rumors have it."

"What do you mean, taken with her? A young woman with flaming red hair and freckled skin looked wide-eyed at the other twenty-one men and women around the table.

"Number Twenty," Number One said to her reproachfully. "We've known for months now about the two changers that snuck aboard *Pathfinder*. One is the woman we're talking about, Caya Lindemay, who is in protective custody. The other is her older sister, Briar, who is not incarcerated for some unfathomable reason and is working at the hospital on cube eleven."

"That's not the whole truth about Briar Lindemay," another woman, Number Eight, said. "She's also known as Red Angel. This is why we haven't approached her. Everyone aboard reveres and loves her for her empathic abilities. Untouchable."

"What about the Seer? The one in custody?" Number Twenty asked. "Can she be obtained?"

Number Two snorted. "Not likely. She has President Tylio's ear and sources claim they spend a lot of time together, which Tylio's schedule lists as 'counseling.' This is one of the most dangerous parts of this whole mess. Tylio is perilously influenced by her."

The people around the table looked suitably dismayed.

The door opened and a woman stepped inside. They all stood immediately and greeted her with reverent nods.

"Sir," Number One said politely. "We weren't expecting you."

The woman, their ultimate leader, referred to only as Grand Superior and the reason they were there in the first place, strode up to the empty chair next to Number One. "Sit. I just met with the president, and I have some disturbing news. Her cabinet of ministers and military advisors is ready to pass and enforce a law that will make it virtually impossible to move around freely aboard *Pathfinder* without being detected by their new and extensive surveillance. "

"Is she insane?" Number Eleven whispered. "Wasn't this one of the reasons for leaving Oconodos? To get away from the micromanaged society with surveillance at every intersection?"

The Grand Superior nodded solemnly. "That's actually one road we can take, among all our planned strategic attacks. We can spread the word and emphasize how Tylio is monitoring her people as if we are all criminals. How it interferes with our right to privacy, our integrity is under siege, that sort of thing. It will infuriate the Oconodian and Gemosian people, especially our young ones."

"Our network is growing and I have formed four subunits, sleeper cells if you wish, who are ready to do their best for us." Number One smiled. "Before you give the go-ahead, sir, we need to find a way to hatch a viable plan to free the Seer. Until she's in our midst, Tylio will have the upper hand." She pulled up a large floating screen in the center of the oval table. "As our group consists of experts at plotting countermeasures as well as planning attacks, I need you all to work out ways to make this happen."

"Yes, Number One," the cell members said in unison.

The Grand Superior smiled thinly. "Good. Excellent."

Number Two and Number Eleven stood and began outlining their next attack. No doubt, the young changer would envision something about this and report it to Tylio. This was all right, since the closest cells would be there waiting.

Before long, Number One would make sure Tylio's administration had to accept the new order.

CHAPTER ONE

"Madam President?" A male voice interrupted President Gassinthea Mila Tylio's thoughts where she sat at her desk in her office. Around her, the ten large screens showing all sides of the vast spaceship *Pathfinder* gave the illusion of viewports. *Pathfinder* consisted of twenty-one cubes, each holding approximately 100,000 individuals on their way to their new homeplanet, P-105.

"Yes, Commander?" Thea said and leaned back in her chair.

"We have to leave for the ceremony in half an hour, but…once again we cannot persuade Caya Lindemay to follow your orders."

Of course. Thea sighed inwardly but merely nodded to the burly man in the doorway. It was rather ironic that a man his size and with his commanding presence couldn't make a petite young girl join in the awaiting festivities. "I'll talk to her."

"Thank you, sir. And as I said, we need to leave in thirty."

"I hear you, Commander." Thea stood and adjusted her ceremonial robe. "I'll see you at the presidential jumper. Dismissed."

The commander looked quite relieved that Thea would approach Caya herself and strode down the corridor toward the gate where they would board the presidential jumper car ready to take them to the park area. The jumpers consisted of a multitude of huge cylinders crisscrossing the twenty-one cubes, transporting people where they needed to go. The presidential ones were fortified to sustain anything but a black-garnet attack, or so the specs claimed.

Thea left her office and locked the door with her security code and retinal scan. She hurried to the far end of the corridor, where her presidential suite was located next to her main cabinet members' quarters. She had stopped in front of a door and raised her hand to the chime, when she had to stop and take a deep breath. Caya Lindemay had been under house arrest in the luxurious guest quarters for more than six months. She could leave them only while escorted by the presidential guards, which didn't sit well with the young changer. Their discussions regarding this matter had grown increasingly heated.

The door hissed open, and Thea stood eye to eye with the apparition that was Caya. Slender, ethereal, and with her waist-long blond hair flowing around her shoulders as if it were weightless, she scanned Thea very carefully with transparent turquoise eyes.

"I see you're off to the naming ceremony. Have fun." Caya stood with her hands on her hips. "If you're here for a security update, I can tell you I don't see any malicious intent happening there." She turned to leave and the door began to slide shut, but Thea put her hand out, which triggered the sensors and reopened it. To her surprise, Caya had instantly turned around and pressed a hand on the sensor. If Thea didn't know any better, she'd have sworn Caya had reacted with instinctive protectiveness.

"I want you to join me. Us." Thea inspected Caya's clothes. "You don't even have to change." Caya was dressed in a white-embroidered light-blue caftan over white slacks.

"Letting me out for good behavior? That can't be right. I'm barely able to be civil to you these days. So why?" Caya tilted her head. "Let me see. I don't have my sister's knack for clairvoyance, but I can bet you want me there to smooth the waves. Try to show me off as a harmless little girl and make the Oconodians and Gemosians see that I'm not going to burst into flames or throw plasma spheres at them. Or—oh yes—or you think my being there will take the brunt of everyone's speculations about what happened between you and Hadler, your lovely ex-spouse."

Thea flinched. She couldn't stop it. The mention of her former husband who had made her private life a living hell for so many years, said with such spite by the young woman before her, was like a blow to her midsection.

"Thea." Suddenly pale, Caya lowered her hands to her side. She looked very young and also tremendously tired at the same time. "I'm sorry. That was uncalled for, no matter what." The huskiness of her voice showed how the stress and sorrow over the long incarceration was taking a toll on her.

"I suppose you assume I deserve whatever harsh words you fling at me." Thea's back was rigid now; she was trembling and could only hope her lifelong training made her reaction invisible. She had aimed for greatness from the age of ten, when her father saw her potential as a leader. This ambition had taken her on different paths, some rewarding, some heartbreaking. And some of the heartbreak had seemed to happen over time, like fate had chipped away at her soul little by little until one day she would wake up and find most of it gone.

"No." Caya sighed and ran a hand over her face. "That's a lie. I do have moments when I think you deserve horrible things for keeping me locked up in this...this golden cage. I'm going crazy in here. Yes, Briar comes by almost every day. As does Adina. Since they became officially betrothed, at least I don't have to worry so much for Briar. Meija and Korrian visit too. And some of the Vantressa family when they can sneak past their megalomaniac matriarch. How she can be Adina's mother, I don't know. So I'm not lonely that way."

"But you're still a prisoner."

"And I did nothing wrong!" Caya held out her hand, anguish now written over her face. "You—you say you keep me here because threats have been made and it's for my own safety, but, please. Please, Thea. Madam President. I can take care of myself and—"

"No. Don't ask me. I will not be responsible for any changer-hating individual taking your life." Stirrings of sheer nausea at the thought of anyone snuffing out this precious girl's existence due to stupid fear made Thea sound harsher than she intended.

"All right." Going very still, Caya closed her hands into tight fists. "Will my sister be there?"

"Yes. She and all your friends are invited to the presidential box."

Caya nodded slowly. "Fine. I'll come. At least I'll see other people for a bit. Perhaps I'll get some readings on something useful as well. Who knows?" She stepped into the corridor and the door closed behind her. "What? No guards?"

"The corridor is monitored remotely. They're only seconds away." Thea knew she had said Caya could join the naming ceremony as she was, but her hair needed tying back. "You need a hair ribbon."

"Oh, right. Wait." Caya pushed her hand into a deep pocket and pulled out a long, dark-blue silk one.

Thea took it from her and motioned for Caya to turn around. She pulled the blond masses of hair back and arranged them into a low ponytail. As she tied the ribbon securely, her fingers tingled at the feeling of the silky strands. A surprisingly spicy scent emanated from Caya's hair, and this together with her otherworldly beauty made Thea yank her hands back before she dug her fingers deep into the golden treasure.

"There. Good to go." Thea motioned for Caya to follow as she strode toward the presidential jumper gate.

The guards knew better than to react openly to Caya's presence. They merely saluted their president and treated Caya like she wasn't there. As they took their seats, joined by four of the most seasoned presidential guards, Thea had to exhale in relief. She hadn't enjoyed pulling rank or being subjected to such resentment, but having Caya come with her was yet another step in the right direction. If Caya, as well as her sister Briar, were to have any kind of normal existence when they reached their new homeplanet, the people needed to see them for what they were. Changers, yes. The sisters possessed the mutation that gave them extraordinary powers, but in their case they were harmless to others. Nothing about them was violent or malicious. Instead, they had saved lives and would continue to do so if allowed.

Briar Lindemay was revered already. She was Red Angel, a moniker ordinary people had given her when they knew her as a nurse ready to risk her life for her patients and possessing a level of empathy for them that superseded anything they'd ever known. She was untouchable. They regarded her younger sister Caya, however, as a stowaway changer, which in part was true, but it also meant they feared she hadn't showed her true self with her full arsenal of powers. The Oconodian people had grown up fearing the violent changers: the ones that spewed fire, threw plasma spheres, altered people's minds, hypnotized, and created explosions with their powerful minds. Oconodos had eventually become a society ridden with fear and demonstrations, and when the last few years before the Exodus operation to leave the planet to find a new home had commenced, Thea had been forced to issue martial law.

Remembering how she had felt when it turned out the young woman she'd come to take quite an interest in was a changer, Thea closed her eyes briefly. Caya had gone into convulsions during a presidential ball, right there on the dance floor, and foreseen Hadler Tylio's death in a terror event. Thea had wanted to remove herself from the ballroom and distance herself from the writhing young woman, but she hadn't been able to move. Instead she had knelt next to Caya and kept her safe until her sister reached them. When it turned out Briar was also a carrier of the changer gene and every bit as powerful as her sister, Thea knew she had reached the point of her presidency that would define her as a person and politician forever.

The jumper stopped, and the loud background noise of excited people slammed into them when the doors opened. Thea stood and followed two of her guards. The others moved in, two steps behind Caya. As they entered the lane leading to the presidential box at the large park area at the center of cube one, Thea felt the usual pull at how beautiful it was. The engineers and botanists had created a real park with actual vegetation and grass. At the center stood a semicircular stage that Thea would soon enter to announce the name of their new homeworld. Protective transparent shields would keep her safe from potential terrorists, but she wasn't worried about herself. Caya was the true target. Her intelligence officers had confirmed that the chatter among the population hinted that most of them feared her and her abilities.

"How many people have gathered here?" Caya spoke quietly.

"Last estimate, 110,000 including the official cube representatives from the different enclaves. Thea cast a glance forward. "Look. There's your sister with Adina and Admiral Heigel and her spouse."

"Meija." It looked like Caya might forget herself and rush forward to greet her sister and their friends, but she dug her teeth into her lower lip and remained between the guards. "It's been too long."

"We've all been insanely busy after that last attack. Not finding the culprits in a timely manner—"

"If you're going to use this moment to twist my arm, I might as well go back." Caya's light, transparent eyes fired off lightning bolts. "I can't force images to appear. How many times…"

"That wasn't my intention at all. Come on. Let's join your sister before she leaps over the railing and drags us in."

As they entered the box, the presidential march played, and the gathered Oconodians and Gemosians stood and sang the ancient lyrics.

Along the path where hills turn into mountains,
Where brooks grow into rivers
And raise the mighty seas,
I dream about the plains of Galamanor
And the colors of the skies
Above the purple beetles' trees.

As always, the song made Thea momentarily homesick. Yes, for her entire life, the threat of growing numbers of hostile changers had cast its shadow over the Oconodian homeworld, but no other planet could possibly be as devastatingly beautiful. Not to mention how brave its people were. Most of them had never even contemplated entering a spaceship. The military or freighter crews were usually the only ones who traveled in outer space.

Thea continued up onto the stage, where Interim President Bymento of the Gemosians and his wife, Dalanja, met her. He was a sparsely built man, low-key in the way he spoke and carried himself, while Dalanja was exuberant and glamorous. Thea had learned over time that the president's soft-spoken manners hid an iron will and a brilliant intellect, and his wife was not shallow at all, but sweet and loyal to a fault.

"Mr. President. Mrs. Bymento."

"Madam President." The Bymentos greeted her, he cordial and correct, she with obvious warmth. "This is a great day."

"It is." Thea motioned to the conductor of the orchestra, and the musicians began to play the Gemosian anthem. Thea hummed along in the ancient Gemosian tongue, as did the vast crowd below the stage. When she glanced at the couple next to her, she saw how Bymento's features had softened and Dalanja had tears leaking from the corners of her eyes.

"Thank you," Bymento murmured as the music ended. "I did not expect that."

"Sir. We're one people now." Thea allowed her eyes to fall upon Caya, where she sat with her sister Briar's arm around her shoulders and Meija Solimar on her other side. The social anthropologist simply patted Caya's knee and then smiled up at Thea, who could have sworn Meija winked at her.

Thea pulled her self together and, after a deep breath, stepped up to the sound system. "My fellow Oconodians. My friends, the Gemosians. This is a very special day. It's not a mere naming ceremony, even if it is important what we will call our future home from now on, but in fact, this is the official day when we merge our two people. We will no longer be known as merely Oconodians or Gemosians. As we continue on our journey toward our new homeworld, where we will be met by the advance team that is working so diligently to receive all 2,100, 000 of us, we will do so as one. If and when we face adversaries, we will meet and combat them as one nation. When we reap the fruits of what we sow, we will enjoy them as one. The Oconodians will not be superior because we were originally in the vast majority. Nor will the opposite be said of the Gemosians. From now on, there is no 'them.' There is only 'us.' We are capable of so much more when we work together side by side."

Thea looked at her colleague to the left of her. "President Bymento has shown great leadership skills, and until we can hold the first democratic voting procedure on our new homeplanet, he has agreed to act as our vice president." She held her breath now, waiting for protests to erupt among the Gemosians. When that didn't happen, she almost lost her train of thought.

"Now the moment has come to reveal the name suggestion that sixty-five percent of you voted for. P-105 will from now on be called *Gemocon*!"

The park area erupted in cheers, and people stomped and clapped so hard, Thea feared this sound might affect *Pathfinder's* course. She smiled, relieved and with a sense of accomplishment, as she had dreaded their respective people would hate the merger of Gemosis and Oconodos. As it turned out, people really did like the name. A new calmness flooded her, and she laughed out loud until her eyes met Caya's. Then Caya nodded where she sat, still with her head on Briar's shoulder. Why this gesture made Thea finally relax fully, she wasn't sure, but if Caya had hated the name, she wouldn't have been able to.

As the ceremony continued with performances by dancers, singers, and actors, Thea returned to the president's box with the Bymentos. She sat down just in front of Caya, which she didn't like at all. Thea wanted to watch her young clairvoyant changer, make sure she didn't do anything to set off alarms or alert the guards. Instead, she had to sit there, straight and in control, when her entire being was wrapped up in Caya's scent.

Afraid Briar might inadvertently read her thoughts, Thea used some meditation techniques to empty her mind of thoughts of Caya. She knew Briar, the Red Angel oracle, did not invade someone's thoughts if she could help it, but she was still perfecting her gift and might stumble into someone's personal contemplations without meaning to. Thea could not risk Briar discovering just how much time during her waking as well as sleeping hours she had Caya on her mind.

CHAPTER TWO

Caya sat among the people she loved, watching President Tylio give her speech, followed by the Gemosian interim president Bymento's. He addressed mainly the Gemosian but made sure everyone knew he was pleased to assume the office of vice president.

"His wife is actually quite lovely," Adina said. "She comes off as trendy and glamorous, but when I talked to her at the presidential dinner, she was so much more than that."

"I know," Briar replied. "She came to see me for a few sessions, and as it was her initiative, I figured I might learn from the experience. I mean, until then, I hadn't had any one-on-one meetings where I've tried to use my gift."

"I know you can't say what you talked about, but was she pleased?" Caya hugged her sister's arm against her, eager to get as much closeness while out in public as possible.

"She was. We've had more sessions and I've learned a lot." Briar looked down at Caya, who easily spotted the sorrow in her eyes. "It's so good to be out here with you and Adina and our friends. I just hate—"

"Shh." Caya placed a finger on Briar's lips. "We know I have to go back after this is over. I'm doing all right in those quarters. You know."

"I know. I don't worry for your physical wellbeing. I fear for your mind. You must miss everyone when we cannot visit."

"I do." What Caya didn't tell her sister was how frustrated she was, how angry and upset and filled with resentment for being held captive by the woman on the podium. Gassinthea Mila Tylio, who insisted they should be on a first-name basis, hadn't budged when it came to Caya's incarceration. Yes, her friends and family could visit as much as she and they wanted, and the Creators knew that the president came by at least every other day. Caya also knew she could page Thea on her private communicator at any given time if she had a vision of some impending doom. That, somehow, didn't make Caya feel any better.

Thea went up to the sound system again and waited until the applause after Bymento's speech died out. Caya regarded her with that strange emotion she had felt ever since she first met Thea. Adina, her sister-in-law, had been hospitalized after a severe red-garnet burn, and together with Briar, she had saved the entire neonatal ward at the hospital and potentially more than that. Caya had visited Adina together with her sister Briar when Thea and her entourage entered the hospital room. Something had happened then that defied everything Caya had ever hoped to experience. Thea had commented on what she called Caya's unusual eye color. Caya never knew until then that she and her sister's eyes held the rarest transparent turquoise hue. Thea had seemed mesmerized then, and Caya had caught her getting lost while looking at her on several occasions. She knew Briar had picked up on it, but apart from looking mystified, she hadn't commented.

Now, Thea locked her gaze on Caya, again, and began to speak.

"*Pathfinder* has passed its half-journey mark. According to Admiral Korrian's calculations, we have traveled past the buoy put in place by the advance team that came here two years ago. They of course traveled much faster than we do and reached Gemocon in a little more than a year. If all goes well during our second half, we'll be there in about four hundred days. The advance team is working hard mapping out the territory where we'll set down our cubes when the time comes. Admiral Caydoc, the woman who lent her name to this park area, sends me constant updates via the buoys they left like breadcrumbs for us to follow. The latest message also showed some footage—we have yet to receive live films—and we're happy to be able to show you. Can we project the photos, please?"

A large screen lowered from the tall, sky-like ceiling. As soon as it clicked into place, photos of the advance team began to appear. Caya looked wide-eyed at pictures of machines digging, people pulling wires and other equipment. Far away, she saw tall, snowy mountains and, at the foot of them, bright-green woods. The possibility of feeling solid ground beneath her feet in the near future made her tremble. Then reality caught up with her and she stood so fast, Briar fell away from her and onto Adina, who barely caught her.

"Caya?" Briar frowned and struggled to get to her feet.

"No. You stay. I'll—I need to go back to my quarters. My prison. You stay here and enjoy your freedom and the wonderful prospects all the advance team's hard labor has to offer a free person." Caya pivoted and signaled to the presidential guards that she wanted to leave. They looked confused for a moment, but eventually two of them stayed as the other two flanked Caya.

"Please. Just wait until Thea is done up there. She'll want to—"

"But I don't. I don't want to do anything. Yes, she might plan to treat us all to dinner, or some other festive event, but it won't matter. Once it's over, you, Adina, Korrian, and Meija will return to your quarters, where you can come and go at your leisure. I, on the other hand, will return to the presidential guest quarters. No fancy dinner or entertainment will change that. I can't stand it, Briar. Don't you see?" Caya's throat hurt, and the idea of being in Thea's presence as if she were on an equal footing with everyone else made her nauseous.

"I do. I actually do." Pale now, Briar pulled Caya into a firm embrace. "For a moment, before you shut me out, I did look into the bright light that is your soul, and the solitude there hurt."

"You read me?" Caya hadn't thought it was possible for Briar to penetrate her defenses. She rarely let her guard down, but of course, in Thea's presence, Caya lost her bearings.

"I had to. You scare me when you are this…this vehement. This is not the little sister I recall."

Caya wondered if Briar was being deliberately obtuse. "Back then, I wasn't incarcerated. Well, at least not to this degree."

"And you're not incarcerated now." Thea's sonorous voice made them all jump. "You're in protective custody."

Less affected by Thea's commanding presence than the others, Caya placed her hands on her hips again. "Of course. It's all for my own good. Why can't anybody here get it into their heads that if something horrible were to happen to me, I would sense it ahead of time and be able to avoid it?" To Caya's dismay, her lower lip began to tremble, and she pinched her midsection hard on either side to keep from making a fool of herself by showing vulnerability in public.

"She does have a point, Caya," Meija Solimar said, her gentle voice pensive. "Perhaps your gift doesn't work so well when it comes to your own safety? So far, your predictions have always been about other people. Even the despicable Had—oh. I am very sorry, Madam President."

Caya knew Meija had almost spoken the president's ex-husband's name out loud in her presence. Glancing carefully at Thea, she saw Meija didn't have anything to fear for her faux pas.

Thea smiled wryly. "Even the despicable Hadler. Yes, Caya. Meija does have a point as well. Perhaps your gift extends to your own safety as well, but for now, my ruling stands. That said, I think Briar and Adina would be heartbroken if you didn't join us for dinner. I have arranged for something out of the ordinary. We're going to have our meal at one of the places aboard *Pathfinder* very few people are ever allowed to go. I'd hate for you to miss it." Holding out her hand, Thea focused her dark-blue eyes on Caya, imploring her. Her blond hair, streaked by white highlights, framed her perfect oval face. Her pink lips kept smiling, but now with a touch of uncertainty and with an onset of nerves that Caya didn't have to have her sister's empathic abilities to sense. Curious now, and also reluctant to hurt Briar in any way, or Adina, who had been nothing but majorly wonderful to her and her sister, Caya sighed and nodded. "So much for my grand exit in a huff."

"Oh, good!" Briar hugged her again, this time hard and rocking back and forth. "I know everything will work out. It has to."

Caya wasn't so sure. She walked between Briar and Adina when they left the park, unable to disregard the long looks and whispered comments around her. People knew who she was. She'd been seen with Thea in public many times, and her face had been plastered across the view-screen transmissions many times after she helped save lives when the saboteurs were active.

Thea and the guards took them through to the presidential jumper that carried them to a set of uninhabited corridors. From there, they rode a lift up through several decks and exited into what seemed to be a small, white hallway. There were two doors, and Caya automatically searched her mind, but she received no warning signals from what she had begun to call her 'inner scanner." Usually the premonitions started with slight nausea and a strange taste in her mouth. She used to get really sick, faint, and have convulsions sometimes, but nowadays she could calm the strange sensations and focus on the imagery flickering through her mind. Every scene that she felt displayed on the inside of her eyelids was for her to interpret, and the way she had developed this skill amazed even her.

The guards opened the door to the left and stood back to let Thea and her guests in. As they walked inside, Briar gasped and Caya just stared. Around them, in full view as if there were no walls at all, space hurtled by at magnetar-drive speed. Silver streaks around them gave Caya a sense of actually traveling for the first time since she had boarded *Pathfinder*. Normally, being aboard the massive ship consisting of twenty-one individual cubes felt like being planetside. The artificial gravity and the attention to detail that the ship's designers had taken made it almost impossible to fathom that she traveled through space. Caya walked closer to the— she wanted to call them windows but realized the walls couldn't be made of regular glass. "Is it safe to touch?" she asked over her shoulder.

"Absolutely." Korrian came up to her. "As you may have guessed, this is a rare component, far too expensive to use on any surfaces larger than this. We have twelve lookout quarters such as these scattered around the ship. That way, no matter how we move the cubes around, a couple of them will be turned toward our surrounding space."

"What's it made from?" Caya let her fingertips slide across the transparent surface.

"A rather innovative blend of transpar alloy and brace-crystalline. The latter strengthens the alloy and emphasizes its transparency. If you look really closely, you can see the facets of the crystalline-like glitter particles."

"Your invention?" Caya looked up at the tall, dark-skinned woman who was a revered hero for her role in constructing *Pathfinder*.

"My invention, but not my idea. Actually, Meija came up with it. She claimed it was vital for some individuals to really grasp that we're indeed traveling through space. Apparently, some people who aren't used to space travel at all can't get a sense of not living in the real world unless they witness the truth themselves."

"It's true," Meija said and wrapped her arm around Caya's shoulders. "As of now, we've had more than eight hundred people visit these lookouts. They need a prescription from a doctor, as this is not a tourist attraction. It's intended for mental-health issues."

"Except right now," Caya said, and glanced at Thea.

"I beg to differ." Thea motioned for her guests to take a seat around the table. "I needed some peace of mind, and I had been here only once before and thought we might just benefit from it." She sat down at the other side of the table, straight across from Caya, who wasn't sure she could manage a single bite if the president was going to scrutinize her like this.

"Well, I'm grateful I was able to see this at least once," Briar said from Caya's right. "The food looks amazing. And fresh! Is this all from the hydroponics chambers?"

"It is. We're starting to see bigger crops finally, and I thought you might like to sample it. Having only food from the dispensers in your quarters can become a bit bland, I'm afraid." Thea placed a napkin on her lap and gestured toward Korrian to start with the plates on her side. Vegetables, fruits, and roots were so beautifully arranged that Caya's mouth watered.

"Oh, look! Water berries." Briar sighed. "I never thought I'd taste those again. Remember the bushes by the brook in our garden back ho—" She blinked and gripped her utensils hard. "I mean, back on Oconodos." Adina placed a hand on Briar's hand.

"Even though we just named our new home today, we can still recognize how much we miss our old homeplanet." Thea spoke softly, her eyes scanning Caya's again.

"And the ones we left behind," Caya said. "I can't stop thinking about what their lives are like now." A nudge from Briar under the table said "not now, not here," but Caya was too agitated to play nice. "I know I'm not the only one who agonizes over what the conditions are for them. I mean, I'm sure the regular population doesn't see all the reports coming through via the beacon system, but even the ones we're privy to tell of such hardship..." She wiped at a tear, but it escaped her and landed on her plate, blending with the pink dressing. "Orphan changer kids living on the streets...it's insane."

"Sweetheart," Briar said, but stopped when Caya put up her hand, palm toward the others.

"I know. I know. I should pick my moments. The thing is," and now she locked her gaze on Thea, "I don't have very many moments to pick. Usually, I dine alone in my quarters, study alone, and when I do spend time with someone, I can tell it's understood that I must cherish those moments, which clearly means I should keep it light and pleasant and not talk about anything real or important." She lost her breath after her long sentence and gasped painfully for air.

"You have a point, Caya." Thea nodded slowly. "We can't share all the messages from Oconodos. It's my responsibility to keep everybody aboard safe, whether it is one changer girl or large groups with family members who remained on Oconodos. If people fear that their friends and family left behind are in any way not faring well, we might face uproars, even a mutiny. I'm well aware that there's an undercurrent of perpetual guilt aboard *Pathfinder*. If I allow it to run rampant, the entire Exodus operation will be in jeopardy." Thea pierced a water berry with her fork. "My job is as simple as it is difficult. I need to get you to Gemocon in one piece and, once we arrive, keep the interim government going until we can have new elections." She lowered her gaze for a moment. "And then I'm free." She stared at the piece of fruit on her fork. "Anyway, I don't want you to feel censored in any way when it comes to topics of conversation in your quarters, Caya."

Caya couldn't find the words to explain that it wasn't just about that. Of course she realized her sister and friends might feel inclined to keep their visits bright and cheery for her sake. This tactic tended to backfire, as Caya needed to talk about the injustice she felt was done to her. Some days she even resented Briar for being free to continue with her life and her career, despite being a changer, an empath, and sometimes a mind reader. Briar's moniker, Red Angel, protected her better than anything else, as she had helped so many people they were ready to airlock anyone who tried to hurt her. Caya didn't have any following. She wasn't even sure anyone but the president and her closest family and friends knew of how her ability to see the future could benefit the people on *Pathfinder*.

"I know," Caya answered now, trying her best to look polite and reasonable. It took more effort than the others realized to calm the resentment and anger to something manageable. "I am grateful I'm not confined to the brig, after all." She knew her acerbic comment was too much as soon as it left her lips. Briar looked at her with such sorrow, and Adina pressed her lips into a fine line. Oddly enough, only Thea looked at her with an open and steady gaze.

"I would never allow for you to spend so much as a second in the brig. You're an asset to this vessel and under my personal protection. I'm prepared to go quite far to stop anyone from exploiting you—or your sister, for that matter."

Thea's passionate words startled Caya. She hadn't heard the president speak like that in a long time. Usually when they were in the same room, Caya kept her distance. She had been an avid admirer of Thea from the moment she first met her. Gushing about her to Briar and Adina, Caya had been ready to give her life to keep the president safe and even protect her from her abusive husband.

It hadn't dawned on her that she'd still be incarcerated at this point and that it would be Thea's decision all along to keep her locked away from the rest of *Pathfinder*.

"Caya knows this, Thea," Briar said quietly. "The thing is, she was cooped up with me for the longest time while I homeschooled her on Oconodos. We were so scared people would find out she was a changer; we were doing…what you're doing now. Keeping her locked up for her safety." She turned to Caya, and tears filled her eyes. "You were just coming into your own with friends and the last year of school after boarding *Pathfinder*. You went jumper-cruising with your friends and you were free. I'm so sorry, sweetheart." Briar's voice broke, and she extended her hand.

Caya stood slowly, knowing if she gave in now, if she took Briar's hand, she would break down and cry…and she feared she might not be able to stop. "I don't think I can—I mean, I want to go back to my quarters now. I'm just bringing everyone down, when this meal and these surroundings should be a celebration. We finally have a name for the planet that will be our home. You all can't wait to reach our destination and begin your new life. I'm not as confident as you that I will find it as wonderful or exciting. I may just switch to new quarters to be confined to, for all I know."

"Caya!" Thea stood also, her shoulders pushed back and with fire in her eyes. "I have never said I'd keep you in protective custody forever. On Gemocon you will most likely be free to carry on with your life and fend for yourself." She looked furious, which made Caya wonder about her wording in the beginning—"most likely." It was a far stretch between "most likely" and "absolutely."

"This discussion is quickly getting old, and it goes on in circles every time without anyone actually listening." Caya bent and kissed Briar's cheek and then Adina's. Glancing briefly at Briar she said, "Thank you for the meal and the view." She raised her hand in a limp sort of wave and left the lookout with her head high, but with tears burning behind her eyelids.

"Caya…" Briar called out but was interrupted by Adina.

"She's upset. Give her some time."

Caya shook her head at the well-meant words. She had all the time in the world, and still her thoughts wouldn't line up enough for her to be able to think things through logically. Perhaps if she refused to have company for a few weeks she might be able to come up with a plan to make life more tolerable.

More worth living.

Chapter Three

W hat proof do you have that this intel of yours is factual and not just speculation, Lieutenant?" Thea sat among the ministers and high-ranking officials, her entire focus on the gangly man in the center of the semicircle.

Lieutenant Diobring squared his shoulders and placed his hands behind his back in the customary stance of a soldier briefing a superior officer. "Sir." He nodded toward Thea. "My team of seven and I have been undercover in disguise for eight weeks. We have covered cubes four, eight, and ten, as some of the law-enforcement officers had heard through reliable sources that something may happen there soon."

"Did they reveal their reliable sources?" Korrian asked. She sat next to her wife, hands folded before her.

"No, Admiral. Not then. They offered." Diobring looked seriously at Korrian and then shifted his gaze back to Thea. "I trust my team with my life, but we still thought it prudent to contain information to a need-to-know basis only. I asked Commander Vantressa to construct a non-connected computer for us to use for this type of intel. The team leaders involved with our operation are the only ones who can access the information, and it takes a joined command of at least two of us to access it."

"I'm glad you approached Commander Vantressa." Thea knew Adina's integrity was beyond reproach. She had stood by Caya and Briar throughout the media's gauntlet and public outcry. Now she was Thea's most trusted advisor when it came to technological and electronic-engineering issues. "So, in short, you're of the opinion that several teams of terrorists can be operating aboard *Pathfinder*?"

"Yes, sir." Diobring pulled out a small device and used it to switch on a set of twelve holographic lights between him and the men and women around the semicircle. A three-dimensional view of *Pathfinder* in blueprint mode appeared and pivoted slowly. "Everywhere you spot a small green light on the blueprint represents a sighting. They are not confirmed, but they're probable. I found this evidence credible enough to bring before you, sir."

"I see." Thea rose from her chair in the center of the table and circled it to stand next to Diobring. She bent forward and scrutinized the blueprint. All the cubes were represented, and none of them were without small glowing green dots. Thea could see how the green dots congregated in three cubes especially. "Don't tell me. Cubes four, eight, and ten."

"Correct, Madam President."

"And now you want to escalate the surveillance, perhaps even go after these terrorists directly."

"If we don't stop them, we won't reach Gemocon in one piece. That's my honest opinion, sir." Diobring clenched his jaw, and it wasn't hard for Thea to see how he was ready and motivated to stop the ones who'd had caused so much pain and suffering since they left Oconodos.

"I hear you, Lieutenant." Thea stood silent for a moment while she considered what her next move would be. No matter what, ultimately the responsibility was hers. "Lieutenant. Give us the room and wait in the common area outside my office. I'm going to confer with my advisors and the members of the cabinet. If they agree with me, I'll need you to accompany me shortly, so stay within earshot."

Diobring stood at attention. "Aye, sir. I'll be outside." He saluted, hand to chin, and then left the room.

"What are your thoughts, Madam President?" Korrian raised an eyebrow at Thea, as if the seasoned admiral couldn't guess already. "Am I assuming too much when I think you want to run his intel by a certain clairvoyant young woman?"

Glowering at Korrian, Thea nodded briskly. "Very astute, Admiral. We won't get much better intel than the lieutenant provided. The next step is to give Caya Lindemay a chance to verify—or perhaps even add to Lieutenant Diobring's facts. She may also advise against it."

"And no matter what this girl says, will you let her have the last say?" one of the ministers, a frail-looking middle-aged woman, asked.

"I have learned to listen to Caya, yes." Thea turned slowly and narrowed her eyes deliberately as she challenged the woman to contradict her. "I believe you were in these halls when the Lindemay sisters saved all of us by issuing warnings and, in Briar Lindemay's case, physically dragging two people to safety while risking her life. Since then, Caya has given us advice several times, which has all been true and thus saved both lives and resources."

"I still find it disconcerting that you are at the mercy of a changer, Madam President," the female minister said. To her credit, she sounded sincere, albeit overbearing enough to make Thea grind her teeth.

"Let me reassure you—all of you—that I'm at nobody's mercy." Giving them her broadest smile, the one she knew made younger assembly members tremble, Thea accepted her official cloak from her assistant, who knew by now exactly when her boss meant to leave. "I know we have more talking points to address, but let's do that tomorrow, or perhaps tonight via communication links. Thank you. Leave in heavenly splendor."

Thea strode out the door, followed by her usual entourage of presidential guards, assistants, and personal secretary. She spotted Lieutenant Diobring at the far end of the corridor and waved for him to join her. He trotted up next to her, about to salute again, but she gestured dismissively.

"No need. We're on our way to visit a person that I hope will be able to add to your intel. This person is somewhat special, and you might not entirely believe in her methods or in my listening to her, but I ask you to bear with me. Can you do that, Lieutenant?" Thea glanced up at the tall man next to her. He was good-looking and in his late twenties, hardened to some degree by his profession, but also with an honest expression.

"Yes, sir. I try to keep all options open to a degree."

"Good to know."

They rode the lift up to the corridor where Thea's private quarters were located, along with the most prominent ministers'. She stopped outside Caya's door, which used to be the president's guest quarters. Now Caya called it a luxurious prison, which wasn't fair. She wasn't a prisoner but kept in protective custody, though Thea didn't know how to convince her of the difference.

"I will enter with Lieutenant Diobring," Thea informed her guards. "Remain here until we're done." She turned to her assistants. "Continue to the workstation at the far end and make sure the computer has transcribed the notes from today's briefings properly. The last few had serious mistakes."

"Yes, sir." The two assistants hurried down the corridor just as Caya's door opened.

Thea nearly gasped out loud but managed to restrain herself. Caya stood there, dressed all in white silk and lace, her hair billowing around her shoulders and down to the small of her back. A white headband kept it out of her face, which made her disdainful expression all the more readily visible.

"Madam President. What a surprise." Caya spoke in a low, menacing voice. "And you brought a guest."

"I did. May we come in?"

Making quite a production of widening her eyes, Caya pressed a hand to her chest. "But of course. These aren't really my quarters after all. I'm humbled that you deign to pay me a visit after all this time."

Thea flinched before she managed to stop herself. It was true that she'd kept her distance these last thirty-some days. Wary of Caya's vitriol, she had been relieved that she didn't have to call upon Caya for official reasons. Until now.

"Stop it, Caya. That's enough." Thea stepped into Caya's quarters and motioned for Diobring to follow her. The door closed behind them. "This is Lieutenant Diobring. He has some information we need to share with you. His team and others are about to go into a situation blind, and if you can shed some light on any of it, it could save lives."

"I see." Suddenly looking tired and older than her twenty years, Caya motioned to the couches by the far wall. "Please, have a seat." She looked back and forth between Thea and Diobring as they sat down. "Life and death, hmm? Nothing like a bit of pressure to make one's day interesting."

Thea understood what Caya meant. To put such a burden on her narrow shoulders was inhumane, to say the least. If Caya hadn't been as gifted as she was, but instead a normal girl about to start her courses at university, like the rest of her peers, Thea would have gladly used any other means. But now that Caya could do more for their tactical advantage than several covert units combined, Thea couldn't allow herself to go soft.

Caya sat down on one of the couches, one seat away from Thea. Her transparent, turquoise eyes shifted between Thea and Diobring, their expression guarded and just one degree away from hostile.

After confirming with Thea that he really was meant to brief Caya with the latest intel, Diobring spoke for a good ten minutes. Once he was done, Caya unfolded her arms and turned to Thea. "And what does this have to do with me?"

Thea disregarded Caya's attitude and spoke matter-of-factly, which was how she knew she would get through to Caya. "You can imagine the damage covert groups could do to individual cubes, not to mention their inhabitants. Of all the scenarios possible, covert operatives are bad, but potential sleeper agents are worse. Is it possible for you to see anything?"

"Excuse me, Madam President," Diobring said. A frown marred his strong features. "What's going on here? What is Ms. Lindemay supposed to 'see'?"

"I can tell that your president has conveniently forgotten to tell you that I'm a clairvoyant changer." Caya looked expectantly at Diobring. "This is news to you, right?"

"It certainly is." Diobring's expression had gone a lot colder. "I didn't want to believe the rumors of stowaway changers. Are you telling me this girl is one?" He refused to look at Caya.

"She is. As is her sister. You did promise me to keep an open mind. Caya has saved this ship on several occasions, and now I hope she can help us find out more about the hostile plans you have almost uncovered."

Diobring pressed his lips together and turned back to Caya, clearly uncomfortable. "Very well."

"Let me try." Caya sighed and moved a little farther from Thea. She closed her eyes and pressed her palms against her knees. Rubbing slowly back and forth, she hummed just below her breath.

Thea had seen Caya do this several times, but she didn't think she'd ever seen her look this pale, her complexion transparent as the air around her seemed to sparkle.

"Creator of all things," Diobring whispered, and Thea shook her head, gesturing for him to be quiet. He nodded absentmindedly, clearly enthralled by what was going on.

"Everything is blue. Dark blue, almost black." Caya spoke with a low, husky voice, very unlike her normal melodious tone. She opened her eyes, startling Thea, as that normally didn't happen. "The woman is fragile. White skin, freckled, hair fiery red. She's wary, afraid, and she has good reason. Something, no, someone, knows she's not entirely devout. Her life is in danger. She's not going to survive longer than three days from now unless you take action." Caya curled up, hugging her knees close to her chest. "She's in a dark alley. I'm not sure which cube. She's on her back, half hidden among a set of…barrels, I think. H-her injuries are extensive… oh, Creator…it's bad. So bad." Caya's eyes filled with tears as she turned toward Thea. Dazed, Caya gripped her hand, which made Diobring stand, but Thea stopped him with a short gesture. She held on firmly to Caya's cold hand.

"Go on," Thea said quietly.

"Her throat is slit. She's lying in a large pool of her own blood." Caya shook now. "And the police and the military surround her now. They begin to move her when—oh, no! No!" Arching her back so violently it had to be a spasm, Caya sobbed furiously, pressing her eyes closed. "Her body…her body was a trap. Thea. Something around her, or underneath, exploded. So much destruction and death. You have to stop them. Save them." She gasped with each breath. "And save her. If you don't, there's no turning back. People will once again blame the changers."

"Changers are behind this?" Diobring rose, pulling at his communicator.

"Sit down, Lieutenant." Thea heard the crack in her voice and so did Diobring, who sat down as if she'd whipped his ankle with an energy rod.

Caya sat up straight. Her tears ran all the way down her neck, but her voice was once again fierce. "I don't think so. I don't know. It really doesn't matter at this point if you don't find this woman and save her. Once they get to her and her secret is out, it'll be too late."

"Can you describe her more than red hair and freckles?" Thea slid closer and tried to take Caya's hand. To her dismay, Caya flinched and pressed her back against the armrest behind her.

"Maybe. She is thin. Very thin, almost emaciated."

"Wait. Let me record your words." Thea reached for her bag and pulled out her personal, highly encrypted recorder. While working with the settings, she glanced up briefly at Diobring. "Get your team together again, Lieutenant. Only use the core officers, as we cannot afford to bring anyone not properly vetted."

"Certainly, Madam President." Diobring stood and bowed toward Thea and Caya. "I hope we meet again during less ominous circumstances, Ms. Lindemay." Diobring smiled cautiously and then left the guest quarters. It didn't escape Thea that Caya had returned his smile. She couldn't remember when Caya had last reciprocated any of her smiles.

"All right. It's recording. Please continue."

Caya tore her longing glance from the door as it closed behind Diobring. "Right. Yes. So, she's very thin, has shoulder-blade-long, copper-red hair. Her freckles are evenly distributed across her face, neck, and lower arms. As for the rest of her body, I have no idea. In my vision she wore a soft-grey trouser suit with white hems, lining, and lapels. I got the feeling she was dressed quite formally. Perhaps she holds some official capacity?"

That was an astute observation. "Anything else. Lips, teeth, eye color?"

"Brown eyes. Short, straight nose. Narrow, peach-colored lips. Didn't see the teeth." Caya rubbed her temples. "Short, well-kept nails."

"Thank you. That's a good start. If you have any more visions, regarding this woman or anything or anyone else, please let me know right away."

"Sure. I'm at your beck and call as always, Madam President," Caya said, her lips tense. Standing up, she began rounding the table between the couches as if she couldn't stand to be in close proximity with Thea a single second longer.

"Caya. Please." Without realizing her intention, Thea gently grabbed Caya's right wrist.

CHAPTER FOUR

Caya stopped instantly and glowered down at Thea, who looked up at her with narrow, ice-blue eyes. The woman wielding such power over every single person aboard *Pathfinder*—including Caya—gazed at her as if she wanted to say something but didn't know how to begin. This was of course ludicrous, as there was not one single day in the year when Gassinthea Mila Tylio wasn't the smartest, shrewdest person in the room. She exuded intelligence, and that trait, combined with her brilliant and calculating political prowess, was enough for Caya to know for certain that Thea always held the winning cards in any game.

This didn't stop Caya's skin from tingling where Thea held her in a firm but gentle grip.

"Sit back down, Caya. It's been too long since the naming ceremony." Thea rubbed her thumb against the back of Caya's hand. "I know I'm hardly your favorite person at the moment, but I still want to know—"

"What I'm up to? What my days are like? What if I were to tell you I'm going insane, little by little, cooped up in here? Would that matter to you at all?" Caya slowly sat down, close enough for their knees to touch.

Thea leaned closer. "If you were to tell me you're not faring well here, I would do anything beneath the stars to change that, short of endangering your life."

"Ah. But of course. Naturally. You're the judge and jury on that particular topic, right?" Caya pushed back against the much-too-old frustration. Thea had let go of her wrist, but her skin still buzzed from the unexpected touch. Normally, Thea knew better than to initiate such things. Perhaps she really was afraid deep down, thinking that Caya might affect her subconsciously?

Not sure of her own motive, Caya took Thea's hand in hers. It was obvious how this shocked the president. Her eyes went from narrow to wide within a fraction of a second. "What are you doing?" Thea asked in a low growl.

"Trying to make you see reason if that is at all possible." Caya held Thea's hand gently. Caya hadn't counted on her own response when Thea remained motionless with her hand in hers.

Images began to flicker behind Caya's eyelids, forcing her to close her eyes tight as she clung to Thea's hand. Visions of a young woman, looking much like Thea, but perhaps at age sixteen, maybe eighteen, streamed through Caya's mind. "What the...?" Caya gasped, and now she clung to Thea's hand. Now the vision was clearing up, and Caya could tell the very young Thea stood by a middle-aged man, pale and upset.

"Father. I refuse. I'm going to the capital." Young Thea pleaded, but defiance shone from her eyes. "I was accepted to the university there. You can't keep me here."

"I can cut off your funds, you ungrateful child!" The man, tall and burly as he stood up, raised his hand. Caya cried out as he hit Thea's cheek, sending her to her knees.

"Caya?" Thea's older voice reached Caya through the haze of the vision, but she had already been whisked away to another scenario. This time, Thea was older, perhaps in her mid-twenties, and a much-older Hadler stood next to her on a tall staircase outside an impressive building. Caya recognized the governmental building, as no other structure on Oconodos was made of bronze-veined marble. At first Caya thought it was a vision from happier days, but then she spotted Hadler's iron grip of Thea's upper arm. She wanted to yell "Let go of her!" to the despicable man Thea had married, but it was futile. Instead, she saw how Thea stealthily rubbed her arm when Hadler finally let go. Another whooshing sound and Caya's vision morphed into Thea looking her current age. She stood by her desk in her office when Hadler stormed in, apoplectic and spitting as he cursed her with foul language. To Caya's amazement, Thea didn't look afraid any longer. Instead, she stepped well within Hadler's personal space and poked him in the chest with two fingers as she hissed some inaudible words to him. A white flash broke the tableau into spinning shards, and now Caya gasped out loud and wanted to stop the visions from crashing into her mind. Here Thea was on her knees in a ballroom, and before her on the floor was Caya, writhing in what looked like a seizure. Thea held one of her hands on Caya's shoulder, the other raised to keep the shocked spectators away. "Give her enough room to breathe!" Again, the vision changed, and this time, Thea was alone in her living-room area sitting curled up in the armchair and holding a pillow as she stared into nothing. Thea's lips trembled, and just before the last vision faded, Caya thought she heard her whisper, "She hates me."

As the mist disappeared from her mind, Caya became aware of still holding Thea's hand.

"What did you see?" Thea spoke quietly and used her free hand to stroke up and down Caya's lower arm. "Anything about what Lieutenant Diobring spoke of earlier?"

"No." Caya was still shocked at her visions; she needed time to process them.

"Then what?" Thea held on to Caya's hand with both of hers.

"They weren't the usual visions. You know, of the future. These...oh, Creator of everything, these were like small scenes from the past. I've never had that happen before. Not even when it comes to Briar." Caya let go of Thea's hand, and for a moment the lack of connection actually brought her a stab of physical pain. She whimpered and curled up much like Thea had done in her vision.

"What's wrong? Talk to me." Thea looked startled and slid forward, raising her hands.

"No!" Caya flinched. "Don't. Don't touch me."

"But—Caya, I wasn't going to hurt you." Hurt tinged Thea's words as she lowered her hand and placed them on her lap in a heartbreakingly awkward gesture.

"Not your fault. Not this time." Caya attempted some gallows humor, but it fell flat as her words made Thea go paler.

"Then tell me what was in your vision."

"It was more than one. It was like a series of scenes from... from someone's life. I think I'm not far off when I interpret them as pivotal moments in their life."

"So it was about someone you know." Thea studied Caya's expression, and it wasn't very hard to detect the moment Thea figured it out. "It was about me? My life. My 'pivotal moments'?" She tightened her hands into fists.

"I can't control where my visions take me, Thea. You know that. If I could, I'd stay as far as I could away from you and your life. I would never invade anyone's privacy, least of all yours."

"Yes. You've made it bloody clear that you don't want anything to do with me." Thea stood. "I want you to tell me everything about your visions about my past. I need to know if it is something your mind conjured up or not."

After that volley of hurtful words, Caya only wanted Thea to leave. "I don't—"

"No! What you fail to understand is that I *need* to know. This is not optional, Caya. Tell me." Thea sat down again, back straight and her hands clasped. Two bright red spots burned on her cheeks, which was rarely a good sign.

Reluctantly, Caya gave a brief recount of the tableaus she had witnessed. With each one, she received confirmation about their accuracy by merely watching Thea's expression and how she grew increasingly ashen. "I take it you really did live through those moments?" Caya winced at her words, but she had to make sure.

"Yes." So tense now, she looked like she might shatter at the slightest touch, Thea rose and walked over to the food and drink dispenser. Punching in a few commands, she grabbed a glass and placed it under the spout, filling it with a green-tinted liquid. After she knocked it back, Thea put the glass on the counter and returned to Caya and sat down. "This is a first? Seeing someone's past like this?"

"Yes. I've only had visions of future events so far. I'm not sure what I did different this time."

"You held my hand." Thea gazed down into her lap and untangled her fingers. "Can that be it?" She examined her hand and then looked at Caya's.

"I don't thi—wait." Frowning as she tried to remember if she'd ever had any physical connection apart from with Briar when a vision hit, Caya had to conclude that she hadn't. Back on Oconodos, while being homeschooled by first her parents and later Briar, her changer status had been a well-kept secret. It had taken her family quite a bit of time to realize she wasn't just having seizures. Initially, they were afraid of her having a brain tumor or some other cerebral illness, but when they learned that she had the genetic makeup of the feared mutation, her parents almost wished she had been ill instead. As she grew older, Caya realized her parents had to have suspected the mutation as they had the test done in secret. When the Exodus operation commenced years later, Caya's genetic results would have made it impossible. Briar had promised their parents to get them to safety, and when the time arrived to get the tests done, she used the same contact that had once helped her father to have them both changed. They didn't know even Briar had the mutated gene, as her tests had given a false negative when they were younger. If Briar hadn't been as meticulous as she was in changing both their test results, as they were sisters and had to look like sisters even genetically, she would have been found out long before she herself knew.

"Caya?" Thea broke through Caya's reverie. "Can it be the case?"

"I think so. Yes. Damn it."

"There's only one way to figure it out." Thea extended her hand. "Try again."

Caya didn't want to. She really, really didn't. Mustering courage, she slid forward. "If we're going to do it, let's do it properly. If holding your hand gave me so much..." She shrugged as her cheeks grew warm.

"What do you mean?" Thea tilted her head. "Oh. Right." She lowered her proffered hand. "How do you want to do this?"

"Want?" Snorting, Caya scooted even closer and wrapped her arms around Thea. She found it so ironic that she was holding the woman she had such conflicting feelings about for scientific reasons and nothing else. Thea was softer and curvier than her strict dress code and commanding persona suggested. Where Caya had expected to find a thin, wiry frame, she instead held full breasts and a narrow waist above slender hips. Just as Caya was about to let go since she had never felt more self-conscious in her life, Thea slowly raised her arms and wrapped them lightly around Caya's shoulders.

"Anything?" Thea murmured.

"Please, Madam President, give a girl a chance to adjust, will you?" Perhaps it was their close proximity that made some of Caya's hostility dwindle. That first month or two of Caya's protective custody, they had been able to banter and enjoy each other's company. Back then, Caya had just been relieved that Briar and Adina were all right, and in love, and she'd thought her stay in the guest quarters would be temporary.

"All right. Do take your time."

Caya was about to snort again at Thea's arrogant tone when Thea suddenly leaned her cheek against her temple. Unable to stop her entire system from responding, Caya gasped. "Thea…" She meant to say they had to stop, but then more images poured over her, flooding her mind, and acute vertigo made her cling to Thea as if outer space had tried to suck her out through an airlock.

"Thea?" A stunning blond woman dressed in an ankle-long, flowing, off-white dress came into the room where a little girl with the same hair color sat playing with a large tablet. She moved her little fingers deftly as she made her small hovercraft move across the screen. Now she looked up, a big smile on her lips.

"Mommy!" She let go of the tablet and rushed toward the woman. "Daddy said you weren't coming until tomorrow." The little girl, yes, of course it was Thea. Caya could clearly see the resemblance between the child and her mother.

"I know, darling. I just couldn't wait to see my best girl." The woman hugged young Thea to her. "Tomorrow is your eighth birthday. I couldn't miss that."

"But—but Daddy said the doctors wanted you to stay and get stronger." Thea looked up at her mother, her long hair cascading down her back. She was dressed in blue shorts and a white shirt, which Caya recognized as parts of a school uniform. She saw Thea had kicked off her shoes and taken off her socks, as they were right beside the tablet on the floor.

"I feel stronger just for being with you and your father," Thea's mother said and rocked her daughter back and forth. "You're more important than anything else to me."

"Now, Thea. Don't tire your mother out." A tall, dark-haired man stepped into Thea's room. He had a becoming, well-trimmed beard and was dressed in an old-fashioned blue suit. He put an arm around Thea's mother. "Rionna? I thought we agreed you could come home today if you stayed down here. You're not well enough to climb the stairs."

Thea looked alarmed, but Rionna placed a kiss on the man's cheek while still holding onto her. "Don't be such a worrier, Mattner. I'm perfectly able to climb one set of stairs. What do you think I've done during my physical-therapy sessions? Have them carry me through the exercises?" Rionna chuckled. "Now, I could smell the food being prepared. Let's not disappoint Ms. Dimin. No doubt she's been cooking up a storm."

The vision blurred, and then Caya found herself in a large foyer. Black-and-white marble walls stretched up toward a skylight that showed it was evening or night. Young Thea stood clinging to the banister halfway up the stairs, whimpering. "Mommy. Mommy…"

"Stay there, Thea," Mattner called out from behind Caya. She turned and gasped at the sight of Rionna. Thea's mother lay on the floor, her head in her husband's lap. Her skin was as white as the marble. "Rionna. Wake up. Wake up. Wake up!" Mattner's voice rose to a roar. "Damn the Creator, wake up!"

Thea's whimper rose until she was screeching for her mother. She passed Caya and threw herself next to her. Taking Rionna's hands, Thea kissed them and hugged them to her. "She's so cold, Daddy. She's so cold." Crying fat tears now, Thea suddenly hit her father on the arm closest to her. "Make her wake up. Make her warm again. She's too cold." She hit him over and over again, her voice getting hoarse from crying. "Mommy…mommy…"

Caya was crying along with Thea, her heart breaking for the child and remembering when she and Briar had lost their parents. At least they had each other, but who had taken care of Thea once her mother was gone? Had Mattner been as loving and nurturing as his wife? Caya studied the man's expression through her tears. Thea was still hitting him with her little fists in her anguish, but he wasn't even looking at her. He was holding his dead wife, and Caya had the distinct sense that what love he had been able to share with anyone had died with her. Slowly the scene faded and Caya was back in grownup Thea's embrace, crying so hard she was shaking.

"Caya? Please? What's the matter? What did you see?" Thea rubbed her hands up and down Caya's back. "I'm so sorry. We shouldn't have tried this again so soon. Let me page Briar—"

"No. No. I'm all right. Or I will be." Trying to pull herself together, Caya was reluctant to let go of Thea. She wasn't quite sure if she needed the comfort of her embrace or she had just witnessed what had to have been the most traumatic event in Thea's life.

"Of course you'll be all right. Just breathe." Thea rocked her. "That's it. Breathe."

Slowly the impact of the vision receded, and Caya pulled back enough to wipe at her wet cheeks. "I think I soaked your jacket." She felt foolish now. Young Thea's pain hadn't been hers. A small, inner voice insisted that her feelings for Thea were the reason for her strong reaction. Not ready to confess any type of strong feelings for the woman who wielded such power over her life, Caya let go of Thea completely and slid back so their bodies didn't touch anymore. She didn't want to risk any other inadvertent visions from Thea's past until she knew what triggered them.

"Never mind the damn jacket. What did you see?" Thea moved as if to take Caya's hand again and winced when Caya shook her hand and backed off some more. "That bad?"

"I witnessed your mother coming home from some hospital the day before—"

"—my eighth birthday." Her complexion grey, it was Thea's turn to pull back. "Oh, Creator of mercy." She covered her eyes for a few moments with a trembling hand. "What exactly did you see?"

"How much she loved being back home with you and your father—especially with you. Then you and your parents were in a foyer and your mother was dead." She could find no easy way to say it. No well-meaning, cautious words would help minimize the pain Thea had felt the night her mother died.

"It was actually the next day. I mean, it was past midnight and I couldn't sleep because I was so happy to have my mother home—and for turning eight. I had wished for a hover bike, and my father had hinted that I might get one. More than that, though, I had wished for my mother to get well and come home, which happened in part, I suppose." Thea spoke with calm, measured words that were completely contradicted by the pain in her eyes. "I heard my father yell my mother's name from downstairs and ran to see what was going on, afraid she was ill again, but she wasn't. As you saw, it was much worse. She had left the bedroom my father had installed for them downstairs and probably fainted as she was walking up the stairs. She fell down and broke her neck. I learned many years later that she would have perhaps lived another ten or twenty days if she hadn't fallen. Her condition was rapidly deteriorating, and she knew it. That's why she came home even if she wasn't well enough. She wanted to be with her family." Thea's expression hardened. "The autopsy results showed her condition clearly, but that didn't stop my father for blaming me for her death."

"What? But why?" Caya came close to taking Thea's hand again. "That's insane."

"You would think so, wouldn't you? Remember, she was going upstairs even after promising him not to. In his mind, that was my fault. If I hadn't been so selfish and excited about my birthday, my mother wouldn't have ventured up the stairs and fallen down when her weakened state caused her to faint or get dizzy. I believed him for years."

Caya sobbed and wiped at her tears. "That's just so wrong. Your mother loved you more than anything. She loved your father too, I could tell, but you—she adored you. I think—and this is just a hunch—that he was jealous. And when she died, he couldn't handle the grief, or the shock...or both. It's what I felt from him during my vision anyway." Caya wiped quickly at her tears again. Her skin was starting to feel raw from all the crying.

"You may well be correct," Thea said and sighed. "I think we proved our theory regarding how your visions of someone's personal past occur. At least to some degree." She smoothed down her hair. "I apologize that you had to witness the birth of my dysfunctional relationship with my father," she said, her tone stiff.

"Thea. Don't. I need to make a few things clear because I can tell you're about to bolt, and knowing you, you'll stay away and send your minions to deal with me until we reach Gemocon."

Looking affronted, Thea folded her hands on her lap. "Do go on." She raised her chin in a clear challenge.

"I promise never to tell anyone, not a single soul, what I learned and what I saw during my visions about your past today. If you never want to mention any of it again, I'll respect that. I know I'm often furious with you for my situation, but, that said, I don't want you to stop coming to my quarters. The only thing worse than being furious at you—is being angry with you and never seeing you again. I'm probably not making sense at all, but please. Don't withdraw behind President Tylio, the public figure, even if you only stop by when you need something from me." Caya tried for a smile but knew it probably looked more like a weird grimace.

Thea studied her quietly for a good minute, and Caya held her breath for nearly as long. "Very well. I trust your work ethic. I always have since that day when you had a vision at the presidential ball."

As that had been one of the first visions, Caya realized she hadn't read too much into Thea's expression when she had warded off the crowd around them with such fury.

"All right." Caya slumped against the backrest of the couch. "Good."

Thea stood and adjusted her jacket. "I will let you know when we find the young woman in your vision. I pray she's all right."

Caya nodded. "Me too."

Thea walked to the door and was about to push the sensor to open it when she stopped, still with her back toward Caya. Lowering her head, she spoke in a barely audible voice. "I did get the hover bike. Our cook found it hidden from my prying eyes in the pantry later in the day and gave it to me." Tugging at the hem of her jacket and resuming her trademark proud posture, Thea cleared her throat. "I never rode it." She slammed her palm against the sensor and walked out the door.

Caya curled up on the couch and pulled one of the blankets around her. She was cold and tired, having depleted all of her energy. Thea had lost her mother and her father's love in one instant. Something told Caya that the woman who had just left her quarters had never celebrated any of her birthdays again. Had she perhaps been looking for a father figure of sorts when, at twenty-two, she had married the much-older Hadler? It made horrible sense. To think that he had turned out to be an abusive cheat of a husband, not worthy of someone as amazing and beautiful as Thea, infuriated her.

Closing her eyes reluctantly, as she was afraid of what any potential dreams might entail, Caya hugged a pillow close to her chest under the blanket. She could still feel Thea's arms around her and her cheek against her temple as she finally drifted off to sleep.

Chapter Five

Thea looked up as the door chime to her office pinged. "Yes, enter."

The door hissed open, revealing a tall woman dressed in the black uniform commonly worn by *Pathfinder*'s military security detail. Striding up to Thea's desk, the woman moved with feline grace that gave her a decidedly lethal expression.

"Madam President, I'm Commander Neenja KahSandra. You requested my presence?"

"Ah yes, Commander KahSandra. Please, have a seat." Thea motioned for one of her visitors' chairs. "You come highly recommended both by my military advisors and the civilian law-enforcement brass."

Unfazed, the commander merely nodded. "Good to know."

"I have a special assignment for you that requires your expertise. I will personally update and elevate your security clearance if you agree to change units for the rest of our journey."

"That sounds intriguing, sir, but I'm very happy where I am, patrolling the outer perimeter of *Pathfinder*."

"Which won't do the ship a lot of good if we're blown up from inside." Thea knew she sounded terse, but she needed the commander to understand just how important this was.

"Have you received such intel, sir?" Commander KahSandra's forehead furrowed. "I haven't seen any such reports lately."

"Hence the elevated security clearance, Commander."

"I see." Commander KahSandra relaxed marginally. "I take my oath to do my duty in protecting *Pathfinder* and its passengers very seriously. I'm prepared to change units if it is required."

"Good. I have read your dossier," Thea said and tapped her tablet, pulling up KahSandra's records. "You're a martial-arts expert, have an engineering degree, and, what tipped the scale in your favor, you're also one of the best explosive experts in the fleet."

KahSandra merely nodded.

"Fine. Use my tablet for your retina scan and fingerprint confirmation regarding your elevated status."

KahSandra accepted the tablet and performed the maneuvers. Thea studied the younger woman closer. She kept her long black hair in a low braid, and her black, straight eyebrows framed stark features that made her more handsome than beautiful. Her amber, slanted eyes regarded the world with a hint of suspicion.

Thea took the tablet back and checked the confirmation. "Excellent. From now on you answer only to Admiral Heigel and me. You will partner with Lieutenant Diobring, and together you will work with his handpicked team to uncover potential sleeper cells set on destroying *Pathfinder*—or at least parts of it."

"I know of the lieutenant but have never spoken with him. What will he think of sharing his team with me?" KahSandra tilted her head.

"Are you that concerned, or is it merely a polite question?" Thea raised an eyebrow and was delighted when KahSandra did the same.

"The latter, in a sense. From a point of professional courtesy, I wouldn't want to step on the lieutenant's toes. As I outrank him, he might feel blindsided by my presence, which could have a detrimental effect on our collaboration."

"Diobring knows he's getting more manpower. Yes, formally you outrank him, but he also has knowledge of the task at hand that you don't, which puts you on even ground. If you're as clever as your dossier suggests, you will find a way to work with Diobring and his team without causing havoc."

"Certainly, Madam President."

"You can start by going to the officers' mess hall and introducing yourself. The team is there, and an informal setting might be best—" Thea was about to ignore the beep from her communicator when Caya's emergency signal followed. Thea held up a finger to Commander KahSandra and slapped the communicator sensor. "Thea here, Caya."

The communicator was eerily silent for a few moments, and Thea stood. "Caya? Do I need to join you?"

"No. I'm all right. Can you talk?" Caya's voice was strained, which twisted Thea's midsection into a knot of worry, for her and for what it could mean.

"Yes. I'm here with a member of the fleet who has the appropriate clearance."

"They're targeting the hospital again. Somewhere on the third deck, I see guards…either unconscious or dead." Caya gave a muted sob. "White garnet. I think it's white garnet. It's burning through the different systems, and patients in the emergency wards are suffering as their equipment is compromised. The staff is trying to stop it, but they burn their hands off as they yank out the computer parts. They can't stop this. They need to evacuate on deck one to four. Anything less and I can't guarantee they'll make it." Caya's swallowed audibly. "And of course Briar is working. She's not on any of those wards, but you know her…she will sense the distress of the ones affected and want to assist. Please, Thea. Send help."

"I'm already doing that." Thea tapped furiously on her tablet. "I'll initiate everything from here and then get back to you. If you see anything other than what you've told me, page me instantly. I'm setting my communicator to auto-connect for you."

"All right. Just hurry."

Thea could hear how distraught Caya was, but she was in full presidential mode, and her duty to the ship came first. This didn't mean she was made of stone. A small but very important part of her yearned to run to Caya and see for herself that she wasn't heading for actual seizures again.

Commander KahSandra stood, ready to spring into action. "Sir?"

"Walk with me." Thea headed for the door, barking orders to her staff as she went. "Have Diobring and his team meet, fully equipped, by the jumper gate. Have them bring one extra set of protective gear and an emergency engineering kit. Page Admiral Heigel and have her do the same. Initiate Code Z for my cabinet members and the Assembly. Time for them to hit the deck." Code Z was the guideline for how to keep the political and public servants safe during an attack or catastrophe. Thea knew technically she needed to join the cabinet members in the built-in bunker in the center of cube one, but she hadn't so far and wouldn't this time either. She needed to be visible and strong—not hide, no matter what her military and civilian advisors thought.

Diobring and the men and women in his unit stood ready when Thea, her guards—which had doubled in numbers to make up for her stubbornness—and KahSandra reached the jumper gate. Diobring took one look at KahSandra and nodded briefly. "Sir," he murmured and tossed her a bag. KahSandra donned the safety gear fast, including the engineering kit that she hooked on her harness.

"Commander KahSandra will fill you in on your way to cube eleven. You will return the courtesy toward her regarding what we know of the sleeper cells and the woman in jeopardy. Admiral Heigel and her team of engineers will meet you as you step off the jumper. We've trained for this. I'll be on the bridge. Go in safe and heavenly splendor." Thea stepped back and watched the team board an emergency jumper car.

She hoped this wasn't the last she saw of them.

Caya felt like a caged animal, ready to chew through the bulkhead to get out. She had tried reaching Briar several times but hadn't succeeded. Calling Adina again, she nearly wept when she heard her sister's lover respond.

"Caya? What's up?" Adina asked, and Caya could hear her walking rapidly.

"I paged Thea. The hospital is being targeted again. Briar is supposed to work today and she's not answering. I need to go there—"

"Hold on. I haven't received any alerts." Adina's steps stopped echoing. "When did you have your vision?"

"Fifteen minutes ago, maybe? Thea is acting on it. She's sending help. I just need to be there to help locate Briar if she's doing some of her heroic stuff."

"Oh, damn." Adina's voice was a mere whisper. "Can you find her, I mean, mentally? Can you reach out to her?"

"I've tried!" Caya howled the words. "I'm too far away. If you come get me and vouch for me, I can get closer and try to connect. She's usually the one to find my mind, but I have to try." Frantic now, Caya began to change into a dark-grey hooded coverall.

"All right. I'm on my way. Thea might demote me to crewman, but I don't care. If Briar needs us, that's all that matters." The sound of Adina's steps indicated that she was running. "I'll be at your door in about five minutes. Good thing I had to give a lecture in the government building."

"Hurry!" Caya rushed over to her cabinet and pulled out an emergency-kit case. This was yet another thing Thea knew nothing about. Caya and Briar had put together a bag with emergency supplies of all kinds in case Caya ever needed to disappear. The bag held everything she would need for five days, including a set of fake identity cards. They wouldn't fool a thorough scan, but the rudimentary scanners used by law enforcement routinely would be deceived.

Tapping her foot just inside the door, Caya waited impatiently for Adina to arrive. When the door chime finally rang and the door opened, Caya was about to jump out into the corridor when she saw Adina's warning gaze. Outside, Thea had clearly put one more guard on duty since Caya's vision.

"Adina, welcome." Caya knew her smile was more of a grimace.

"I thought I'd ask you to join me and Briar for some dinner at our place." Adina ran a hand through her short, dark hair. "It's been a while."

"Sure. Will you be able to vouch for me?" Normally, any of Caya's outings needed to be cleared in advance and logged.

"Absolutely." Adina turned to the guards, and whoever saw her insignia probably recognized her on sight. "I'll take responsibility for Ms. Lindemay. She'll be back in a couple of hours. I'll page the lieutenant in charge of your shift when I know the exact ETA."

The guards exchanged a glance, but it was clear that Adina's rank made them wary of asking questions. "Feel free to page the president if you think you need her confirmation. I believe she's busy though." Adina looked casual.

Caya nearly gasped but realized Adina was gambling that they wouldn't dare disturb the president with such a routine matter.

"No, that's all right, sir. I will need your retina-scan signature."

"Of course." Adina performed the procedure put in place to keep Caya safe. "There. We better hurry, Caya. Briar's waiting."

"I'm ready." Caya stepped outside and hurried after Adina before any overly conscientious guard objected. "That was bold."

"Don't kid yourself. That was the easy part." Adina lengthened her steps. "Let's hope we don't run into Thea on our way out the door. I had confirmation on my way here that she's on the bridge, but you never know. For having the ultimate office on this ship, she sure likes to micromanage at times."

"For good and bad," Caya said. She might well argue and be furious with Thea, but she didn't like it when anyone else said anything unfavorable about her. "Who knows under what conditions I'd be held if she didn't micromanage my situation? Or Briar, for that matter."

"True." Adina didn't elaborate, but the way she pressed her lips together told Caya she was a force to reckon with if anything or anyone threatened Briar's wellbeing. Right now, that wellbeing might hang in the balance unless Caya reached her sister. The closer they got to the jumper gate, the harder it became to keep up their speed and not run into people. Passengers, politicians, and military personnel milled around them, and Adina took Caya by the hand.

"We can't get on the regular jumpers. No official traffic is going into cube eleven right now. We need to procure a military cart." Adina motioned for a door close to the entrance to the gate, where a growing crowd of passengers stood. She swiped a card and allowed the retina reader to confirm her identity again. The door opened and she pulled Caya with her. "Hurry. If the general public thinks they can get in and find a transport in here, we'll never be able to close the door."

Caya squeezed through and saw how Adina closed the door behind them just as people came running. Hands banged on the door, making Caya cling to Adina's hand. "Why are they so agitated?"

"Rumors spread fast, and even though Thea no doubt put the lid on this pretty fast, some may have been leaked. Now people either want to go home or to the hospital and get their loved one out of there." Adina let go of her hand and crossed the track as she moved to the opposite bulkhead.

Caya felt as if every palm and fist hammering at the door hit her midsection. What if she had interpreted the vision wrong—or if the vision had come to her too late? It could mean the end for Briar and many other people, most of them sick or injured already. She heard a scraping noise and turned in time to see Adina flip open a hatch and reveal a very small runner, meant for four people.

"Get in. I'll program it in transit. Otherwise it won't cross the border to cube eleven."

Caya took the left seat. Knowing they'd be going much faster than in the usual jumpers, she strapped herself in with the six-point harness. Adina did the same and began giving verbal commands as the jumper began to move. It shook slightly before it reached maximum speed, and the tunnel walls became a blur. Caya gripped the seat, fearing they might crash at any moment. As they neared the gate of cube eleven, Caya half expected the guards there to stop them or the automatic brakes to disengage the magnets that kept them moving forward, but they blasted straight through the gate, not even slowing down.

They reached the hospital area and Adina steered manually until they came to the main gate. "Hmm," Adina said. "Something tells me we need one of the side entrances. Hold on." She whipped the mini-jumper around a corner and moved it into a side track.

The side entrance wasn't as inundated with people trying to get in, but Caya could tell they would have to struggle. She was the one grabbing for Adina's hand as they weaved in and out among the people. How could rumors spread this fast? The answer was self-evident. During the first attacks, nobody had been prepared, or even worried, that such things would occur aboard a ship of salvation. Here they were all hoping for a new, safe future for the Oconodians and the Gemosians. Why would anyone want to destroy that? Now, after several attacks, of learning about changers having snuck aboard, the passengers on *Pathfinder* didn't take things at face value. When they learned of a rumor regarding something happening that might impact their loved ones, they didn't sit around waiting for the authorities to deal with the situation.

"To the left. I need to reach the guards or we won't get inside." Adina gasped and tossed Caya in behind her as a group of men approached, shouting "Open the door" to the security personnel in charge. Feeling a hard shove against her back, Caya fell to her knees. She knew she had scraped them badly against the floor but bounced back up before she was trampled.

"Hold on!" Adina pulled Caya in under her arm and literally dragged her over to the closest soldier. "Open the door, but keep the weapons trained on the crowd. Do you have reinforcements coming, Ensign?"

"Sir. Yes, sir!" The young woman already had her rifle in a ready-to-fire position, her index finger mere millimeters from the trigger sensor. "Two units from cube four are inbound. Get behind me, sir. Ensign Cioma will open the door for you on my signal. Be prepared. We can't do this too many times, or they'll storm us."

"Understood, Ensign. Be safe." Adina glanced down at Caya. "I'm so dead when Thea learns of this."

"Me too." Caya gripped Adina's hand again. The door opened before them, and they almost fell through it. As it hissed closed behind them, they heard the wheezing-popping sound of weapons being fired.

"Oh, no." Caya whipped her head around, staring at the door.

"She's firing above their heads the first time around. Hopefully the teams from cube four will get there soon."

Caya hoped so too. She glanced around. They were in the far right wing of the hospital. People scurried around on the inside as well, but not nearly as many as on the outside. The communication system kept repeating for people to evacuate unless they were unable to do so for medical reasons.

"I need somewhere a little bit quiet, Adina." Caya looked for a door to an office or even a cleaning-supply closet. "I can't focus with so much movement around me."

"This way." Adina pulled Caya along and opened a door located just around the corner. It was indeed a minor office area that had apparently been evacuated.

"This all right?" Adina locked the door behind them.

"It's fine. Now, I need you to be very still until I know if I can reach her."

Adina merely nodded and sat down on the closest desk.

Caya pulled out a chair and sat also, barely noting her torn coverall and bleeding knees. She pressed her palms to her chest and closed her eyes. Thinking of her sister, Caya envisioned them together when she was little and they lived in the traditionalist house in a small town. They would sit on the porch or in the garden, have homemade juice or tea made from the charka trees by the river. Longing so desperately for her sister, Caya began to hum the melody Briar had always sung to her on those days when they both missed their parents, or when Caya had one of her nightmares that were preludes to visions. Only Briar's voice could soothe her back then.

"Caya? Caya?" Briar's voice was like a whisper in the wind, but it was there. "Caya?"

"Briar. Where are you? Are you safe?" Caya focused so hard to maintain the connection, she could feel sweat run down her back.

"I'm fine. You had a vision about what is happening?"

"I did. I'm here. First floor. With Adina." It was getting harder to maintain the contact.

"At the hospital?"

"Which floor? You on?" Clutching the armrests tightly, Caya began to slump. "Tell me."

"I'm on the third deck. A team of soldiers is already here, and I'm trying to assist."

Caya felt Adina's hands cup her shoulders and hold her upright. It was as if Adina's love for Briar and deep affection for Caya helped her regain her strength and focus. "We're coming to help you."

"But—"

"On our way." Caya snapped her eyes open, gasping for air. She grabbed Adina's wrists and pulled herself up. "Third deck. Soldiers in place searching. We need to hurry."

CHAPTER SIX

The third level of the hospital was eerily quiet. The staff moved patients in hover chairs or beds, soldiers searched every part of the wards meticulously, and nobody spoke above whispers or murmurs. Adina and Caya moved down the corridor, Adina now with her sidearm in her right hand.

"Can you sense her?" Adina glanced back at Caya.

"No. I don't function like that. She should be able to sense me though, unless someone in great pain or distress drowns me out." This had happened before. Briar was getting better with each passing day when it came to tuning out the noise around what she really wanted to home in on. Still, it was hard to filter out someone overwhelmed with emotions or in excruciating pain.

"What's going on? Where are you taking me?" An old woman clung to the railings of the hoverbed, staring at the soldiers with frightened eyes. She was Gemosian and so emaciated, it pained Caya to see her thin, transparent extremities. She was dressed in a light-blue shirt that matched her starkly blue-veined skin in a distressing way. Part of Caya wanted to reach out to the woman, but she feared if she touched her she might be inundated with the woman's long history. Was this to be Caya's future—fearing the touch of other people?

"Don't worry, ma'am," Adina said, as if she had read Caya's mind. "You will be well cared for at another unit until we sort everything out. Just relax. You're in good hands."

The old woman tilted her head and looked at Adina and then at Caya. As she gazed into Caya's eyes, she suddenly smiled, which looked completely out of place. "Ah, yes. She awaits you in room four. You best hurry on, little miracle girl. Time is of the essence."

Caya gaped at the woman slumped back against her pillows as she was whisked away by the staff. "What—what was that about?"

"I have no idea, but I suggest we might as well find room four and check it out." Adina hurried down the corridor, twice as fast as before. Caya kept a lookout for the room numbers located above the door frames. When they reached a fork in the corridor, Caya spotted room four on the far right.

"There," she called out, then began running.

"Wait!" Adina caught up with her. "Stay behind me. I'll go in first."

"Adina?" a familiar voice said, and Briar poked her head out through the open door to room number four. "I heard your voice." She ran up to them and pulled them both in for a quick, strong hug. "I believe that room four—"

"—is where they placed the white garnet." Caya nodded. "We have to discuss how you managed to use an old lady as a conduit just now, later." She walked with Briar to room four, only to have Adina yank both of them back by tugging at their coveralls.

"You're not going in there, in case you're correct." Adina stepped in front of them and motioned for someone behind them to approach. "I'm Commander Vantressa. I need this room swept before you continue to do anything else."

"I'm Commander KahSandra," a melodious female voice said from behind them, and a stunning woman circled them, followed by eight soldiers. "This is Lieutenant Diobring and his team. We're reporting directly to President Tylio, and she said nothing about you being here, sir."

Caya studied Commander KahSandra and wondered if they were really going to waste time by arguing who was in charge of what. Exchanging a glance with Briar, she didn't have to mentally connect with her sister to realize she was thinking the same thing. Caya saw Briar nod discreetly, motioning with her head toward room four. As Adina and KahSandra faced off over what needed to be done and in what order, Caya and Briar moved stealthily along the wall until they managed to slip inside room four.

"Creator...can you smell that?" Caya crinkled her nose. She was sure she had never encountered that exact odor before. Something chemical and tinged with metal, it made her nauseous.

"I can't smell anything other than regular hospital scents." Briar frowned. "What are you talking about?"

"That foul, sickly sweet smell. Surely you have to notice it?" Caya spoke in a whisper to not alert the ones outside the door of their whereabouts. "It's from over here." She walked to the left part of the room, where the heads of the beds had been before they were evacuated. A multitude of cords, hoses, and different outlets confused her at first, but then she realized the odor came from an outlet marked TPN. "Here. It's from here. What's that?"

Briar joined her and sniffed at the outlet. "You have to be wrong about this, sis. That's where we hook up patients that need complete nutrition via infusions. Total Parenteral Nutrition."

Caya thought fast. If what they were looking for, the white garnet, was in the TPN system, and infused into someone...This couldn't be true. "Either way, the guys in the corridor need to bring their scanners. If I'm right—"

"The whole hospital needs to shut down their TPN lines." Pale now, Briar hurried to the door and called Adina's name. Soon the entire room was filled with KahSandra and Diobring's team.

"How the hell did you slip in here?" Diobring growled.

"Never mind that," Briar said calmly. "Scan this room for white garnet. Even trace amounts can be lethal, so be careful."

"What does she know of white garnet?" Diobring muttered as he and his team took out their scanners.

"More than you, Lieutenant," Adina said and rubbed her lower arm.

Caya shuddered at the memory of how Adina had been seconds from having her arm severed by the volatile substance only days after *Pathfinder* launched. Briar had saved her by adding a neutralizer, something that was standard fleet issue now in the shape of small aerosol canisters. Adina had hers already prepared to administer.

Commander KahSandra pulled out her scanner, a larger, more elaborate tool than what the soldiers had on hand. She ran it up and down the wall, starting by the corner, and when she reached the tubes and outlets, it began to sound a low hum that increased until it literally howled.

"Here." KahSandra pointed at the TPN outlet, and it was her turn to go pale. "I'm reading concentrated amounts, but no corrosion, which doesn't make sense."

"It actually does." Adina joined her. Briar put her arm around Caya's shoulders and approached them carefully. "White garnet has a very slow impact on silicon-lined tube systems like these." She was already tapping furiously at her tablet. "I'm issuing an alert to all medical facilities on *Pathfinder*. Caya's vision showed only this ward at this hospital, but we need to be prepared."

"What happens if someone gets this into their system mixed with the TPN?" Caya asked, nauseous at the mere idea.

"I've never even heard of anything like that," Briar said.

"Sir." KahSandra turned to Adina. "We must study the blueprints and make sure we know exactly where this TPN line has outlets."

"I can tell you that if you're prepared to listen," Briar said calmly, but her turquoise eyes glimmered dangerously.

"Ma'am—you are a civilian—" Commander KahSandra stopped talking when Adina raised her hand.

"Before you step into what you're about to say with both feet, let me inform you that this is Briar Lindemay, also known as Red Angel. She's saved my life twice, and when she speaks, those of us who know her and her abilities also know when to listen."

"Yes, sir," KahSandra said, her lips tense.

"Anyway." Briar motioned toward the TPN outlet. "This goes from the basement straight up through the walls. Each line has its own canister down there. They should all be checked, naturally, but for now, it is this one, and on all the levels."

"What if someone has already been infused?" Caya asked. "I mean, it's early afternoon. If you're on TPN, surely you get some of that stuff at breakfast?"

"Damn." Adina slapped her communicator. "Commander Vantressa to Admiral Heigel."

A brief moment later, Korrian responded, sounding agitated. "Heigel here. What's up?"

"Admiral. A quick question. What will white garnet diluted with Total Parental Nutrition do to a body?"

"What?" It was obvious the question shocked the otherwise seasoned admiral.

"We have a reading suggesting that this is happening through a certain room on the wards directly above each other on the hospital, cube eleven."

"Madam President, you need to hear this," Korrian said, and soon Adina's tablet showed the *Pathfinder* logo and then Korrian's and Thea's faces. Caya stepped to the side, trying to become invisible. If Thea saw her here—it wouldn't be a good thing. And it would distract them all when they needed to focus on the crisis at hand.

Korrian rubbed her forehead with her thumb and middle finger. "Diluting it with any harmless fluid would slow the volatile process. It might even give us a chance to stop this before it goes any further. Let's hope we've caught it in time."

Caya tuned out the discussion, and then a vision of the old, emaciated woman she'd met in the corridor flickered through her mind. Every thought of trying to stay out of Thea's view vanished. "And if it has already entered a body? What would that look like?"

"Depending on how much it has been diluted, it will eventually turn the individual into a living, breathing explosive device." Korrian's voice was hollow. "They would no doubt look close to transparent, as all their veins would be emphasized…dark blue.

Caya groaned and walked over to Briar and Adina. "Adina. The old woman from before. She was from this room. Wasn't she, Briar? You must have seen her and used her, involuntarily or not, as a conduit for reaching out to me so I could find you."

"Yes. The little old Gemosian woman. She was so afraid." Briar blinked.

"We need to find her." Caya was about to rush after the old woman when Thea's voice boomed over the comm system.

"Caya? How the hell can you be in cube eleven?"

"I can explain, but not now. We don't have time. There could be more patients with explosive TPN in their systems. It's not only about this unit. I was wrong. It only *starts* here, but if other people in the hospital have white garnet in their veins, the entire cube, and ultimately *Pathfinder*, is in jeopardy." Caya rounded Adina and met Thea's furious glance. "We need to locate all patients who have been subjected to poisoned TPN. You need to figure out what we're supposed to do with them when we find them."

"She's right," Adina said. "We don't have much time. Depending on the amount of white garnet mixed into the TPN, we may have an hour, or we may have only minutes. Either way, we need to hurry. Commander KahSandra and Lieutenant Diobring's team will accompany Briar and Caya to where they are caring for the ones evacuated. In the meantime, I'll take my engineering team downstairs to test the TPN containers. From there, we should be able to use the computer to track who has been given the nutrition and how much."

"We can do that from here." Korrian looked grimly at them from her tablet. "Just take the samples and let me know the concentration of white garnet. I'll do my calculations accordingly."

"Yes, sir." Adina gave Briar a quick kiss on the cheek and hurried out the door. Caya heard her gather her engineers and disappear down the corridor.

"I can show you which ward received the evacuated patients. Follow me." Briar began to run and Caya bolted after her.

"Quick. Take my hand. I need to make sure we're not forgetting something." Caya reached for Briar, who squeezed her hand as they ran.

"What are you thinking of?"

"Help me extend my range of visions. If the ones behind this had a backup plan and placed white garnet somewhere else apart from in the TPN containers, we need to know, or we might be walking into a trap."

"Clever girl." Briar nodded and massaged the back of Caya's hand with her thumb as she hummed under her breath.

Caya was glad Briar was guiding her, as it was damn near impossible for her to half run and focus on visions at the same time. They simply didn't have time enough for her to stop and seek out seclusion for this. Images scattered, fractured, and reassembled at a furious pace, but no matter how she searched the patterns and examined every part of them, she couldn't find any evidence or hint that the culprits had tampered with anything else. Instead she saw shadowy figures stir with long rods in what looked like metal barrels. She saw them open and close three barrels standing side by side in a room with green walls. When she couldn't find anything else, she let go of Briar and nearly fell over as she was tossed out of her vision, rather than slowly easing out of it like she was used to.

Tapping her communicator, she paged Thea. She could have chosen to talk to Korrian, but the admiral was probably busy carrying out her end of the frantic search. "Caya to Commander Vantressa."

"Caya. Adina here."

"Look for three containers in a green room. As far as my vision allows me to see, those are the only containers they managed to reach. I think the lockdown may have prevented the terrorists from reaching more, if that was their intention."

"Thank you. We're entering the level in question now. Where are you?"

"About to enter the ward where the evacuated are kept." Briar spoke into Caya's communicator. "Be safe, Adina."

"You as well. Vantressa out." Adina's clipped voice showed them how close to disaster they all were.

Behind them, Commander KahSandra paged Korrian asking for information regarding which patients they needed to locate.

"Korrian here. You have eight patients that have received TPN within the last four hours. I put four hours as a safety margin, as I don't think it would be likely for anyone to survive white garnet in their bloodstream any longer than that. I'm sending the list to your tablet as we speak, Commander."

Briar and Caya stood on either side of KahSandra, reading the names. "We can find two of them each." KahSandra waved to Diobring to join them and handed out two names to each of them. "I think you better look for your little Gemosian lady and this young boy." She pointed out the names on the list to Caya, who began moving between the beds.

It didn't take her long to find the old woman. She was pale, and beads of sweat had formed on her forehead. Despite that, she was shivering under her bedcovers.

"Ma'am?" Caya said and loosened the break on the hover function. "I'm going to move you to another location, where we need to treat you. You are having a bad reaction to the TPN solution."

"I think something worse than that is happening to me." The woman looked up at her with her amber eyes appearing like they were on fire. The whites of her eyes were grey-tinted, which made her look like a storybook wraith.

Caya moved the hoverbed over to the door leading out of the ward, where two of the team lined it up with the other beds as Briar and the others located their patients. The young boy was easy to find as well, as he was the only one that young among the evacuated. Like the old Gemosian lady, he was pale, blue-veined, and possessed the same grey-tinted eyes.

"Good job, everybody," KahSandra said and looked at the two rows of four connected hoverbeds. "Admiral Heigel sent me coordinates to a place where emergency medical teams will meet us and exchange their blood volume. Engineers will come and jettison the containers of tainted blood from *Pathfinder* as we work." She motioned for them to start moving.

Caya helped Briar guide the long train of four beds by holding on to the last one. The Gemosian woman looked up at her, smiling gently. "I'm Gioliva."

"I'm Caya. Over there is my sister Briar."

"Red Angel." Gioliva nodded. "She is the revered one. You are the oracle. Some people fear you."

"I know." Caya swallowed hard. "I wish they didn't. I'm harmless."

"That may be." Gioliva coughed and grimaced. "Your power to foresee the future and recollect the past is enough for some to feel threatened. They lack basic honesty themselves, which makes it impossible for them to perceive how strong your sense of integrity is."

Baffled, Caya struggled to keep up with the hoverbeds and listen to Gioliva at the same time. "How do you know this?"

"I don't know how. I just do. One moment the knowledge wasn't there—and then it was. I think it has something to do with your sister. Her power of empathy and insight is amazing."

"Yes." Caya wiped quickly at unexpected tears. "Just rest now, Gioliva. We're going to take care of you."

"You may not be able to rid us of the poison in time."

Horrified at how perceptive Gioliva had become, Caya didn't know what to say. "We're sure going to try. This team consists of the best."

Gioliva merely nodded and closed her eyes. Caya was secretly relieved. Gioliva's whites had now turned almost black.

CHAPTER SEVEN

Thea gripped the edge of the computer console with both hands. How the hell had Caya managed to leave her quarters? Thea knew it hardly mattered right now when so many lives hung in the balance, Caya's being one of them, but she was going to have someone's head when the crisis was over. That head might just be Caya's own if her explanation wasn't satisfactory.

"You're going to make permanent indentations if you squeeze much harder, Madam President," Korrian said absent-mindedly. She was standing next to Thea reading from her tablet.

Thea loosened her grip and clasped her hands behind her back. "Where are we on the TPN containers?"

"I'm receiving the initial reports from the samples Adina and Commander KahSandra have examined. Good thinking of the engineering teams to place basic testing kits in all major structures in each cube. Saves time." Korrian tapped on her tablet, read some more, tapped again, and then put it down with a low growl. "Damn."

Thea waited impatiently. She wanted to shake Korrian, demand information, but she could see the older woman needed to collect her thoughts. Eventually, Korrian turned to her, and the expression on her face made Thea uneasy. "The white-garnet ratio in the TPN is high. Eight point two percent. I've sent orders to jettison the containers immediately. I'm sure Adina has already started the procedure to do just that. But that's not our biggest problem. The eight patients need to go through dialysis instantly, but the dialysis technology is not calibrated to handle white garnet. The instruments need to be adjusted, and that takes time."

"Do we have personnel ready to do that?"

"Yes. I deployed chemical engineers to the hospital as soon as Adina alerted us. According to her initial report, if Caya hadn't actually smelled the white garnet on the TPN outlet, it would've taken us even longer to figure out this…this horrendously evil plan." Korrian leaned against the computer console, her face pale. "I don't know, Thea. I might be getting too old for this."

"Korrian?" Worried, Thea grabbed one of the hover stools and tugged it closer. "Have a seat, Admiral. You're not too old. You're simply reacting like the rest of us. I'm struggling to understand how anyone can do this to another person."

"Yes. And to sick people on top of everything." Korrian rubbed her forehead. "Where would we be without Briar and Caya? We wouldn't know of these sinister new methods if their visions and other abilities didn't show us in time."

Korrian was right. Intellectually, Thea completely understood and appreciated the advantage of having benevolent changers who were all about using their powers for the good of the *Pathfinder* passengers and crew. That said, she was still furious at how stubborn and careless Caya had been when she left her quarters like she did today. Yes, she was with her sister and Adina, but what if someone had recognized her as the normally incarcerated changer?

"Madam President?" Fleet Admiral Orien Vayand, the highest-ranking military officer aboard *Pathfinder,* approached them. "We need to call the military leaders and your cabinet. This new attack means—"

"Is still underway. I'm not leaving the bridge until the hospital in cube eleven is secured. That includes the eight patients as well." Thea raised her chin, knowing Vayand, who was a stickler for protocol, didn't like it when she went off script, something she did every now and then when required.

"Of course, Madam President." Vayand nodded briskly. "I will gather the military chiefs and follow the outcome from the situation room. Let us know when you are ready to join us, and I will have my aide de camp assemble the cabinet members as well."

"Sounds excellent." Thea was taken aback for a moment. Vayand usually was much more rigid and disapproving when she didn't immediately conform. He was a reactionary kind of man, used to how his military career had evolved under the previous, male, president. Now, Vayand seemed unusually subdued, his light-grey eyes looking wary. Perhaps the ruthlessness of the latest attack had gotten to even this seasoned old bear of a man? "Orien." Thea lowered her voice and stepped closer. "This is a dark day in our history. We will get through it, but as I have subordinates that remind me to eat and drink, I expect you to listen to yours when they suggest the same for you. People look to us, not just the ones working for us, but the entire ship. We need to remain calm and strong. That means taking a few minutes when we can to do what we feel we must. For me, that is following the outcome of our effort from the bridge. Please do what you feel is best for you right now. I need your strength."

Vayand eyed her with an expressionless face. "I suppose I can use some of that tea."

Thea smiled faintly. "It really does help." She nodded to the food and drink dispenser at the back bulkhead. "Tea, spicy, six-eight-four."

"Even better with a shot of mogot-brandy." Vayand smirked and walked over to the dispenser. After getting his mug of tea, he raised it to Thea in what she surmised was a silent way of thanking her before leaving the bridge with his entourage.

"Now that was interesting," Korrian said, sounding more like her normal self. "Bringing Vayand down to a level where he actually sounded less pompous and more...real. Amazing."

"Oh, stop it." Thea drank more tea as Korrian checked her tablet again.

"Fuck!" Korrian pushed her fingers into her steel-grey hair.

"What's going on?" Thea stepped closer, fear clawing in her chest.

Korrian looked devastated. "The dialysis process is taking too long. They have one machine ready to go, but two patients."

Thea had to sit down. "They need to sacrifice one of them?"

Korrian tossed the tablet across the bridge and then gripped the sides of the computer console hard with both hands. Bending her head, she breathed deeply before answering. "Yes, but how the hell do they choose?"

❖

Caya sat next to Gioliva, holding the birdlike hand in hers. The woman looked up and over at her every now and then, but mostly she slept. Sometimes, she shuddered and a small grimace of pain or discomfort appeared on her weathered features.

"Are you *sure* we can't give them anything for the pain?" Caya asked Briar, her voice broken. "Anything?"

"No. I told you, sweetheart. With all those foreign agents in their bloodstream, we can't risk adding anything else."

Caya remembered what Briar had told her the first time she asked. If they added yet another chemical to their system, they could set the white garnet off, killing the patients—and perhaps setting off an explosion. "I'm so sorry, Gioliva. You will feel better once you're hooked up to the dialysis machine. I promise."

"Child." Gioliva didn't look frightened, as she had done earlier while she was being evacuated. If you disregarded her odd-looking black eyes that made her green irises look quite diabolical, she seemed serene. Gioliva's voice was strained, and she coughed a few times before continuing. "It really doesn't matter. I've had a long life."

"That's ridiculous. You have many good years left now that we're not far from our new homeplanet. You've gone through hell to get there. Don't give up now." Caya took both of Gioliva's hands. "Just hold on until the machine is ready."

"Caya? Can you come over here?" Adina showed up in the doorway.

"Hang on, Gioliva. I'll be right back." Caya hurried over to Adina and knew instantly something was very wrong. People buzzed around them, running between patients and the dialysis technology.

Two of the patients were ready, and orderlies pushed the hoverbeds to adjoining wards. Everyone worked in silence, which gave the entire unit an eerie feeling, accentuated by the soldiers standing on watch, weapons ready. "What is it?"

"We are starting the dialysis procedure on the fourteen-year-old boy now," Briar said quietly. "It's very last-minute, and we might be too late with him, but everything took longer than we thought."

"But someone said earlier that there was only one machine ready to go. All the others were occupied. I thought he was already being treated. What—" Caya could hardly swallow, let alone speak. "What about Gioliva?"

"She won't make it." Briar wiped at her damp eyelashes. "She's very old and frail to begin with." She sobbed and took Adina's hand. "I'm so sorry, Briar. I know you've taken such good care of her."

"This is crazy. This is just...it isn't right. Just because she's old, she's not...she doesn't count? Is that what you're saying? I've been with her all this time, trying to make her comfortable while she waited, and now you tell me she's not getting her chance?"

"We've asked for additional dialysis machines, but it's taking too long to bring them from cube six, which has the only hospital with the model that can be calibrated for white garnet."

"I fucking hate white garnet!" Caya took a step back and hit her hip on a cart loaded with medical supplies. Furious, she shoved it aside, sending the items on top of it flying across the floor. "This woman. She's the loveliest person you can ever hope to meet. She's been so brave and strong. She deserves to be saved. These terrorists, the ones doing this, they don't get to kill little old ladies that never did anything to them!" Caya was crying now. Briar took a couple of steps toward her and extended her hands.

"Sweetheart. Come here."

"No. No! I'm not a child that needs you to comfort me and blow on my scraped knee. I need to go sit with Gioliva. She should have someone with her." Caya had turned to walk back to Gioliva when Adina's voice stopped her.

"Only for a few moments, Caya." She sounded as stricken as Briar. "We're monitoring her condition as well as the increasing instability of the white garnet in her bloodstream. As you have seen, it is affecting her, one organ system at a time. Once it penetrates the barrier between the arteries and her brain tissue, she'll die. And when she dies, when her heart no longer keeps the blood and the white garnet moving, the white garnet will solidify back into its usual gel form, and the intended explosion will occur."

"Briar?" Caya knew she was chalk white. She could feel her own blood leave her facial capillaries. Briar had a similar look and could only shake her head in sorrow.

"So, what will happen?" Caya trembled but stood so straight her back hurt. "What will you do with her?"

"We're going to transfer her to an empty cannon casing." Adina walked up to Caya and cupped her cheek. "Of course we'll wait until the very last minute, as we're hoping for the dialysis machine from cube six to get here, but when…if, she dies, we need to jettison her instantly. You may not have noticed, but cube eleven is now halfway detached from *Pathfinder*, making it possible to jettison the containers downstairs as well as Gioliva if required."

"I'm going to be with her until the very last second. I've given her my word." Caya didn't want to look at her sister or Adina any longer, or she would lose her resolve. As she returned to Gioliva's side, the old woman looked dazedly at her, her eyes nearly taken over completely by the foreign agent in her body. "Are you in pain, Gioliva?" Caya kept her voice low and soft.

"It's not so bad," Gioliva said, and coughed. "As long as I don't keep my eyes open too much."

"Don't you have anyone we can notify?" Caya had asked once before, but Gioliva maintained she had outlived her entire family.

"No, child. I'm not going to put anyone else through this. I'm quite content, and as I believe in the afterlife, I know I'll meet my husband, my children and grandchildren, on the other side. Don't begrudge me that, child." Gioliva raised her right hand and motioned for Caya to come closer. "Listen. I'm not sure how I know this, child. You were put on this ship for a reason. Perhaps stopping the evil minds behind this particular attack was one reason, but something tells me, this is just the beginning. You have much to learn and even more to do before you're ready. Listen to those who love and care about you. Use your head and your heart when you do your duty toward the people of Oconodos and Gemosis. Do...do..." Gioliva's voice faded and she slurred her next words. "Change... cour—course. Danger. Too many. Too—" Gioliva's hands lay still and she was barely breathing.

"Briar!" Caya cried out, but her sister and two physicians were already there.

"It's happening faster than we realized. Fetch the pod. She needs to get into it now."

Adina was already bringing the pod. Someone had placed a blanket in the stark, empty metal-alloy case normally used to deliver missiles from *Pathfinder*'s cannons. The physicians lifted Gioliva gently and placed her in the pod. They let her keep the infusion, as it stabilized her system.

"Damn. This is a dark day." One of the physicians, a man in his sixties, wiped his forehead. "I never imagined I'd let a patient down this badly, only to jettison her."

"We should do it right away," the other doctor, a young woman who looked apprehensive and frightened, said. "She's unconscious. She won't know the difference."

"You're not touching her," Caya growled. "You're not even laying a finger on her until she's truly dead. You don't know. The dialysis machine could get here in time."

"Hardly likely," the female doctor said and glowered at Caya.

"You don't *know*." Caya put herself between Gioliva and the doctor, placing both hands on the old woman's sternum. She closed her eyes and willed the visions to appear. Gioliva deserved to have someone remember her, her family and her life, no matter what.

Chapter Eight

Thea stepped off the presidential jumper at the gate by the side entrance of cube eleven's hospital. She couldn't count how many times she had been here to visit wounded, including her former husband. It was when she visited Adina just after *Pathfinder*'s departure that she met Caya and Briar for the first time. Adina had been wounded by white garnet at the time, and Briar had saved her. Thea would never forget how Caya's translucent, aqua-colored eyes that seemed to glow from within had mesmerized her. Of course, back then Thea wasn't aware Caya was a changer, which was fortunate, as she most likely would have sent her back in an escape pod.

Now Thea entered the hospital surrounded by no less than twelve presidential guards. Korrian and Meija had arrived minutes earlier and waited in the lobby, and now they accompanied her as they moved toward the formerly evacuated wards. Adina and her team had confirmed the danger was over regarding the TPN containers and the affected patients. Upon hearing this, Thea had insisted on visiting the scene herself. A small inner voice suggested her motives might have a lot to do with Caya, but she had pushed the realization out of her mind and gone into full presidential mode.

Thea walked into the ward. Seven patients were sedated and hooked up to elaborate machines that cleaned their blood and inner organs. Health-care professionals scurried around them checking monitors, all the time casting worried glances toward the doorway at the far end of the room. Muted lighting set the ambience of serenity and calmness, which Thea surmised benefited the patients when they woke up. She frowned. Wasn't there supposed to be eight patients?

Thea had prepared to greet them and commend them on their bravery when she noticed loud voices coming and going. She turned her head toward the doorway that attracted the concern among the staff, realizing the shouting came from there.

"What's going on?" Thea asked, turning toward a woman tapping information into a tablet by the closest patient's bed.

"Madam President," the nurse said nervously. "I'm not sure. I think it has something to do with the last patient of the eight. Some controversy, I believe."

Thea motioned for the guards to get out of her way. "Korrian. Meija. With me." She strode toward the doorway and entered another room, which appeared to be the hub of this ward. Two men stood pressed up against the wall with a bulky machine between them. In front of them, teeth bared and tears streaming down pale cheeks, Caya looked formidable when she gestured wildly and raised her voice so much it nearly broke.

"Too late! Can you understand that you were too late getting here? She's already gone, and if you'd had the sense to use emergency transport instead of the regular cargo jumpers, she might have stood a chance. What the hell were you thinking?"

"Caya?" Thea stepped closer. "What's going on?" She directed her question at Adina and Briar, who stood just behind Caya, looking ready to grab her if she actually launched herself at the two men.

"Madam President." Briar sent Adina a glance, and her lover nodded and put an arm around Caya, who instantly shook it off. Adina remained close.

"We waited as long as we could." Briar spoke in a low voice. "Gioliva's vitals became unstable, and eventually we had to break Caya's connection with her. If these guys had used their heads and procured emergency transport, we might have saved her. Caya was connected to her, trying to stabilize her and keep her calm, but eventually it was becoming too dangerous for her. Gioliva started showing symptoms of complete system failure, and we knew if she wasn't jettisoned immediately after her heart stopped beating, the white garnet would gather and eventually explode. We had to pry Caya away and bring her to the jettison tube." Briar stroked her face with her hand. "Thea. It was bad. Really bad."

Thea glanced over at Caya, who looked like she was about to explode. "Can you take her back to her quarters, Briar?"

Briar shot her a glance that seemed to question Thea's sanity. "I'm grateful if I can persuade her to not kill the orderlies from cube six. They arrived minutes after we had to let Gioliva's body go. Too late."

"Damn." Thea wasn't sure how to proceed. She really wanted to take Caya away from everyone who was staring at her, judging her, but Thea feared Caya's aversion toward her might just make things worse. The crowd of patients and hospital staff was slowly growing, and this she could put a stop to. KahSandra and Diobring rounded the corner just in time. "Commander KahSandra. How about some crowd control before things get out of hand?" Thea didn't raise her voice, but KahSandra nodded and began ushering patients back to their rooms, together with the rest of their team.

As the crowd thinned, Thea began to walk closer to Caya. The two men she was directing her fury at had scurried off with everybody else, and now only the usual inner circle was left.

"Caya?" Thea hated sounding so stern as the young woman looked like she'd been to the deepest crevices of hell. "We need to go back."

"Back." Caya didn't make it a question but more of a statement as she slowly pivoted to face Thea. "She's gone. I had her. I lived through her and kept her going and—Thea?" Blinking, Caya seemed to have a hard time focusing her eyes. "What are you doing here?" Her voice was husky from crying and shouting, and it made Thea's skin tingle.

"I'm here as I wanted to convey my appreciation for everyone's courage. Including yours." Still in presidential mode, Thea hoped her words would set the tone for Caya as well as help her pull herself together enough to go home to her quarters.

"Courage? Yes. A lot of courage." Sounding dazed, Caya swayed where she stood. Thea was closest to her and took two long steps forward and wrapped her arm around Caya's shoulders.

"Don't faint on me now. You need to sit down." She looked up at Briar, who was also struggling to keep herself together. No doubt the poor woman's empathic ability was on overload after so much drama. "Briar. I need a room where Caya can sit down and have something to eat. I suggest you and Adina find a similar room, as I imagine you also need to...recharge."

Briar's expression softened, and she motioned with her hand. "There are some visitors' rooms down that corridor. I'll have someone send for some fruit and chilled herbal tea."

"I can do that," Meija said and put her arm around Adina and Briar. "You two go have a rest. Madam President? Same for you and Caya. Your guards will keep everyone safe and undisturbed. I'm sure Korrian will be able to answer any and all questions the bridge or cabinet members might have for now."

"Come on, Caya. Let's go sit down." Thea nodded gratefully at Meija and managed to take Caya with her. Caya moved as if the gravity plates in the deck had malfunctioned, making it hard to move her feet. Thea kept her arm around Caya's shoulders, knowing if she let go, Caya might either bolt or sink to the deck.

One of her guards scanned the room quickly and held the door open for them.

"We'll be right outside, Madam President." Steadfast, he looked at her and took up his position next to the door.

Thea nodded curtly. "We're expecting a food delivery in a bit."

"Yes, sir." Her guard closed the door behind them, and suddenly it was quiet. Almost too still after all the shouting.

"Come on, Caya," Thea said, finally able to let go of her public role. She rolled her shoulders to rid herself of the ache that had accumulated since she heard of the impending attack. She guided Caya to the two-seat couch and nudged her to sit down. Hoping Caya wouldn't throw herself into yet another rage, Thea sat down and turned, facing Caya. She rested her elbow against the top of the backrest, leaning her head in her hand. Thea was exhausted. Watching this miracle of a woman so lost in her frustration and pain wrung what little energy Thea seemed to have left.

"Talk to me," Thea asked quietly.

Caya raised her head and turned it slowly to face her. "She's gone. I tried to keep her, but I couldn't."

Frowning, Thea did her best to understand. "What do you mean, keep her?"

Caya rubbed her temples with trembling fingers. Her hair lay like a cloud around her all the way to her waist, tousled and messy. Dark-blue circles under her eyes made her transparent irises seem as colorless as water. Caya normally exuded good health and strength, even when she was upset and angry at Thea. Now, she looked like a whisper-thin apparition, fatigued and without hope. The latter frightened Thea most of all.

"I failed to hold on to her. Her soul. Her mind. Her *life*! I kept my hands on her body, skin to skin, and she showed me her life. Every high and low. I met every single one of her loved ones, her friends, and, oh, Creator of all things, her tormentors. She suffered so badly at the Loghian refugee camps."

Thea felt her own soul darken at the thought of the Loghian camps. When the Gemosians' homeplanet was destroyed, the Loghian system had offered to help with the 100,000 refugees until *Pathfinder* could pick them up enroute to Gemocon. The conditions had been beyond horrible, and the stories of the atrocities committed against the Gemosians kept surfacing to this day. Thea hadn't met Gioliva, but to imagine anyone mistreating an elderly woman infuriated her. Still, the other part of Caya's words made Thea nearly crumble.

"You bonded with her? Like you did with me?"

"Deeper. I had to hold on to her to try to save her life. I knew if she died, the white garnet would take over and explode. So I penetrated her mind, searched along every single synaptic connection and…for a moment I became her. I lived her life in the time it took for her to fade away. She was so generous with herself, and perhaps her willingness of bond came from a desire to leave some sort of legacy. I don't know. I don't know anything but that I failed her!" Caya shook so badly, Thea couldn't watch her turmoil and do nothing.

"Come here." Thea pulled Caya into her arms. "You did more than anyone else ever could. I think you did too much. You put your safety and your sanity on the line when melding with someone you weren't previously acquainted with—I know, I know," she said and put up a hand, forestalling objections from the woman in her arms. "You did it for all the right reasons. Because you're you. This is what you and your sister do. You save lives."

"But I'm clearly completely incompetent. Gioliva died." Caya pressed her face against Thea's neck. "She died, and they put her in that awful casing and sent her body into space. Just like that."

"I know," Thea said again, her voice hitching. "They had to. If they hadn't, so many other lives would have been lost." *Including yours.* Thea pressed her lips to Caya's hairline above her forehead.

"I do get that," Caya said. "I feel like I'm going to burst. I have all of her emotions, her thoughts, and no one to share them with."

"Then tell me. Share them with me, Caya." Placing two fingers under Caya's chin, Thea tipped her head back and met her intense gaze without blinking.

A knock on the door stopped them, and Caya tensed immediately.

"Madam President? It's your food cart," the guard announced.

"And it's just me bringing it." Meija's melodious voice came through the door. "May I enter?"

"Yes. Please." Perhaps food and drink would help both of them get through this.

Meija came in pushing a hover cart. Several plate covers showed she had played it safe and brought them all kinds of food and beverages. "Here you go, ladies. This will have you feeling better soon, Caya, darling. You too, Thea. I borrowed two of your guards to help me fetch food for everyone on the team. The hospital staff is doing the same for the patients and each other."

"Good thinking." Thea gestured to the armchair next to her and Caya. "Why don't you join us, Meija?"

"No, thank you, dear. I'm going to make sure Korrian eats something. She's been known to skip meals in a crisis situation."

"Tell her I'll page her later."

"Certainly." Meija bent to kiss the top of Caya's head where it rested on Thea's shoulder. "Poor girl. Eat some. You'll feel better if you do." She nodded to Thea and left the visitors' room.

"Here. Some cold tea?" Thea gestured to the cart before them.

"Yes, please. So thirsty." Caya drank greedily from the mug. "Oh."

"What?" Thea watched with increasing concern how Caya put the mug down and then clasped her forehead. "What's wrong?"

"I can't seem to get her thoughts out of my mind. The images from the refugee camp—they're awful. Horrible." Shaking now, Caya gripped Thea's hands. "Did you know how bad it was?"

"I have read reports and seen some vids of some of it. I think what you're experiencing, having captured this woman's memories, must be worse." Caya slid closer. "Tell me about it." She hoped that would help cleanse Caya's mind. Right now she looked like she was bursting.

"You sure? Those memories aren't pretty." Caya's eyes brimmed with tears. "Then again, Gioliva's story is worth telling. It really should be recorded."

Mentally chastising herself for not thinking of this immediately, Thea let go of Caya with one hand, pulled out her tablet, and tapped it to assume voice control. "Computer. Record conversation. Security level one, code Gassinthea Mila Tylio voice recognition and retinal scan."

Caya didn't start right away. She ate some of the fruit and drank some of the cold tea, perhaps realizing it would take some replenishing to get through Gioliva's memories. She still sat close to Thea, who fought the urge to pull her into a protective embrace. What was it about this young woman that made her act not only out of character, but on a personal level that she had vowed to never do after her divorce? Letting someone close left you vulnerable in all kinds of ways. Thea was the president of the people aboard this ship and would be until the next election. That was her first priority. It had to be.

Caya shifted next to her on the couch and now faced Thea head-on. "Here goes." She closed her eyes briefly and breathed deeply and evenly a few times. Wincing, she blindly felt with one hand in the space between them. Thea took it between hers, not surprised at how cold it was. Caya opened her eyes but seemed to look at something far behind Thea's left shoulder. Then she began to tell Gioliva's story.

CHAPTER NINE

Caya half closed her eyes and prepared to let the inner voice that was Gioliva's take over. It wasn't like being possessed because Caya was still in charge, but she needed to share the old woman's personal story or it might get stuck in her mind and heart forever. She had held Gioliva so very close for a long time, allowing her mind to absorb all the memories while trying to keep her alive. The fact that she'd ultimately failed tore at her, and perhaps it would serve her right to carry Gioliva inside her for the rest of her life. That would drive her crazy, and she wouldn't be of further assistance to *Pathfinder*'s passengers—or Thea.

"Be careful, Caya," Thea whispered and squeezed Caya's hand.

Not quite sure how she was supposed to be careful, Caya clung to Thea. She fixated on the wall behind Thea, and then it was as if she transported through time and place, ending up among barracks, where the rain whipped at her face.

"Move!" a gruff male voice says, and she feels a hard hand push from behind. "How the hell are we going to feed all these people?" a man behind her growls. "There are thousands and thousands of them, and that's just in our sector."

"I know. I don't care what these Gemosians say we're responsible for. I sure as hell have never even been close to red garnet. And if they were so stupid that they used it to mine for minerals on their only moon, that's hardly Loghia's fault."

"I hear you, brother. I think it's their own damn fault that their moon blew up and their planet became uninhabitable. That's what happens to ignorant fools."

Furious now, Gioliva pivots, and the two Loghian guards nearly stumble over each other to stop from trampling her. *"Even if you have none, or very little, empathy for the disaster that has befallen my people, you could at least get your facts straight,"* Gioliva says, her voice steady. *"A Loghian state-owned company sold the red garnet, singing its praises and stating, above all, how safe and stable it was."*

The taller of the guards sneers. *"How the hell would you know anything about that, old woman?"*

"Because until ten days ago, I was the head of my family business. One of the biggest construction firms on Gemosis. I know what red garnet can do, as well as white and black garnet. I also know that the manufacturers on Loghia are ruthless and ready to do just about anything for profit."

"Profit, huh? Croy? Did you hear what little old Grandmother here is trying to sell us?" the tall guard says to his colleague. *"If she's such a big shot, why does she look like a street beggar?"*

"Because I was washed up from the ocean onto a tiny island in the sea." Gioliva straightens her back despite the searing pain. She glances down at her clothes and has to agree she looks ragged.

"What do you want?" the shorter guard asks, sounding exasperated. *"You're holding up the line."*

"Not much," Gioliva says. *"Just that you treat us as you would like to be treated if you were in our shoes. None of us is to blame for the red-garnet incident that destroyed my homeplanet. If we recognize this, we might stand a better chance of understanding each other."*

"Or you can shut your mouth and keep walking, Grandmother." The tall guard chuckles at his fast comeback. He pushes her hard again, and Gioliva would have fallen without a man standing just in front of her catching her.

"Don't even bother with them," the stranger, a Gemosian like herself, says, his voice tinged with dismay. *"We've never been on good terms with the Loghians."*

"There is always hope," Gioliva mutters but has to concede that these particular guards may be hopeless cases.

Caya gasped, and for a moment she saw Thea, who looked so beautiful and had a concerned expression. She wanted to say she was all right and ask if she was able to narrate any part of Gioliva's story, but her vision overtook her senses and sent her back to the Loghian refugee camp.

"I can't take this, Gioliva. You haven't eaten all day." Maloah, the young woman Gioliva has befriended, implores her to take back her evening ration, but she refuses.

"You're pregnant, child. You need this to sustain your little one. He or she is going to be born into this godforsaken place and will need what advantages we can offer him."

"But not at your expense." Maloah wipes at her ever-flowing tears. "It doesn't feel right."

Gioliva is hungry. Her stomach hurts, and just surviving on water of undeterminable quality is not a wise strategy in the long run. The fact remains that she is old. Maloah and her baby have hopefully a long life ahead of them if the Oconodians launch their ship in time. They all count the days until the Exodus ship comes to whisk them away to a bright new future. Until then, Gioliva is determined to help Maloah stay healthy. "Listen. Please make me happy by accepting my gift. I lost my entire family. Every single one. So did you, except for the miracle growing in your belly. Please let me help you keep him safe."

"Oh, Gioliva." Maloah hugs her, and she can feel the baby twist and turn within her young friend.

Back in the visitor's room, Caya fumbled blindly for her cold tea. Thea held the glass to her lips, and she drank, suddenly so parched, she can hardly speak. "Th-thank you."

"Are you sure you can go on?" Thea put down the glass and cupped her cheeks. "This is taking such a toll on you, I can tell."

"Have to." That was all Caya managed to say before she was within Gioliva again.

"Next group!" A female guard barks the order, and Gioliva steps forward together with nine other naked women. Once a week, their barracks go through an inspection. The Loghian claim it's for their own good, but Gioliva doubts it. She sees it as a way for their "hosts" to wield their power and emphasize their superiority.

Now the female guard strolls along the line of shivering women, inspecting them. Maloah stands next to her, looking terrified as the guard stops in front of her, tapping her chin with her sting-rod, every guard's favorite weapon for controlling crowds of Gemosians. Gioliva has heard rumors how painful a sting delivered by such a rod is and how it can actually damage someone of Gemosian descent. Loghians and Gemosians look alike on the surface, but the internal makeup is different enough that such weapons as the sting-rods, which are harmless to Loghians, can be lethal to sensitive Gemosians.

"I can tell you haven't far to go," the guard says now, smiling in a way that makes Gioliva highly suspicious. "You know, having an infant in a camp like this is going to be very hard. Too hard on a girl your age. You have no husband or even family. You won't be able to apply for work in our djorgo-fields. As you know, this is something every able-bodied person must do. Once you've given birth, you are considered able-bodied. We have an agency that places Gemosian newborns with loving Loghian parents."

"What? Give my baby away, you mean? I will never do that!" Maloah starts weeping. "You can't make me."

"Of course not. But you have to be in the field, tending to the djorgo. Your child will starve and freeze to death when you're gone—"

"That's a scare tactic," Gioliva says, furious. "You might have to go into the fields, but you are not without a family. You have me, and I may not be able-bodied, but I'm strong enough to take care of your baby. We will find a way to extract your milk, and I will feed it to your child. Do not *agree to give up your child. This scruple-free*

excuse for a woman—" Gioliva saw the sting-rod swing toward her and knew this would be painful.

Caya fell forward into Thea's lap, moaning at the memory of how the tip of the sting-rod sent fire along every single nerve ending throughout her body.

"Caya! This has to stop. I can't bear to see you suffer like this." Thea stroked Caya's hair back and bent over her. "Please."

"There is only one more part I need to share. I have to, or it might linger with me forever. And Gioliva deserves it. Bear with me, Thea. I beg you." Caya gripped the fabric in Thea's caftan, wrinkling it in her fists as the last vision gripped her.

The little boy sleeps in Gioliva's arms when the strange men storm into the barrack. Gioliva knows instantly it is one of the brutal gangs she's heard of from other people at the food and water stations. Gangs that bribe the guards to turn their heads while they ransack the barracks. They most often do it during the day, when only small children and the sick or elderly are present and everyone else is out in the djorgo-fields.

She quickly tucks Maloah's two-month-old son under the bed, where they have a basket for this purpose, and covers him lightly with a blanket. Praying to gods she often has had reason to question during her long life, she begs for the child to stay asleep and not make a sound. Gioliva has never wanted to believe in the rumors of stolen Gemosian infants, but now she's not about to risk it.

"Line up over here," the man Gioliva surmises is the leader roars. "Don't get in our way and you won't get hurt."

Gioliva highly doubts that but steps out into the aisle, standing at the foot of her and Maloah's bunk bed. She can't remember ever being this afraid. Glancing at the other elderly in the barrack, she hopes they won't cave and tell the looters about the baby. She is even more worried about the eight young children. They won't understand the importance of keeping quiet about the youngest of them.

"So. What do we have here? The men start overturning mattresses, feeling through the blankets for anything hidden. "Damn, it stinks in here. Don't you people ever bathe?"

Used to such insults, nobody in the barrack responds. Clearly it rarely dawns on anyone not living under these conditions that water is a rare commodity, not to mention soap.

"No valuables to speak of, Boss," one of the female gang members says and holds up a small pouch. She eyes the closest child, a three-year-old girl. "This one might bring in a few lodiochs."

Gioliva goes rigid. The little girl's parents are in the djorgo-fields, and all the elderly take turns looking after her and the other children in the barrack. In return, the ones working the djorgo-fields share some of their slightly bigger rations with them. Gioliva refuses to take any food allotment meant for Maloah. She needs to help keep Maloah strong enough to work and feed her child. Now Gioliva looks on in horror as the threatening woman takes the thin little girl and roughly bends her head back with a fist full of curly hair.

"She's pretty for a Gemosian. Teeth are good. These clothes are dirty but of good quality. She must stem from a good family—that will increase her value even if she's a bit old."

"Leave her alone." Gioliva doesn't realize she is the one speaking with such a thunderous voice until the words are out.

"Shut up, old woman," the female looter says and lifts the girl, who now realizes something terrible is about to happen and howls for her parents.

"Put her down," Gioliva says and walks toward the woman holding the child. Thinking frantically of what to say to save the child, she places her hands in the Loghian position for warding off evil spirits. "It isn't safe for you to be that close to her."

"What the hell are you talking about?" The woman runs her eyes up and down Gioliva's slight form and then back to the girl. "She looks healthy enough."

"Looks can deceive. The camp physicians are testing her for a multitude of viruses. As you must be well aware, Loghians are highly sensitive to some of the Gemosian common viruses. This young girl is coming down with something, and she's in the most infectious phase. It hasn't quite broken out yet—but it will." Gioliva does her best to sound ominous and truthful but isn't sure the woman believes her.

The little girl's eyes well up with tears, and as if on cue, her soft little flat nose starts to run as well. The woman drops her unceremoniously on the ground and backs up fast as the child begins to scream. Gioliva hurries to pick up the girl, pressing her close to her. Her heart thunders as she fears the commotion might wake up Manoah's baby.

"Let's get the fuck out of here. And get rid of that," the leader says and points at the pouch of small valuables. "If one of them has some of those pest viruses, we can't risk using anything in here." The woman groans and tosses it on the nearest bunk bed. They leave, slamming the door shut behind them. The baby gives a startled cry under the bed.

Gioliva prays the other children's crying will drown out the baby's wailing; they have all joined in now, frightened at how close one of them came to being abducted. Gioliva holds the girl close to her still as she retrieves the basket. Earlier, she has made knots on each corner of his blanket, and now she tucks one of them into his mouth, hoping he will suck on it. The tiny boy twists his head back and forth and draws a deep breath to launch another displeased howl when the little girl sticks two small fingers into his mouth. His eyes wide, the baby grabs her hand and holds it tight while sucking at her fingers.

Gioliva kisses the girl's head. "How did you know to do that, child?"

"Manoah told me he likes my fingers." The girl shudders. "He can't cry. The bad woman might hear him and come back and take him away—and me too."

Gioliva hugs the children to her, vowing she will give her life rather than let any Gemosian child be torn from their parent and sold on the black market.

Shaking, Caya pushed up, drawing deep breaths. "She did that today. She gave her life to save the others. And she gave of herself to me when I held her and all the time I tried to keep her stable. I calmed her, kept her breathing slowly, tried to help her not panic or give in to the pain as the white garnet traveled through her system. I thought if I could help her remain calm, I'd buy her time."

"You did more than anyone could ever ask of you." Thea stroked Caya's shoulders and captured her gaze. "Please don't blame yourself. This woman, Gioliva, was clearly extraordinary. I wish I'd been able to meet her. And thanks to you, I did, in a way." Thea held Caya gently by her arms. "You are fearless. This is not the time for me to go into how you frightened me today, or punish you, but I want you to realize I didn't take it lightly when I discovered you were not in your quarters." She raised a hand, making Caya shrink as she could tell Thea was struggling to harness a slow burning anger. "You and I both know there was an elevated risk for you to run into someone with a sinister motive." Squeezing her eyes closed, Thea sighed. "But you didn't. Instead we are all grateful to you and Briar for helping save a lot of people, the hospital—perhaps even the entire cube."

"It's not over. This is only the beginning. We haven't found the redheaded woman yet. I'll have to prepare myself for more visions as her fate may have changed because we interfered today." Caya was so tired now, she could barely move. She merely sat there, half slumped against Thea. "Don't you have places to be, people to brief, minions to scare witless?" Caya attempted a faint smile in case Thea didn't realize she was joking.

"I certainly do, but right now, being here with you is more important." Thea pushed an errant lock of hair from Caya's forehead. The touch was whisper-light but still created what felt like a mini bolt of lightning along Caya's nerve endings. This time, the touch had nothing to do with her clairvoyant capabilities, but rather the way Thea had locked her eyes on Caya. When had her expression gone from concerned and reassuring, to this dark, opaquely unreadable gaze?

"I want you to rest before you attempt any more visions." True to form, Thea wasn't asking.

"Sometimes the visions find me no matter how I try to forestall them." Caya worked every day on harnessing her ability to read the future, most of all because she wanted to learn to control it, rather than the other way around. She was getting better at it, but still, some visions forced themselves on her.

"I know. Just don't feel pressured into thinking we all depend on your abilities."

"I'm truly not that presumptuous," Caya said and had to smile again. "But if I can save even one soul for doing the right thing at the right time, I'm going to do it. It's my fate, Thea. No matter what you think, or how you try to protect me, my fate will find me, and my destiny will create a way for me to follow."

Thea looked taken aback. More than that, she seemed stricken. "Are you saying you know your own future? Have you seen your own lifespan?" She pressed her lips together, and Caya wondered if this was to keep them from trembling, but that was assuming too much, surely.

"No. I have never seen my future, other than in relation to visions about other people. That said, I still know, beyond any doubt, that my path is set. I may change minor things, but my destiny is pushing and prodding me along."

"And as you cannot see your own future, you risk everything to save others. Even people you've never met before."

"I should try to find the redhead. I'm just not sure I can manage another vision right now." Caya wished she could, but fatigue made her limbs so heavy she couldn't help but slump against Thea.

"Don't even think about that right now. You need rest. More food and lots of sleep." Thea pulled her closer, her arm around her shoulders. "We'll go back to the governmental building in a little while, but I really want you to relax for a moment first. And honestly, I can use with a few minutes to gather my thoughts." She smiled wryly.

Caya couldn't resist. Leaning against Thea, inhaling her flowery, sweet scent and just letting go of everything she had just been through, felt way too good. She let her head rest against Thea's shoulder, feeling her hair tickle her cheek. This took her back to when Thea was her biggest crush—her first crush, to be truthful. That really hadn't changed, but so much animosity and resentment had gotten in the way, Caya hadn't allowed these softer feelings to emerge. She glanced up, saw how Thea had tilted her head back against the backrest of the couch and closed her eyes, and this was the most human she had seen Thea in a long time. She was normally so strong and untouchable, and to see her like this softened something inside Caya. If she could just run her fingers through Thea's silver-streaked blond hair or caress her cheek ever so lightly…but that was still impossible. Being here, virtually in Thea's arms, was miraculous in itself. Only hours ago, she had been rude and yelled at the woman she had once wanted to please more than anything else. Now they were here, having avoided a disaster—and what Caya needed to do was prepare for more visions to help save the redhead who would lose her life if she didn't.

Caya sighed and shifted against Thea's shoulder. The president raised her head, her eyes once again sharp and probing. "What's wrong?"

"I suppose I need to get back to my quarters. If we're going to find out about the redhead, I need to prepare my system to not fail me. You're right. If I put pressure on myself for more visions when I'm this depleted, I may get a false result and end up failing even more people."

"Failing…?" Thea placed two fingers under Caya's chin and gently tipped her head back. "You haven't failed anyone," she said firmly.

"Gioliva is dead. I couldn't save her." No matter what anyone said, Caya knew this was true, and it ate at her. Still, Thea's hands against her skin soothed her more than her words did, and Caya managed a faint smile. "I will, however, save the redhead—and the soldiers in jeopardy because of the trap someone will turn her into."

"I believe you," Thea said, her voice soft. She studied Caya's features for several moments, making Caya wonder what she might be looking for—and if whatever it was even could be found in a person's face. "All right. I'm going to return to the assembly and my cabinet members. They will want to be debriefed about what took place here today. New safety measures and security routines will have to be put in place." Thea let go of Caya and stood. "You can choose to go back with me and my guards, or with Commander KahSandra and her team."

Caya blinked. That was a first. A choice. "I don't know Commander KahSandra. I'd rather go with you, if that's all right." Did Thea sense how nervous having a choice suddenly had made her? Choosing to go with Thea voluntarily spoke volumes, from Caya's point of view. If she had chosen to go with KahSandra, she would have stated very clearly she didn't want to be around Thea if possible. Would Thea recognize Caya's former feelings for her stirring again—or would she be oblivious to them?

Thea actually looked a little stunned, and then she smiled, a quick broad smile that melted the first thin, icy layer of many around Caya's heart. "Very well then—let's go."

Chapter Ten

Thea stood behind her desk, needing the barrier between her and Adina. She wasn't sure reminding herself of their friendship on a personal level was a good idea. It made her all the more furious.

"Explain to me what possessed you to bypass the presidential guards and take Caya out of protective custody without notifying me...hell, anyone?"

"You have every right to be angry, Madam President. I take full responsibility." Adina, her chief engineer and part of her inner circle, answered calmly, standing at attention.

"That's beyond the point. You know how dangerous it is for Caya to be out among the general public with all the changer hatred raging. Still you risk her life by taking her to a hot zone where we know contraband has been put to its most horrendous use yet." Thea leaned forward on her palms. She wanted to shake Adina, make her understand just how close she was to getting air-locked—at least in the back of Thea's mind.

"Correction, sir. We didn't know anything more than Caya had already told us. And it was her presence, and Briar's, that made it possible for us to save the hospital, its patients, and potentially a big part of cube elven. We can only speculate what eight white-garnet explosions would have done to the ship. Not to mention the three canisters on the lower decks."

"I know this!" Slamming her left palm hard onto the top of her desk, Thea was grateful for the sting it left behind because focusing on that kept her from throttling Adina. "I'm fully aware how much we owe the Lindemay sisters. They're not the culprits here—you are."

"What would you have said if I had checked in with you before taking Caya with me to save her sister? That was our objective before we actually got there. We were just going to go in, find Briar, and get her to safety while security did their sweeps. It was only when we came within close proximity to Briar that they discovered the different clues that led us to the white garnet. They did that together." Adina sighed. "Yes. I was wrong to trick the guards to let her go with me, but as protective as you are about Caya—I'm equally ready to do just about anything to keep Briar safe." Her chin held high, Adina did look contrite but also unapologetic when it came to some of what she'd just said.

"What do you mean?" Thea straightened and clasped her hands behind her back.

"Madam President, Thea…" Adina held out her hands, palms up. "I'm not being presumptuous, I swear, but it's been fairly obvious ever since you decided to not send Caya, or Briar for that matter, to the brig, that you care about her. When she lashes out at you like she's done quite a bit the last few months, it obviously hurts you. That's why you're so furious with me now. I disobeyed orders, but if it were only that, you'd take some professional actions, perhaps even demote me, yet this," Adina said, motioning with a hand back and forth between them, "is personal."

"That sounds fairly presumptuous to me," Thea growled but felt entirely naked, as if Adina had peeled every single protective layer from her. "And yes, this is both professional and personal. As much as we left Oconodos to leave the changer issues there behind us, clearly there were ways for some people motivated enough to come aboard anyway. Fortunately for us, the Lindemay sisters are not only benevolent, but they're beyond ready to assist—to a fault."

"Tell me about it. Briar has worked double shifts for the last two months to set up her private clinic as a counselor. I rarely see her, and when I do, she's too tired to do anything but eat and sleep." Adina smiled wryly. "Yet I'm so proud of her. She's taking her Red Angel status to a whole new level."

"I didn't realize she had gotten that far in her efforts." Thea tugged at her fingers behind her, a habit when she needed to hide her emotions. "I do admire her. I also worry Caya may demand more strongly to move back to your quarters or, worse, to quarters of her own. She doesn't enjoy Briar's amazing reputation."

"I know. Some know she's Red Angel's younger sister, but not everyone does. Perhaps we need to make that public? I mean like a proper interview."

"And draw even more attention to her?" Thea shook her head. She wanted to hide Caya until they reached Gemocon. What they would do about her status then, she wasn't sure, but at least they wouldn't be as cramped for space there. "No. Not yet, anyway."

"Forgive me, Thea, but surely you realize the harder you tie her down, hold her back, the more she will plot different methods to regain her freedom. She just barely had time to make some friends for the first time. She went jumper hopping and got a sub-ink without telling her sister. After living like a secluded sorceress on Oconodos from the day they realized she was a changer until *Pathfinder* launched from the space-dock, she's understandably been acting out the way she does."

"Hmm. You have cleverly changed the topic of our conversation from you going against explicit orders to how I manage Caya's protective custody. What do you think is a fair punishment for what you did today, Commander?" Thea emphasized Adina's title to make her realize they were still in official mode.

"Any retribution you come up with will be fair, Madam President," Adina said and returned to standing at attention.

"If I can harness my anger, and yes, my anguish at finding out what you two did, I just may be somewhat fair. But you're far too valuable to this ship as its chief engineer, and I know Briar would read every last thought I'll ever pass through my brain if I did anything she deemed unfair." Thea snorted and motioned for Adina to take a seat. "At ease."

"Probably true." Adina looked pensive. "I really am sorry we had to worry you so badly, Thea. I can imagine how you must've been absolutely furious as well, especially as you were on the bridge and we were in the thick of it all."

Thea wasn't sure she liked that Adina compared how Thea felt about Caya to how she felt about Briar. Adina and Briar were deeply in love and committed to each other. Nobody in their presence could ever mistake them for being anything but each other's soul mate. Was Thea really that transparent? Did her staff gossip behind her back about her protectiveness when it came to the young changer that a lot of them thought ought to be in the brig—or worse, air-locked? Thea knew the gossip press and the entertainment channels were always ready for any such tasty snippets for their transmissions. Rumors grew fast on a ship as densely populated as *Pathfinder*. For anyone to think a young, beautiful woman had swayed the president was noteworthy enough. If someone got the idea she was making herself vulnerable to the influence of a changer—it would be disastrous.

"We could do something in between, which would actually make our situation marginally better overall." Adina leaned forward, looking energized. "It would make it possible for Briar and Caya to spend more time together, and it would also get Caya out of her quarters on a regular basis. Properly protected, of course," she said and held up a hand.

"And how do you propose we do this?" Frowning, Thea hoped the idea would be doable, as she vividly remembered Caya's calm but sorrowful glance as Thea said farewell and left the guest quarters. For a moment, Thea had gotten the impression Caya was about to ask her to stay longer but stopped herself.

"Watching Caya and Briar pull their abilities together today gave us a hint at what they can learn to do in the future if they're given the opportunity to work together. So, what if Caya joins Briar at her clinic? I mean, we have to ask Briar, but I can't imagine her saying no. This way Caya will slowly, but surely, be known as Briar's sister. The public will see them interact and that Caya is just as caring and honest."

Thea started to decline the suggestion, but she forced her mind to consider the idea and found it brilliant. This might be what they needed to bring some peace of mind to not only the sisters, but also to Thea, who badly needed it as she feared she had only seen the beginning of the second wave of the white-garnet attack.

"Fine. If Briar finds it beneficial to have Caya with her during her sessions, and if Caya is interested, of course, I'm not going to stand in their way. I want to emphasize that Caya goes nowhere without at least three guards."

"Yes, sir." Adina smiled broadly. "I can't wait to tell them the good news. Or perhaps you want to tell Caya yourself?"

"Why would I want to do that?" Thea waved away the suggestion with a flick of her wrist. "You can tell her."

"I think you should deliver the good news for once, Madam President." Wincing, Adina rubbed the back of her neck. "That didn't come out right. I'm sorry. I only meant—"

"That from Caya's point of view I've been nothing but black smoke? That about sums it up, I suppose." Rapping her blunt nails against her desk, Thea gave it some thought. Perhaps it was a good idea after all, for her to offer positive news rather than increasingly more restrictions? "Actually, I will tell Caya." Thea narrowed her eyes deliberately; well aware of the effect it usually had on people. Adina looked suitably awkward, but not pale and sweaty like some of her male peers.

"All right, Commander Vantressa. Go share the news with Briar. I look forward to reports from her regarding their work method and development."

"Yes, Madam President." Adina saluted and left the office.

Thea turned the chair to face the largest view screen that showed the video feed from one of the top-mounted cameras. In the far distance, stars created silver streaks, and she never grew tired of watching the beautiful pattern they created. Some boasted faint colors, sparkly and transparent, much like Caya's eyes. Covering her face, she had to draw deep breaths to calm herself. She wanted to page Adina and revoke Caya's permission to join Briar. Who knew what type of people might seek out help only to use it to get revenge on a stranger? Chastising herself for reacting so strongly to any matter regarding Caya, Thea pulled her hands from her face and smoothed down her hair. It was time for her weekly screen conference with her cabinet members. In the beginning of their journey, they had all come to cube one from their respective home cube, but after several terrorist attacks, she had decided it was too hazardous for them to be in prescheduled transit so often.

Thea cast a glance into a small mirror she kept on her desk. She didn't like how pronounced the dark circles under her eyes had become lately. Poor sleep and constant worry about the terrorists' next move gave her far too many sleepless nights. She had tried sleep medication, but it dulled her senses for the entire day. Thea applied another coat of makeup. "Better," she murmured and began the logon procedure. As the new Gemoconian symbol she'd had a group of reputable artists create began to twirl, she adjusted her iconic ten-row pearl necklace, donned her presidential persona, and pushed all other thoughts aside as she saw the grid of live transmissions. It was showtime.

"Look at this place. It's lovely." Caya stood in the center of Briar's new office. In fact, it looked very little like an office. Instead, it consisted of a small computer console in the far left corner next to a food-and-drink automat, a set of three comfortable armchairs, and a two-seat couch around a low, oval table. The walls were painted in a discreet lilac color, and all the furniture featured different pastel-green hues. "Very calm and serene, which I'm sure serves its purpose."

"Yes, it's supposed to anyway." Briar adjusted the chairs before engaging the lock on them. Most furniture aboard *Pathfinder* was outfitted with magnetic locks. "I'm both baffled and delighted that Thea allowed you to come to the first session with me. Is she starting to mellow some regarding your protective-custody status?"

Caya rested her hip against the desk and crossed her arms. "No. Not really. I think she understands more how I feel now, but she's not convinced I'd realize the potential danger I might be in if I was free to come and go as I please." She crinkled her nose. "After the hospital incident, we have at least been civil, not that I've seen a lot of her. She's busy as we're getting close to the Gemocon sector, I assume." In fact, until yesterday, Caya had seen so little of Thea during the two weeks since the latest white-garnet attack that she would almost welcome a fight just to be in her presence. She could have used a few more opportunities to talk about Gioliva and the residual memories that fluttered to the surface occasionally.

"I can tell you miss her." Briar came over and hugged her. "I was afraid she'd demote Adina after she brought you to the hospital without guards."

"If she hadn't, guards or no guards, you would've been killed, as would a lot of other innocent people. I'm not being conceited. It was when you and I worked in tandem that we managed to find out what was going on."

"Yes. I think that's why my darling is still a commander and you're here now. Thea seems to be really trying to make you happy, even if I'm pretty sure this is killing her."

"What do you mean?" Stepping closer to her sister, Caya frowned. "Why would it?"

"Oh, come on, sis. Thea and you share this amazing connection that not even I can put my finger on. Sometimes I think the two of you are destined for each other like Adina and I are." Briar shrugged. "Other times, I get the feeling she knows you're destined for even greater things and that she goes with her instinct when she insists on keeping you safe. Perhaps it's a bit of both."

Gaping now, Caya pointed at Briar with two fingers like she had when she was younger and wanted to make a point. "You're crazy. She's the president, and it's her job to look out for her citizens. I'm also a useful asset, and she's all about creating opportunities for *Pathfinder*. Keeping me close isn't about anything personal. Well, not the way you're implying, anyway."

"You might be a little blind when it comes to Thea. I mean, you've been angry for a long time, though I admit you seem to have found your equilibrium since the latest attack. So, I'm thinking, perhaps not so blind regarding Thea after all."

"We did talk a lot at the hospital, and I thought she heard me for the first time in ages. It calmed me down, I suppose." Caya wrapped a lock of her hair around her hand. "I'm taking things one day at a time and just pray she doesn't go back to being completely unapproachable again."

"So far so good." Briar smiled. "And speaking of that, I think we're ready for our first client. Let me go get her and also inquire if it's all right that you're here."

Caya nodded and watched Briar go to the door leading to the waiting area. After a few moments she returned with a tall, slender woman in her forties.

"Caya, this is Ameeli. We're on a first-name basis here only to assure privacy. Ameeli, this is my sister Caya. As I told you, she is also a changer, but she receives visions regarding the future. She has also been instrumental in enhancing my empathic ability, and if it is all right with you, we can use this gift in this session with you."

Ameeli, a beautiful woman with blue-black hair and grey eyes, was dressed in flowing trousers and a silk tunic and wore her hair in a tall bun. Now she took Caya's hand and squeezed it gently. "Hi. This really means a lot to me as I've tried just about everything and felt I'd run out of options even before we boarded *Pathfinder*."

"Why don't we all sit down and you can tell us as much as you are comfortable sharing?" Briar gestured toward the sitting area.

They sat down, and Ameeli looked back and forth between them before she began. "I'm married. My husband and I have been together for fifteen years and have three children." Ameeli smiled tremulously. "Two of them are here with us aboard *Pathfinder*. One...our firstborn...remained on Oconodos."

CHAPTER ELEVEN

Caya steeled herself against the gasp that wanted out of her mouth and the jerking of her muscles that would betray her reaction. What could possess them to leave one child behind? She could think of only one thing.

"Our firstborn is our only son, and it hurts so much to think we're adding to the distance between him and us with each minute that passes. My husband claims I cosigned the documents with him, but..." Ameeli began to weep. "But I don't remember doing that. He says I fainted afterward, but..."

Briar held up one hand and pushed a box of tissues toward Ameeli with the other. "I think you need to tell us why you had to leave your son, Ameeli. We won't judge you for having to do so. We just want to help."

Wiping her cheeks, Ameeli nodded. "Our son, Jonno, is fourteen years old, and he's a changer." Ameeli's entire body taut, she couldn't quite face Briar and Caya. She looked ready to shatter at any moment. "His dormant gene made itself known when he was six. We did everything we could to keep him in public school, but it was impossible. Jonno is a fire-starter. He had to be restrained on a daily basis until he was ten years old and able to control his curse."

It was nauseating to hear anyone aboard *Pathfinder* talk about a changer's ability as a curse.

"What do you mean by restrained?" Briar asked, her voice mild. Caya knew her sister well and saw how she had schooled her features into a nonjudgmental expression. She was merely there to listen and be a sounding board for the woman before them.

"Just that." Ameeli wiped at her cheeks with the tissue. "Jonno was dangerous to himself and others. A mere flick of his fingertips would create these tiny blue flames, and even if they were small, they could do a lot of damage in the hands of a scared and excited little boy." Ameeli pulled up her left sleeve and showed her lower arm. This time, Caya couldn't keep from gasping. Scars, some like small craters, some like long, superficial lines, marred Ameeli's skin. The pain this woman had to go through was indeed twofold. Leaving her son behind and sustaining such physical pain and damage by him through the years was a cruel fate.

"I'm so sorry." Briar took Ameeli's hand. "May I read your emotions, Ameeli?"

"Sure," the woman said and clung to Briar. "I was hoping you'd be able to counsel me."

"I will try." Sending Caya a glance, Briar then closed her eyes for a moment. Usually, she didn't have to close her eyes to enter a person's mind, but she said it helped to focus initially. "I can feel your strongest emotion." Briar smiled gently and opened her eyes. "Your love for your children is your strength but also the cause of your greatest pain." She waited and looked into Ameeli's eyes. "I would say the other feeling is a blend of two tough ones. First, you experience perpetual guilt for leaving Jonno behind on Oconodos. He is constantly on your mind, and you can rarely go through even so much as an hour without thinking of him. Even when you are together with your girls and your husband, Jonno's image is imprinted on your mind and in your heart."

"What kind of mother would I be if it wasn't?" Ameeli blurted out and yanked her hand away. "I miss him!"

Briar quietly took Ameeli's hand back between hers. "It was just an observation," she said. "We're not judging you in any way. I promise."

"It's true." Caya thought it best to reassure Ameeli from her end as well, so her presence didn't become detrimental to the purpose of the session.

"The other emotion that comes at me in waves is resentment. I can't see why you feel this way. Can you tell me?"

Ameeli blinked, looking puzzled. She stroked her hair back with her free hand and then shook her head. "The guilt part is obvious, but resentment...I don't know. I mean, I can somehow sense what you mean, but I don't know."

"Does it have anything to do with your husband?" Briar asked cautiously.

"Cryon? No. He's a good father. He's great with the girls, and he's struggled with and for Jonno as much as I have. More sometimes, as I had to take care of the girls when they were babies. If we'd known about Jonno having the gene before he was six, we might not have dared to have more children, but they were born when he was three and five."

"I think you need to unlock the mystery of this strong resentment. It would be easy to chalk it up to your heartbreaking situation as a whole, but I don't read it that way." Briar massaged Ameeli's hand gently. "I think there's more to it, and perhaps it is the key to your deep anxiety."

"I can't imagine what it might be. My husband and I are heartbroken over Jonno, but we both agreed to sign over custody to the Council of Mutant Affairs."

This time Caya barely contained a flinch. A majority of the changers feared and strongly criticized the Council of Mutant Affairs, which was one of the reasons the Exodus operation had been expedited and launched a decade sooner than originally planned. The members of the Council, all of them changers, stood for a policy that on paper looked reasonable but in reality was not. They worked for equality, or so they claimed, but did nothing to address the security issue regarding the changers possessing volatile abilities. Fire-starters, plasma-chargers, freeze-clouders, and acid-smokers could roam freely. Gangs formed, and it was rumored that privately sponsored leagues of mercenaries were gaining ground on all continents. The latter had caused Thea Tylio to demand the Exodus operation to commence as soon as she was elected president. Some said this was how she won the presidential race in the first place.

"That must have been difficult for you." Briar stroked the back of Ameeli's hand.

Ameeli's expression changed into one of confusion. "I suppose. I honestly can't remember much of that day. Cryon says I have blocked the memory since it was so painful. Evidently it was my idea to sacrifice Jonno to save our girls and help them have a better future." Ameeli's tears began to fall again. "No wonder I've blocked it. What kind of mother can even contemplate doing something like that, right?"

Briar exchanged a pointed glance with Caya, who nodded. She also had started to think there was more to this story—probably blocked just like Ameeli said, but the reason wasn't clear.

"Listen, Ameeli. My sister is clairvoyant, and mostly she can see the future in her visions. She found out only recently that she can see brief parts of someone's life, their pivotal moments, if she's allowed to hold their hand. If you want to, she can try to see if we can unblock your missing memory." Briar smiled encouragingly. "It's up to you. There is always a risk with unlocking things the mind rather would not remember."

"I can't feel much worse than I already do." Ameeli looked cautiously at Caya. "That's an amazing ability."

"Thank you. Nothing I can take credit for. I just try to use it for good." Caya moved over to the two-seat coach and patted the cushion beside her. "Actually, I have a better chance to have a vision if you will allow me to hug you."

Ameeli looked stunned. "Hug me?" She looked back and forth between the sisters. "I—I'm not sure."

"I can tell you're apprehensive, but that you also harbor a longing for someone to touch you. Has it been long?" Briar asked the question in a very low voice.

"Yes." Ameeli drew a trembling breath. "I haven't been able to embrace anyone except my girls for the longest time."

"From the day when you let Jonno go?" Caya guessed.

"Yes. I think so." Ameeli took the seat next to Caya and wiped her hands against her trousers. "All right. Let's try it. If I flinch, it's not a reflection on you."

"You will be fine. I won't let you down, Ameeli." Caya slid closer and carefully took the slender woman into her arms, holding her in a gentle embrace. "Just relax. I have you."

Ameeli trembled violently at first, but as they merely sat there and nothing seemed to happen, she relaxed and let her forehead fall onto Caya's shoulder.

Caya closed her eyes hard, willing her mind to search for something connected with Ameeli. She saw flickering images of children, little girls with dark curls running on a lawn, a house with a lush garden, and flowers in abundance. She searched along the perimeters of the harmless memories, and suddenly a jagged lightning bolt set a bed on fire. A young boy with short, wavy hair, looking so much like his sisters it pained Caya, stood a few meters away, grinning.

"Jonno!" Ameeli, dressed in a nightgown and a robe, rushed into the room with a fire extinguisher and put out the flames. "Please, darling. You need to take your medication. The doctor assured us you would be able to control yourself if you take it three times a day."

"I hate the doctor. I'm not sick." Jonno glared at her, and small flames danced in his pupils. "I can control it, Mother. I can."

Gesturing at the bed as she opened a window, Ameeli sighed. "You just set fire to Dimina's bed."

"Because I wanted to," Jonno growled, his voice angry. "She teased me. Called me a freak."

"Oh, darling. She's just six years old. All siblings tease each other."

"I don't. I use my powers instead. It works much better." The young boy laughed now. At the sight of his mother's tears, he didn't seem remorseful at all—instead he had a chilling smirk on his face.

The scene dissolved, and then Caya stood in the center of a posh office. A large desk made of rare umbra-wood dominated the room. Behind the desk a man in his forties sat, sorting through documents on a tablet.

"Cryon and Ameeli—and young Jonno. I am delighted that you've managed to agree on this decision. It will lead to a great future for your Jonno, and he will be able to live among his own where he can thrive and learn how to use his talents to serve our cause." The man stroked back his long, blue-grey hair, and now Caya spotted his gills. Ah, so this was Council Chairman DeLorogan. The infamous water-dweller was in equal parts feared, admired, and loathed, depending on who you asked. She had seen him only on news vids back on Oconodos. Now she virtually stood right beside him, next to Ameeli.

"I'm still not sure." Ameeli, sounding dazed. "I don't want to give up on him."

"Come on, darling. Just sign as we agreed back home. Just sign and Jonno will be all right."

Jonno stood on the other side of his mother, and to Ameeli's surprise he didn't seem as if he was very excited about his new prospects. "Mother? Does this mean I can't visit? Ever?" He frowned.

"Of course you can visit," DeLorogan said and winked at Cryon. "Right, Cryon?"

"Eh. Sure, son. As often as you would like. Sure."

Caya didn't think he sounded truthful, but it was Ameeli's reaction that shocked her.

"How can he visit when we'll be aboard Pathfinder?" Ameeli asked, slurring her speech some. "That's impossible."

"Pathfinder?" Jonno looked back and forth between his parents. "What's she talking about, Father?"

"Great, Ameeli. Now we're going to have a scene as well. Wasn't it enough I had to medicate you for you to see reason?" Cryon glared at his wife. "Just sign so we can get out of here."

"Yes. Better make it quick. Far less painful for Jonno that way," DeLorogan said and pushed the tablet toward Ameeli. "Just a retinal scan and a fingerprint, Ameeli. It's a quick procedure once all the bureaucracy is taken care of."

"But..."

"Ameeli!" Cryon took Ameeli's listless hand and pressed her index finger on the screen. DeLorogan held up a cordless, orb-like *retinal scanner, and Ameeli blinked slowly as the light pierced her right pupil. Cryon performed his part, and as the machine scanned his right retina, Jonno began to weep. The young boy knew what was going on now, Caya could tell. Distraught, she wanted to stop what was happening and let Ameeli take her son home, but she was a helpless observer.*

She watched some people come in and sweep the boy up in a fireproof cloth and carry him off. Cryon looked ill at ease but mainly relieved. Ameeli stood motionless, her eyes glazed with tears that clung to her eyelashes.

"Give her another dose of the rhesolyde. It will make her limited amnesia permanent. You gave her the first dose yesterday morning, right?" DeLorogan hardly glanced at the wailing young boy, but instead focused on the swaying woman next to Cryon.

"Just as you informed me, yes." Cryon rubbed his forehead with the back of his hand. "If she remembers, she's going to hate me, take the girls from me."

DeLorogan smiled knowingly. "Trust me. I've seen this done more than fifty times this last year. No matter which spouse is reluctant to let go of their changer child, this medication is safe and reliable. In the old days they used it in much smaller dosages for burn victims to suffer through treatments and then forget about the pain afterward. It became obsolete when new technology replaced it. We find it works well for our purpose."

"What if the authorities find out?" Cryon looked taken aback. "I mean. If someone tells."

"Who will tell? You who used it on your unsuspecting wife? I wouldn't think so. You have done what is right for your son and what is humane for your family. You can leave this planet now, knowing your son will inhabit it with his changer family—and his descendants after him—all of them changers. It is simply a paradigm shift when it comes to who survives. We, the changers on this planet, especially the leaders on the council, are prepared to give boys and girls like Jonno a future without drugs and incarceration. You are now prepared to create a future for your family."

"*I thought you said he would be thrilled to be among his own,*" Cryon said, looking at the door where the staff had left with Jonno between them. "*He was crying.*"

"*He will be content. Give him some time to realize who his real family is. Not by blood, but by common traits and by the common genetic mutation. He has all the traits of a leader and the ability to put the fear of the Creator into any adversary.*"

Cryon looked dazed, and Caya got the impression he regretted everything but knew it was too late. He put his arm around his trembling wife and pulled her with him. "*Come on, darling. Let's go home. The girls are waiting for us.*"

"*Our girls. Yes. And Jonno?*" Ameeli looked up at her husband, her eyes still filled with tears looking like they were never going to fall.

"*Jonno will be fine. He's with his friends, remember?*"

"*His friends.*"

"*And this was your idea after all, Ameeli,*" DeLorogan said as he walked them to the door. "*You persuaded your husband that this was best for Jonno. Don't you remember?*"

"*Yes?*" Ameeli glanced at the tall man over her shoulder. "*Yes, of course. I wanted Jonno to have friends, to stay with his own kind. That was my decision.*"

"*And you wanted your girls to be safe and have the opportunity to leave Oconodos aboard Pathfinder.*" DeLorogan smiled broadly. "*See? You figured it all out. You knew what would be best for everybody, and you made your husband see that. This was all your doing, Ameeli. That's all you have to remember.*" He turned to Cryon, who had watched the exchange with widening eyes. "*Keep reminding her of this last part when you give her the last injection. If you do it this way, you will never have to fear her blaming you. You can look forward to a calm, normal family life when you reach your new homeplanet. That's what all of this was about, right?*"

"*I don't...Yes. I suppose it was. Yes.*" Cryon walked out with his arm still around Ameeli. Caya ended the vision before she choked on her fury.

As if she felt the vision was over, Ameeli pulled back from Caya but held on to her hands. "That's the most anyone's held me in ages. If nothing else comes from this session, the kindness you radiate is healing in itself. I suppose you are aware of this already?"

"What? No?" Caya glanced at Briar, who merely smiled and shrugged. "But thank you for telling me. I do believe that physical touch in a noninvasive and nonthreatening way is good for all of us."

Ameeli nodded and reluctantly let go of Caya's hands. "Did you see anything of importance in your vision?" she asked shyly.

"I did. I want to make sure, though, that you are ready to examine things you may not recall or that caused you great pain in the past. Remember that you have to go home and find a way to work past it."

Briar moved from her armchair to sit on the small table closer to Caya and Ameeli. "We will schedule as many sessions as you need to get through it."

"But—I know this first one is free of charge…Will it be very expensive if I need more sessions?" Ameeli lowered her gaze. "My husband is wealthy, but I personally don't have enough credits of my own to use for therapy."

"Oh, Ameeli. I didn't inform you properly. Caya and I don't charge anything for our sessions. We do this on a volunteer basis. Don't worry about paying us for a single sec."

Ameeli looked stunned. "Free? Completely?" She clearly could hardly believe her ears.

"Absolutely." Briar patted Ameeli's knee. "Now. Do you wish for Caya to describe her vision?"

Ameeli turned her attention back to Caya, as if searching her face for clues. "Yes. I cannot go on like this. I feel like I'm losing my mind."

Caya tried to look calm and assertive, but in truth, she dreaded telling Ameeli about her husband's treachery. Looking for the best way to share her visions, she concluded that the straight-up truth was the only option. No way of sugarcoating it would make it less painful for Ameeli. Taking Briar's cue, Caya assumed a warm and calm tone as she described what she'd seen Jonno do as a little boy and what Cryon had done toward Jonno and Ameeli—and also against the two little girls who would never truly know their brother. When she finished, Ameeli was quiet and didn't show any emotions. Briar's eyes had darkened to an opaque forest green, which let on how furious she was.

"How could he?" Ameeli spoke to nobody in particular. "He lied to me. Every day since we left Jonno with that horrible man, he's lied to me. Cryon stole Jonno from me and took away not only my rights as a mother, but Jonno's right to decide for himself." So rigid now, she looked like she might shatter, Ameeli shouted the last words. "For each word you spoke when telling me the truth, my memory returned. Not intact, not completely, but enough." Tears began to run slowly down Ameeli's cheeks, but her back straightened and she unclenched her fists, wriggling her hands at the wrists as if to get the blood flow back into them. "He put all that guilt on me. He indoctrinated me into thinking I took the decision to leave our firstborn behind while we moved onto a carefree existence without changers." Ameeli winched and caught herself. "I apologize. That came out wrong."

"Don't worry. That's what most people aboard the ship are after—including us."

"But you're changers yourselves?" Ameeli looked relieved to turn the focus of the conversation on to Briar and Caya.

"We knew I was a clairvoyant changer. That's it. We had no idea Briar was an empath." Caya caressed a few tears away from Ameeli's cheek with the back of her curled fingers. "We wanted to live in peace, without fearing for our lives, just like you and your husband."

"He never looked at Jonno the same after we found out he had the mutated gene. It was as if Jonno wasn't truly his son anymore. Cryon dotes on our daughters and on me too. He never mentions Jonno unless I bring him up first."

"I would wager he carries just as much guilt as you—maybe more." Briar went back to her chair and sat down. "Do you think he would be interested in a session either with you, or alone?"

"I doubt it."

"He might, if you mean to confront him with your true recollection of what took place at DeLorogan's office," Briar said.

"I may want to hold off a couple of days and get my bearings. Perhaps a few more memories will appear now that Caya has unlocked these."

They sat and spoke quietly about Jonno, the chance of more memories floating to the surface, and how Ameeli intended to approach her husband, for another half hour. As they stood to say farewell, Ameeli hugged them both firmly.

"You are amazing women, nothing short of miraculous. I'm not saying that because you have gifts, though they are very useful, but because you radiate such love and kindness. You make me think you have no hidden agenda, no other purpose of doing this than to help. I'm so glad I came."

"So are we, Ameeli. Don't hesitate to refer us to anyone you think might benefit from seeing either or both of us." Briar walked her to the door in the waiting area.

Returning to Caya, Briar beamed. "How's that for a flying start, sis?"

Caya was as pleased as Briar but couldn't quite muster the energy to be as positive.

"What's wrong?" Briar walked up to her, cupping her cheek. "Was it too much for you, all at once?"

"What? No." Caya shook her head. "No, the session has been a success so far. That's how I feel anyway. It was just, I became really nervous about barging into her life and then offering her a truth she may not be ready for. I'm apprehensive about doing this with other people. What if their emotional issues work as the only glue holding them together?"

"Yes. I'm aware of that risk. However, I firmly believe knowing the truth and working on your situation in accordance with it is the only way to truly heal. If you balance your health on the murky tightrope of living a lie, it's going to backfire. With a vengeance."

"Like our situation did for me?" Caya asked, but regretted her stark tone when Briar flinched.

"Yes. You could say that."

"No. No, no. That's unfair of me." Caya hugged Briar. "I'm sorry, sis. You kept me safe and, fortunately for me, off the radar of Council Chairman DeLorogan. I owe you my life."

"I think we both owe each other, but who's counting?" Briar chuckled. "But if you're truly concerned it will take too much of a toll on you to sit in on these sessions, I understand. You have enough on your plate being an advisor to—" Briar's communicator beeped. She tapped it and gave her name.

"Briar? Is Caya still with you?" It was Meija, and she sounded out of breath.

"Yes, she is. We just ended a session."

"I've been trying to page you for a while but understood you might be occupied with a client. Caya needs to get back to her quarters, or perhaps Thea's." They could hear that Meija was walking, as her boots hammered against the deck plating.

"What's wrong?" Caya frowned and rushed over to where she'd hung her jacket earlier.

"Oh, it's bad, Caya. It's really bad. That self-serving, mis-ogynistic bastard." The otherwise so soft-spoken Meija sounded absolutely infuriated.

"Who?" Briar asked.

"Hadler Tylio. The idiot has found the most loathsome way to exact revenge on Thea for divorcing him," Meija growled. "He's written his memoirs and sent preview copies to about twenty-five chosen individuals, Thea being one of them, of course. For some unfathomable reason, Korrian and I received a copy two hours ago. We weren't sure what it was about and read the first two chapters. That was enough. If he can be so horrible to her in such a short text, I can only imagine how eviscerated she'll feel after going through the whole damn thing."

"I need to go to her right this minute, Briar." Caya's cheeks went cold, and she knew this meant she was pale as moonlight. "Alert the guards."

"I'm accompanying you." Briar opened the outer door and signaled the guards, who immediately joined them. "I want to see Adina. She may have gotten one too."

Caya half ran toward the closest jumper gate. She hardly dared imagine how Thea felt right now. She might not want to see anyone. Or she might decapitate Caya for assuming too much. Caya didn't care. Hadler was always bad news, but this time, he had overstepped worse than ever before. Caya was ready to throttle him.

"I'm on my way," she murmured as she tried to will the jumper cart to go faster. "I'm on my way, Thea."

CHAPTER TWELVE

Thea paced back and forth in her private quarters. She had attempted to make herself some tea, but that had ended with the mug hitting the wall with a resounding thud. Unfortunately, she hadn't gained a shred of release from the stress that riled her entire system.

"Fuck you, Hadler," she muttered as she pivoted by the large view screens. She stopped and drew a deep breath. "Computer. Set all view screens to forward-facing outside hull cameras." Within a second space hurtled by, and she hoped this view would help ground her. It often did, but not always. Not when it really mattered. She kept pacing, trying to get a rhythm going, a cadence of her heels against the deck. The diversion worked as long as she was outside of the carpeted area, but as soon as her steps were inaudible, the thoughts of her ex-husband's latest stunt inundated her mind.

She glanced at her desk in the far right corner of the living area. Her computer tablet sat where she'd tossed it. The way she had flung it on the desk in utter disgust, it was a miracle that it still worked. Thea had browsed Hadler's, or his ghostwriter's, text, and knew instantly what he was after. Revenge, by stripping her soul bare of any privacy. He knew her well enough to realize this was what she valued most. She was in the public eye from when she got up in the morning until she went back to bed at night. Writing about personal details, twisting facts just enough to stay reasonably within the limits of truth, he might as well have pulled the skin off her back.

She actually felt raw to the touch. Her only countermeasure would be painful, but she had little choice if she wanted to stop the launch of his memoirs.

The door chime rang, making her flinch. She walked over to the surveillance console. "Identify yourself." She was not in the mood to be polite.

"Thea? It's Korrian. I have Briar, Adina, Meija…and Caya here as well. Please let us in. Or at least some of us…"

No. She didn't want to see anyone. Most of all, she didn't want to explain to anyone what was going on, what in the book hurt the most, or how she had ever come to marry such an awful man. She really didn't. Still, her hand moved of its own volition and pressed the sensor for the door.

Thea motioned for them to enter with a grandiose gesture of her right arm. "Why not? You seem hell-bent on sharing my misery."

"Where's your team?" Korrian gazed around Thea's quarters as she stepped inside. "I would imagine you'd need them to perform damage control."

"Oh, trust me. They are." Thea watched Caya enter. Her guards stayed back in the corridor, nodding respectfully toward Thea before she closed the door. "They're just not doing it here. I sent them back to the office. I would have ripped someone's head off if they'd stayed."

"Oh, my." Meija picked up the dented tea mug. "That bad?"

"Worse." Thea couldn't relax. Her entire body was buzzing, and she didn't know where to direct her fury and embarrassment. "I've only browsed through most of it, but it's a pretentious piece meant to defame me. He refers to me as cold, frigid, and yes, naturally, a product of his fine mind that molded me into the successful politician I am today. How he's been the brain behind all my decisions, how I've asked him for every miniscule detail in my speeches…well, it goes on and on. You can imagine. He has conveniently forgotten about the nondisclosure agreement he signed in the hospital as I filed for divorce. He was pretty high on medication at the time, but plenty of witnesses saw him sign everything voluntarily. That said, his lawyers, I'm sure, will debate this fact and find loopholes *after* the book is published and is a bestseller on everyone's tablet!" Thea began pacing again. "The message stated he has sent it to several people already, and I'm sure they've read it. Eagerly."

"He sent it to Meija and me." Korrian stepped into Thea's path and held up her hands in a placating gesture. "We read a couple of chapters before we realized what he was up to. Once your name came up, we stopped. We're your friends, Thea. No matter what he's trying to do, we're not putting any stock in it. He's a pitiful, sorry excuse for a man."

"I know." Thea's stomach was in knots. "You've known me for many years, Korrian. You too, Meija. We worked on the Exodus project long before I was elected president. You know how meticulously I guard my privacy. Now Hadler has written in great detail about private matters that are nobody else's business." She flung her hands in the air. "Some of the things he writes about are half-truths, and he's angling them, making them plausible. This is a nightmare, and I'm not kidding myself. If his memoirs become available to the public, my privacy is a thing of the past. People are inherently curious. The possibility to learn of a public figure from someone who was once close to them will be too tempting."

"He won't get it published. Once your team makes it clear, to whatever publisher that might be interested in his ramblings, how you regard the matter, they're going to think twice about going against the president." Meija joined Korrian. "Don't underestimate the respect people have for you. If they catch on to the fact he's lying or exaggerating to hurt you, or embarrass you, they'll back off."

"We can't be sure of that," Thea growled. "Briar and Caya can tell you how fast rumors spread around the ship. I would imagine the word is already out that there might be a tell-all book in the works about the president." Pain erupted in Thea's stomach, and she swayed where she stood.

"Creator of all things sacred, Thea." Briar and Adina rushed forward and caught her before she lost her balance. "Have you eaten anything? You're very pale." Briar held Thea's wrist, no doubt feeling for her pulse.

"I had tea and crackers this morning," Thea answered automatically, not quite sure why she allowed them to touch her at all.

"That's more than ten hours ago. At least." Briar nodded at Meija. "Can you program the food dispenser, please? Something light."

"Sure." Meija nodded and walked over to the kitchenette.

"Here. Sit down, Thea," Briar said, and together with Adina they guided Thea to an armchair. "We will figure this out."

Thea slowly turned her head and found Caya standing next to her chair. "Please. Tell me about the session today." She couldn't take more comments and reassurances regarding Hadler at the moment. "Did it go well?"

"I think so. A good start at least. We'll see when our client comes back for a new session—unless she cancels." Caya spoke quietly and knelt next to the chair, leaning against the armrest. "Briar is brilliant when it comes to putting people at ease, and that made it possible for me to use my vision to actually find out the truth for her. It was hard. Infuriating, actually, but it might be the start of acceptance and for our client to forgive herself and her spouse."

"Forgiveness." Thea thought of the concept. Would she ever be able to forgive Hadler? The man had gone from a well-meaning father figure of a husband, to a demanding despot who never stopped complaining to her and about her. When his verbal abuse became physical, it hadn't seemed like such a stretch, and Thea had always thought she could tough it out, deal with it. It took seeing him through the eyes of the Lindemay sisters for her to realize how wrong she was.

"I want to hold you right now, but I'm so angry at that bastard I'm not in full control. I might snap into a vision, and you'd hate for that to happen in front of everyone," Caya murmured, instead patting the armrest as if the touch would transfer to Thea. She glanced toward the others, but they were busy over by the kitchenette and dining area getting some food ready.

Thea wasn't sure how to interpret Caya's words. Did the young woman pity her, or was there something else behind her words? *I want to hold you right now.* Thea felt so raw at the moment, she couldn't think straight. It didn't sit well with her that she actually would have loved for Caya to hold her. Despite her petite frame, Caya was strong and vivacious. The times they had been in close proximity, Thea had sensed how her entire system aligned several times and her world had righted itself. She had chalked that up to Caya's gifts as a changer, but now she wondered if that was all it was.

"Thea?" Caya tilted her head.

"I'm all right. Or I will be once I know where I stand with this. Hadler wrote about things my father shared with him. I knew early on to keep my innermost thoughts to myself around Hadler, but my father saw him as his peer and good friend. He freely discussed everything, including private things about my childhood and adolescence." Thea pressed both hands against her stomach. "No doubt Hadler kept extensive notes through the years."

"The bastard." Caya's eyes darkened to a greyish green. "He never deserved you. Not for a sec."

"I would agree if I didn't sound completely conceited." Thea leaned back against the chair and covered her eyes with her hand.

Caya carefully placed a hand over Thea's other one. She closed her eyes briefly. "I know you're going to stop him. You already have a plan. It's bold. And you—"

"How do you—?" Thea yanked her hand away from her face and sat up straight in the armchair, gripping hard at Caya's hand.

"Easy there, Madam President." Caya put her free hand to her lips. "Shh. I'm not in deep-vision mode. This is just an educated guess based on what I know about you and what I can sense from a mere glimpse at the future. It's all right. Don't get upset," she whispered and rubbed her thumb over the back of Thea's hand. "The others might overhear and wonder. I have a suggestion that might help."

The gentle touch from Caya was a new sensation. Caya actually asking to share an idea before going berserk all on her own accord was equally new. "I'm listening. Tell me." Not thinking about if it was advisable, Thea took Caya's hand between both of hers.

"I could go with you to meet with him." Caya waved to forestall Thea's protest. "I could hold on to him long enough to find something in his past to use against him."

Thea slumped against the backrest again. The *things* Caya was prepared to do for her. "I appreciate it, but I don't want you anywhere near him, darling." It took Thea a few seconds to realize what she had just said. Caya's lips parted and she looked wide-eyed at Thea. "Besides, he fears you and your sister so much, he wouldn't go anywhere near you." Trying to shrug her telltale word choice off, Thea wasn't sure where to look. She focused on the top button in Caya's tunic, but eventually she had to meet the other woman's gaze again. She was struggling for something to say to get back on track when Meija called for them to join the others at the dinner table.

Thea ate without actually tasting much of the food. Meija was a brilliant cook. Korrian could get lyrically detailed when she described how Meija used to cook in the traditional way, using a stove and an oven. At such moments, Meija would just huff and say something about how anyone could easily follow a recipe if they took the time.

"What do you think? Thea?" Korrian nudged Thea gently. "We recall the book from all parties, as it is a threat to national security?"

"He will fight it in court, bringing even more attention to the damn thing," Adina said.

"Adina's right. I need to go another route. Actually, I discussed another approach with Caya earlier. She offered to assist, but this is something I need to do alone."

Caya flinched. "Thea?"

"It's the only thing that might work." Thea clenched her jaws. "I need to hit him where it really hurts, and no, I don't mean physically, albeit that has a certain appeal, all things considered." She snorted unhappily. "I want you all to know that it's because I have friends like you that I can even contemplate dealing with Hadler in this manner."

Korrian looked concerned. "You should run whatever this idea is by your publicist and PR team." She put down her utensils and placed a gentle hand on Thea's shoulder.

"They will do their bit, but when it comes to my ex-husband, I'm the unfortunate expert. His many mistresses have no doubt seen only the side of him he showed me while we were engaged. A perfect, old-fashioned, charming gentleman. Once we married, he turned out to be a completely different person. Not even my father, his friend of many years, knew of Hadler's temper or his…ways." Thea swallowed. She wasn't going to give them any of the sordid details.

"Can you at least share with us what you intend to do? I'm not actively trying to read you, but I can sense your, well, nervous energy, coming at me in waves," Briar said from across the table.

"I'm going to remind him of a few of his less-than-stellar moments during our marriage. He doesn't know it, but I've kept a few recordings. Some video, some audio only. I must have had a bit of a clairvoyant streak myself back then when I decided to put such measures in place."

"Are you saying you have surveillance footage of Hadler Tylio's abuse?" Caya pressed her lips together and gripped the edge of the dining table hard with both hands.

Wincing inwardly at the blunt words, Thea refused to let any of her discomfort show. "Yes. And the penalty for striking a member of the assembly, not to mention the cabinet and a president, is a significant number of years in prison."

"Please let me go with you." Caya curled her fingers in and pressed her fists together. "Or anyone else that truly is on your side. Take *someone*."

"My guards will accompany me, and I'll meet with him at his publisher's office. That way I won't have to submit to this charade more than once. I've made up my mind." Thea looked at her half-empty plate. She just couldn't stomach any more food. "I'm going to page my assistant to set up the meeting now. Do feel free to stay and finish your meal. Thank you for joining me here and showing me your support. It's a good feeling to have such loyal friends."

She stood and casually placed a hand on Caya's shoulder as she passed her. Caya tipped her head back to look up at Thea, her transparent eyes large and filled with worry. "I'll see you later."

Belatedly, Thea looked at the others. "All of you." She automatically adjusted her beads and walked toward the door. Slapping her lapel communicator, she barked an order for her guards before snatching up the computer tablet from her desk and exiting her quarters. She knew Caya had sensed her feelings even if she wasn't an empath.

Thea was out for blood.

CHAPTER THIRTEEN

Are you sure you'll be all right on your own? I can stay over." Briar took Caya by her shoulders and looked into her eyes, probing.

"You don't have to read my mind." Caya shook her head. "I'm going to wait up until I hear from Thea. Or at least I hope I'll hear from her. She's been erratic when it comes to connecting with me, but today I felt she trusted me more than she has in a while."

"Perhaps because you didn't curse and kick at the furniture," Briar said and grinned. "Truly, though. I agree with you. I can sense the bond between you has strengthened. Perhaps this is the beginning of a new understanding between the two of you. I imagine she can use a friend after dealing with that monster of an ex-husband."

"Yes. He's bad news."

Adina had stood quietly behind Briar as the sisters said good night. Now she wrapped Caya up in a hug, lifting her off the floor. "You stay safe now. You and Briar did a great job at the hospital, but it brought you into the public eye even more than before. And people can be inventive."

"Yes, I know. I'm safe here in the guest quarters. You know that, Adina." Caya made a wry face. "And yes, I'm being good about it."

"If not, Thea's going to blame me again and bust me down to ensign—or crewman. I'll be scrubbing the jumper tunnels with a toothbrush for the duration of our journey."

"Ha-ha. More like the hull without a space suit." Crinkling her nose, Caya kissed Adina's cheek. "See you in two days. I look forward to our next sessions. Today was difficult, but I think our method might be good for some people, sis."

Briar nodded. "I do too. Good night, sweetheart."

Caya was about to press the sensor to close the door when movement to her left caught her attention. She saw Lieutenant Diobring relieve her usual evening guard. He dug out a small metal cylinder and swallowed it.

"Lieutenant? Are you on my guard duty tonight?" Caya leaned against the door frame as she studied the handsome young man.

"I am, Ms. Lindemay. After you left your quarters without permission, some of your guards were relieved. That means my team will have to help babysit you until the president deems it unnecessary."

"Are you ill? I saw you taking medication." His obvious annoyance didn't bother Caya. Perhaps he was cranky because he was coming down with something?

"A mere headache. A pain blocker usually does the trick." Diobring shrugged. "I suggest you walk inside and lock your door. It's late."

Now *that* annoyed Caya. She would not be talked down to by any of the guards or anyone at all, for that matter. "I suppose I can just page Commander KahSandra and have her send someone to relieve you, as your headache could impair your ability to uphold your duty."

Stiffening, Diobring pressed his lips together. "No need, Ms. Lindemay. You're quite safe."

"Good night then, Lieutenant." Caya shot him what she hoped was a fierce glance and closed the door. She strode into the bathroom and pulled off her clothes. Placing them into the recycling unit, she stepped into the shower. As a guest in these luxury quarters, she could have as long a shower as she wished and waste energy on water to her heart's content, but she never took advantage of that privilege. Only too mindful of the short two-minute showers allowed for regular people aboard *Pathfinder*, she didn't feel it was fair to use any more time for herself. Sometimes, she did take an extra minute to cleanse her long hair, but mostly two minutes was quite enough.

Caya closed her eyes as the cleansing cycle provided a spray of artificially scented disinfectant soap. Once that was distributed, forty nozzles sprayed at her body from four directions, rinsing her. As the soap and water ran through the perforated flooring of the shower stall to be recycled into energy, Caya chose to dry herself off the old-fashioned, traditionalist way, with a towel.

She browsed her garment program and opted for the clothes dispenser to create a long, turquoise nightgown. It felt cool and silky against her skin, which she liked as her visions often made her feel overheated.

Her door chime rang, making her drop her hairbrush just as she pulled it through her rich mane for one last stroke. Annoyed, thinking it was Diobring with more condescending remarks to get off his chest, she strode toward the door.

"What can I do for you, Lieutenant?" she asked via the communicator, not about to open up for him to gawk at her dressed like this.

"Caya, it's Thea." Thea's voice was as stern and noncommittal as always. "May I join you?"

"Of course." Opening the door, Caya stepped back to let Thea stride past her. The other woman had clearly been at her quarters to change as well. She was dressed in what went for leisure clothes when it came to Thea: light-green trousers and a long, ivory caftan. She stopped short when she turned to look at Caya.

"You are on your way to bed. I apologize. It's too late. This can wait." Thea took one step toward the door but stopped as Caya raised her hands.

"I was hoping you'd drop by. Don't go. Why don't I make us something to drink—"

"Yes. Some Lyumine wine would be lovely."

"As my quarters are outfitted with a wine cellar, which I honestly find rather ridiculous, I can probably scare up a bottle or two."

"I find it just as silly, honestly, but in this case, I think wine is called for. I've spent five minutes in the shower to wash my ex-husband away from my very soul. If I have some alcohol as well, I may just rinse him out of my system permanently."

"Can you tell me how it went?" Caya opened the cabinet that held perfectly chilled wine. She found the Lyumine wine and pulled it out, pouring two glasses for them. "Want to sit here?" She pointed at the tall chairs by the kitchenette counter.

"Why not?" Thea gracefully climbed into the closest chair and accepted the glass. She sipped the wine first, tasting it thoughtfully. "I haven't indulged in alcohol more than a few times while in space. Fleet Admiral Vayand once told me, no matter that we're in an artificial-gravity environment, alcohol is inadvisable in large quantities out here. Not that I've ever been a heavy drinker, but I do admit I've used it to numb my senses when…when called for." She grimaced and sipped from her glass again. "I don't assume you've had much experience with alcohol?"

"No. For a clandestine changer to use alcohol…that's not a good idea. After I revealed my identity, I've had some at functions. Never alone. Briar says that's not advisable. Drinking alone. Honestly, I haven't been tempted."

"She's right. I spent some time alone with a wine bottle, or with my housekeeper's homemade brandy, and it only enhances the loneliness."

Caya tasted the wine. It was smooth and silky, so she could understand why others preferred it. "So. Hadler. Did he escape unscathed?"

"Barely." Thea shook her head. "He was at the meeting, bringing three lawyers and his publisher. It was interesting to watch him change from an arrogant bastard to a pale, trembling idiot."

"Did you have to play the surveillance files for them?"

Thea paled. She twirled the glass of wine in front of her, creating a small vortex in the amber-colored beverage. "I thought at first I wouldn't have to. As soon as I mentioned their existence, I could tell he became nervous. If it hadn't been for one of his attorneys, a woman I think is his latest conquest, in fact, persuading him to 'call my bluff,' as she put it, I don't think he would've dared." Thea followed the rim of the glass with her index finger. She smirked, an unhappy grimace. "He didn't want to lose face, I think. Perhaps he didn't believe I had the surveillance recordings, but perhaps he did and gambled I wouldn't want to share them. I don't know."

"But you did." Caya wanted to put her hand over Thea's but knew it might trigger a vision when Thea seemed to feel so skinless.

"I played an audio recording first." Thea shrugged. "Hadler went pale and sweaty at the sound of him calling out obscenities. I think it was after I became mayor of the capital. He had used rude and offensive language with me before, and as luck would have it, when I set up surveillance, he was really true to form." Thea tilted her head. "Do you want to listen to it?"

Caya winced. She truly didn't but had to be careful. If she said yes, she might come across as curious and sensationalizing. If she said no, Thea might think she didn't care. "I'm afraid I'll kill him next time I run into him, but if you want me to hear it, I will."

"Oh, Creators of all things sacred, I don't want you to hear any vile thing from him whatsoever. He has taken, or I have allowed him to disrupt too many years of my life."

"Yes. He has." Caya couldn't keep from touching Thea any longer. She placed a gentle hand on Thea's knee, squeezing for emphasis. "And you know, if you don't want to play any of the surveillance for me, you can still show me. Will you permit me to attempt a vision from your past again, Thea?"

"After drinking wine?" Thea frowned.

"I've had a few sips. Not even half a glass." Caya smiled. "And this is just between us. I'm interested in everything you've been through, good and bad alike. I would never judge you."

"I know that." Thea patted Caya's hand. "Very well. If you insist."

"I don't insist." Caya blinked. "Well, maybe I do, in a way. Just as you insist on keeping me safe the best way you know how. "

"Point taken." Thea rolled her shoulders as if she was about to enter a prizefight. "All right. Do your thing."

"My thing." Caya stood and pushed at the low backrest of Thea's stool. Her mouth suddenly dry, she parted Thea's legs and stepped in between them well within her personal space. She wrapped her arms around Thea's shoulders and held her tenderly. When Thea's arms came around Caya's waist, she heard Thea draw a trembling breath.

Hadler was screaming. He was so furious, his voice had cracked and his words were hardly intelligible. Thea didn't cower, she never did, which was perhaps not very clever, as it made Hadler rage even more. Now he came closer, his fist close to her face as he spat out what he had to say.

"You think I'm blind? You think I'm fucking deaf? I heard how you talked with the Cornian representative, and you contradicted every single one of my suggestions, of every policy I stand for. You made it clear you don't value anything I have contributed as the Presidential Spouse. I demand respect. I demand you take your rightful place as my wife when we're inside the walls of the presidential palace. Here, I'm the ruler. You—you—are my subordinate here. If you can't fathom that fact, Oconodos is heading for trouble. You will listen to me and carry out my policies if you know what's best for you—and for Oconodos. Even your father knew what I had to offer you. Why else would he have given us his blessing?" Hadler gripped Thea's arms so hard that she feared he might break one of them this time. He was a sparse man, but he was wiry and strong, and most of all, his anger and resentment had no limits.

"Hadler. Listen to me. I never intentionally belittle you. I never say one word against you. The thing is, the Oconodians chose me as their leader, as the president that will be in charge when Operation Exodus begins. That means they expect me to carry out what I promised them during my campaign. They didn't elect you. You are my husband, and a lot of people admire you. But as for policy and how the work will be done, they look to me. Don't fool yourself, Hadler—ah!"

Thea flinched as his fist hit her midsection. He never hit her face. He was shrewd enough to know she had to be able to cover the bruises. As she fell to the floor, she saw the sole of his shoe rush toward her.

Caya tossed her head back, tearing herself from the pain of the vision, and opened her eyes. Sweat dampened her temples, and she hated knowing what Thea had endured for so long. "Oh, sweet Creator. Thea. Thea." She kept holding Thea in a firm hug.

"Caya?" Sounding almost drunk, Thea in turn clung to her, trembling. "How did this happen? How could I see your vision?"

"What's—what do you mean?" Caya cupped Thea's cheek, saw the tears in her eyes. "What did you see?" She didn't understand.

"I…I was there. I saw it happening to you—to me…us. I saw it this time. Your vision. Like a video in my head. I mean. I was myself, but I saw it, felt it, like it was both of us. What the hell?"

"You saw my vision? That…" Caya was now shaking too. "That's never happened before. You mean I transferred my vision to you somehow? It never occurred to me that could be done."

"I don't know how else to describe it. You mean it wasn't like that during your session today?" Thea pushed Caya's hair out of her face and wiped at Caya's tears with her thumbs and then at her own.

"No. Not at all. I would've told you." Caya rested her forehead against Thea's shoulder for a brief moment. "During the session I was merely a spectator. I saw what happened to our client, but I didn't live through it like I just did. He hurt you. Us. Hadler hurt us physically right now."

"Yes." Thea shook her head. "I didn't want that for you. I mean, I didn't want you to have to endure that, even in a vision."

"I needed to. I needed to know what living with him was like for you. I pray I never stumble upon him when no witnesses are around." Caya pulled back her lips in a snarl. "And I'm not joking. I hate him."

"Don't. He's not worth it." Thea wrapped her arms and legs around Caya. "Hold on to me, but for the love of the Creator, don't start anymore visions right now."

"Not likely." Dizzy now, Caya stood in the circle of Thea's embrace. They were still unsettled, but for Caya the reason for her tremors had changed. Thea's scent—a mix of flowers, fresh herbs, and something sweet—filled her senses, and Caya wanted to bury her face in Thea's neck and inhale it over and over. This would, of course, not be welcome. She had to be grateful that Thea needed her close like this right now, no matter the reason. Caya could hardly believe how natural the closeness felt, and all she cared about right now was the way Thea was holding onto her. Gentle but firm, and apparently not in a hurry to let go.

"When I'm close to you, it's as if I can forget about everything else for a moment," Thea whispered. "It's like you ground me, in a strange way. Once I lost faith in the ones I used to trust—my father, Hadler—I never allowed myself to get this close. I knew I was a good judge of character when it came to my professional life, first as a judge and then as a politician. On a personal level, I lost my confidence when it came to friendship. As for a lover? I never even attempted anything remotely romantic. I decided that was over and done with for me…until I saw you for the first time."

Caya was sure she must have misunderstood. "Thea?"

"I know, I know. I infuriate you more often than not, but during times like these, when we can set aside our differences, I…I need them. Like now, I need this. Your touch. Believe me, I'm not crazy. I know very well that I'm too old for you and you're meant for great things, and I would never stand in your way. Not ever. That's why I've been so adamant in keeping you safe."

What? Caya's mouth fell open. What did Thea mean exactly? Afraid to ask, but not afraid to act, Caya let her hands move in gentle circles against Thea's back. "I didn't know you realized I'm on a destined path. Clearly I'm an idiot to not understand that's what this whole setup is about." Gesturing vaguely around the guest quarters, Caya sighed. "I still don't agree with the whole protective-custody reasoning, but I do get it from your point of view." Caya pressed her cheek against Thea's temple. "What I don't understand is what you said just before that. About giving up on having a lover or on romance?" Caya tipped her head back and tried to read Thea's expression.

"You don't know?" Thea looked honestly surprised. Blushing faintly, she rubbed her hands against her trousers.

"No. But I want to. Surely you realize that. Our connection, everything we've been through together so far has showed us it's special. Rare. I have never transferred a vision, not even to Briar, who is my empath sister!" Caya held Thea by her shoulders, on the verge of shaking her. "Am I totally misunderstanding you? Perhaps you weren't talking about me in a romantic concept at all?"

Thea took a deep breath as shadows came and went in her eyes. "Yes, I was."

Caya's heart skipped so many beats, she was afraid it might not resume its steady rhythm, but then it did, only to hammer painfully against the inside of her ribcage. "And you think you're too old."

"I do. I mean, I am."

"And I don't. Think you're too old. I think you're gorgeous. Sexy. Alluring. And tons of other adjectives to that effect."

"Are you sure about that?" Thea murmured, nuzzling Caya's cheek. "There have been occasions when I've thought you felt the same way, or is that wishful thinking on my part?"

Caya thought she might go crazy while trying to navigate the minefield around this woman. "Are you asking if I've ever wanted to be physically close to you?" She felt heat radiating off Thea's slender frame.

"Yes. In a way. I mean, the times we've been in close proximity, I've sensed reluctance in both of us to let go." Thea drew a gentle line with her index finger along Caya's jawline. "Even when you hate me—"

"I *never* hate you. Not even when I'm the most furious and frustrated do I ever hate you. I could never. Not for a sec." Caya noticed only after the fact that she'd placed her palm against Thea's sternum, between her breasts, for emphasis. It didn't seem to bother Thea.

"That's…good to know." Letting her index finger caress Caya's lower lip, Thea tilted her head. Her shoulder-long hair fell to the side, some of it having escaped the chignon, and her eyes were dark, narrow slits. "I've longed to be alone with you, no one to interrupt us or interfere. It seems the people surrounding us are either protective of you or of me. Or both. It leaves very little room for us to ever finish a conversation."

"Or even an argument." Caya agreed. Well-meaning friends, or staff, tried to keep Caya from, figuratively speaking, strangling Thea—and vice versa. By doing so, they left them no room to ever fully reach a compromise. "I've been acting like a brat. Storming off in a huff. I'm sorry."

"Don't be. I've been arrogant and not quite taken into consideration your past on Oconodos."

"Or I yours."

Thea shook her head. "Not the same thing. You may have known Hadler wasn't a nice man, but you couldn't have known any of the things you were privy to in your vision just now. I, however, had a lot more information about your past on Oconodos, but didn't put it into context when it came to your protective-custody situation. Not the same thing."

"Shh." Caya pressed her cheek against Thea's and hugged her. "Don't. Don't talk about that right now. Let's just do this."

"Do what?" Thea's eyes widened.

"This. This exploration to see if there is an 'us,' if the attraction is real and mutual. We're no cowards, Madam President."

Thea chuckled breathlessly. "All right." She slid her fingers through Caya's long hair, combing it gently. "Amazing. Your hair is like moonlight. It glows."

"It does?" Caya spoke against Thea's temple. "Your hair smells like…like candy. Sweet. Fruity."

Thea turned her head and pressed her lips against Caya's cheek. Blindly, Caya turned to capture Thea's mouth with hers. Missing it, she whimpered, "I'm sorry." She tried to pull back.

"Don't be." Thea framed Caya's face with her hands and kissed her lips gently. Over and over, she pressed their mouths together, changing angles each time as if testing how she liked it best.

Caya could hardly believe it. Thea was kissing her, and not like you kiss a friend or a family member. Thea kissed her with passion and as if she couldn't get enough. Parting her lips, Caya tried to make each kiss last longer. Thea must have sensed her intention because she withdrew some, scanning Caya's expression.

"Are you sure?" Thea asked huskily.

"Very sure." More certain than she had ever been about anything, Caya wound her arms around Thea's neck. "Kiss me again."

"Creator…" Thea shoved her hands back into Caya's hair and tugged her closer. Now she deepened the kiss instantly, her tongue seeking entrance to Caya's mouth, something Caya eagerly granted. Whereas the previous kisses had been passionate and exploring, these were erotic and sensual. Caya had never kissed anyone like this, but she knew instinctively how to respond to Thea. Kissing her was such a thrill, so incredibly exciting, and it made her entire body tense. Oddly enough, it also gave her a sense of finally coming home. Not sure if that was a contradiction of terms, and not really caring at this point, Caya explored all of Thea's mouth as her hands mapped Thea's back, arms, and hips.

"I—Caya, please. You're making me so dizzy, I'm about to fall off the stool." Smiling faintly, Thea kissed Caya's chin and followed her jawline to her earlobe. "May I suggest we move to a more comfortable place? Your couch?"

"No. My bed?" Caya's suggestion made Thea flinch.

"That's...that's too soon, darling. Don't you think so?" Biting down on her lower lip, Thea slid off the stool.

"Too soon for what?" Caya blinked. "You wanted to be more comfortable and—"

"And you suggested your bed. I know you're young and quite innocent. Asking someone to come to bed with you is something you need to think about. It suggests...I mean, it can be interpreted in a certain way..." Thea exhaled sharply through her nose.

Caya wondered just how innocent and oblivious Thea thought she was. She had, after all, grown up in a household with a sister who was an outspoken nurse. "Taking you to my bed might be interpreted as if I want us to make love. Which I do. Are you saying you don't?" She studied Thea's expression closely. "It's all right, you know. If you're not ready for it."

"No. Not at all." Blushing now, Thea covered her eyes for a moment. "I'm trying to be mindful of your youth here, and I fear I only managed to sound condescending." She removed her hand from her face. "I just don't want you to think I assume...things." Thea's eyes seemed darker than their usual light blue, and Caya realized how nervous Thea was.

"I think we need each other more right now than we ever have," Caya said. "I may be inexperienced when it comes to the practicalities regarding sex, but Briar believed in openness and honesty when it came to educating me. Besides, I'm not a child." She pursed her lips.

"No," Thea said, her voice still husky. "You're not." She stood and wrapped an arm around Caya's waist. "Bed it is, then. It's been a long day."

"Yes." Caya was in awe of Thea, of being alone with her and of Thea trusting her this much. Still, she couldn't help bracing herself for impact, half expecting Thea to change her mind, return to her quarters, and leave Caya alone here once again. "What about your guards?" Caya glanced at the door. "Are they going to stand in the corridor next to Diobring?"

"Right." Thea tapped her communicator. "Tylio voice recognition, code eighteen nocturnal. Good night."

"Good night, Madam President," a female voice said. "Moldali and Judio are on the first watch."

"Thank you. Tylio out." Stroking her thumb along Caya's lower lip, Thea stepped closer. "Are you embarrassed they know I intend to spend the night here in your quarters?"

"No. Are you?"

"I couldn't care less what they think, but no. I'm not embarrassed. I suppose we have two sets of guards tonight."

"Like you said," Caya murmured and nipped at Thea's thumb with her teeth. "I couldn't care less."

They stepped into the bedroom, where the housekeeper service had already turned down the bed when Caya had been out. Caya wasn't sure how to proceed and felt self-conscious for hesitating.

"Can you unclasp my pearls, please?" Thea turned her back and lifted her hair.

Caya found the miniscule clasp and unhooked it. She carefully handed the famous ten-string set of beads to Thea, who placed it on the vanity by the bulkhead.

"It's a beautiful necklace," Caya said, "but you're even more stunning without it. This way, I can see your neck." The sight of Thea's revealed skin made Caya's mouth water. She wanted to bury her face against Thea's neck and taste it.

"Creator..." Thea whispered. "You look positively voracious."

"Can you blame me?" Caya nodded at Thea's reflection in the mirror. "You're gorgeous." Still standing behind Thea, Caya reached around her and began unbuttoning the silk caftan. Slowly, she undid the magnetic buttons by twisting them and changing their polarity. The caftan she pulled off Thea's shoulders moved like running water and revealed a camisole so sheer, it made Caya moan. She saw the entire outline of Thea's body, including her full breasts that appeared supported by some built-in Nomobedian lace. Caya's nightgown was made of a similar fabric as Thea's camisole, but she also wore a camisole of such fabric, just not as sheer or elaborately woven as Thea's.

Reaching around Thea again, Caya undid her trousers and pushed them down her legs. She realized she was being forward, but if she stopped to hesitate, her shyness would take over, and she would resort to feeling clumsy and out of place. She told herself if she kept up the initiative, she wouldn't disappoint Thea.

CHAPTER FOURTEEN

A fter helping Thea out of her trousers and her shoes, Caya seemed to lose a bit of her momentum. She fiddled with the neckline of her nightgown and gazed at Thea through her eyelashes.

"My turn, I suppose?" Thea kissed Caya lightly and began to pull her nightgown up along her petite body. Caya raised her arms, and the thin fabric slid easily over her pale skin. Thea stood there breathless, unprepared for the vision of Caya dressed in only her underwear. "Are you cold?" Thea murmured. Her small breasts were in full view, and Thea could think of little else but to warm them with her hands.

"Uh. No. The opposite. I'm warm. Hot." Caya's eyes were colorless and transparent, which made them appear luminescent and bright. Thea knew she would never grow tired of gazing into them.

"Hot. Yes." Thea chuckled. "I'll say." She pushed her fingers into Caya's hair and made the amazing tresses billow around her. Caya's hair followed, floating for a second before it landed around her shoulders, its rich locks reaching the small of her back. Thea couldn't take her eyes off the young woman before her. So beautiful, so deceptively fragile. Thea wanted to devour Caya, pleasure her until she gave in and allowed Thea to keep her safe, body and soul. Her uncensored thoughts made Thea whimper inwardly.

Caya clearly didn't want to be the only one half naked. She tugged at Thea's camisole, but Thea shook her head and showed Caya the tiny beads that kept it closed between her breasts and down her stomach.

Caya cursed under her breath, making Thea chuckle as she unbuttoned the pearls from the lace fabric and pushed it off Thea's shoulders. Caya stopped in mid-motion, gasping out loud.

Thea felt her nipples grow even harder and knew Caya's hungry stare rather than the cool air in the bedroom was causing it.

"Oh...I'm...You're amazing." Caya stumbled on her words as she stepped closer.

Thea raised her hands and nudged Caya onto her back on the bed. Caya gazed up at Thea, who had never seen anyone look so ethereally beautiful. Caya's hair lay in a semicircular cloud around her, and her skin virtually glowed, as if silver coursed through her veins. Thea crawled up along Caya, lowering her head every now and then to taste her amazing skin. "You smell divine. Like flowers and...something else. Something dark." The last part surprised Thea, as to her, Caya was pure light.

Thea couldn't remember ever being in such awe of another person—let alone a lover. She placed her hand on Caya's hip and let it slide down her thigh. Tugging Caya's leg up over hers and that way effectively parting her legs, Caya ended up half on top of Thea, who now smiled broadly. Caya rose on her elbow and looked down at her, lips parted as she gasped for air.

"You like it like this, darling?" Thea pushed her hands into Caya's hair again and spread it like a shield around them. "We're in your magical world now. Kiss me?"

Caya moaned and bent her head, capturing Thea's lips and parting them instantly. Thea met Caya's tongue with her own, eager for her taste and the sounds she made as the kiss went on and on and on.

"I want you naked." Thea nipped at Caya's lips. "Come to think of it, I want us both naked."

Caya moaned and nodded. Thea was quickly losing her composure and pushed at whatever fabric she came in contact with, be it her own or Caya's. She knew they were both naked when the unobstructed sensation of Caya's silky skin against her own made her cry out in pure pleasure.

"Caya?" Thea gasped as she cupped Caya's cheeks. "Look at me." Caya opened her eyes a little more than the narrow slits they'd been just before. "I want you so much. I can't think of anything or anyone I've ever wanted more." Thea hoped Caya understood. Right here, right now, with this young woman, Thea could confess to herself that not even winning the presidency had meant more to her. Skin against skin, and gazing at those otherworldly eyes that held such magic, such secrets, Thea understood the truth of her own statement. She was meant to be with Caya. She was certain Caya had a more important and distinguished purpose in her lifespan, but for Thea, no matter how much political power she wielded, from now on, the most important aspect of her life was Caya Lindemay.

Thea caressed Caya's right breast and massaged it slowly. Its pebbled nipple drew patterns in Thea's palm, and she cherished how the small breast fit perfectly in her hand.

"Oh...oh!" Caya whimpered, and the breathless sound caused a gush of moisture between Thea's legs. She couldn't remember when that had happened in someone else's presence. The last few months, she had guiltily envisioned Caya in a multitude of fantasies while tending to her own pleasure, if nothing else than trying to remain sane. Now, with the actual Caya here, Thea couldn't keep from undulating against her young lover. Oh, Creator. *Lover.* Thea moaned and arched her back. "Darling. I need your hand. Please?"

"Show me," Caya whispered and stroked along Thea's body while at the same time reclaiming her mouth. "I..." She kissed Thea again. "I need you to show me how."

"I will. Here." She took Caya's hand and guided it in between her thighs. "You've made me so ready for you." Thea's voice caught, but Caya's steady gaze helped her, reassured her.

"So wet." Caya's fingers dipped in between Thea's slick, swollen folds. "I can feel it. Amazing." Lowering herself farther onto Thea, Caya whispered the words in her ear, her breath hot against her. "What do I do now?"

"Just caress me. Gently at first. If you want to go inside later, I'll show you."

"I know some...of this," Caya whispered. "I've tried it on myself." She trembled more now, her hips rocking against Thea in a way that made her wonder if Caya was aware of it—and of how she was pushing Thea toward her orgasm.

"What did you do when you pleasured yourself?"

"You don't think that's wrong of me...to mention it, I mean?" Caya ran her tongue against Thea's ear.

"Not in the least. So, what did you do?" Thea's mind was already conjuring up images of Caya splayed on her back, here on the bed, bringing herself to orgasm.

"Should I show you, perhaps?" Caya moved farther down and kissed Thea's neck, just below her ear.

"Yes!" Thea arched her back. "Creator of all—yes!"

"I like it like this." Caya pushed two fingers inside Thea and rubbed the heel of her palm against Thea's hard, throbbing clitoris. Thea began a slow, steady rhythm. Fingers in, palm up, fingers retracting, palm pressing down, over and over. "Feel good?"

"Better...than good." Thea tipped her head farther back, moving her hips in tandem. "Holy Creator...oh...oh...Caya..."

❖

Caya couldn't take her eyes off Thea. Glistening from perspiration, her head tossed back against the pillows, Thea keened unintelligible words as her hips danced faster and faster against Caya's hand.

Caya mimicked the movements, pressing her hips forward. Every time Thea moved, Caya rubbed her slick folds up and down Thea's slender thigh. She knew she was going to orgasm soon and wanted desperately for Thea to join her.

Thea's breasts, bigger than her own, moved with the same rhythm, and the temptation became too much for Caya. She caught the closest nipple between her lips and sucked it deep into her mouth, where she worked it greedily with her tongue.

Thea began convulsing only moments later, squeezing Caya's fingers inside herself hard as she came in wave after wave. "Caya, darling...don't let go. Please."

Caya had to let go of the now-bright-red nipple to answer. "I won't. You're amazing, so ama—oh, Creator. Thea…" Going rigid, Caya arched against Thea, shamelessly rubbing her wetness all over her hip and thigh as she came. She wanted to tell Thea how good it was, how supremely fantastic she felt, and how much she wanted her to never let go, but her vocal cords were tied up in knots. All she could do was whimper and moan as she pressed against Thea's sweat-soaked body. Her fingers were still locked inside Thea, and Caya was reluctant to remove them for fear of losing their new, fragile connection.

Eventually, Thea withdrew, slowly separating them as she moved onto her side. Before Caya began to feel too cold, Thea wrapped her arms around her, holding her close as she pressed her lips against Caya's neck. "What…I never would have guessed, no matter how much my mind conjured one hopeful wish after another. I never would have guessed."

Caya returned the kisses, pressing her lips against Thea's forehead, her hairline, her mouth. "Guess what?" She wasn't quite following.

"That you actually could want me like this." Thea wiped at beads of sweat running down her temples, or were they tears? Perhaps both, Caya surmised and hugged Thea even tighter.

"From the first time I saw you," Caya said, her voice not quite stable. "I was yours from that day onward."

Thea's eyes snapped open and she cupped Caya's face. "And the same goes for me, darling. From the first day."

As they lay there, hearts calming and bodies mellowing, Caya absentmindedly dragged a blanket up over them. Thea hummed gently and kept touching Caya's hair, winding it around her hand. Just before sleep claimed them, Caya thought of how everything was going to seem so different tomorrow. Surely taking this enormous step as individuals also meant they were more on an equal footing now?

CHAPTER FIFTEEN

Waking up alone had never hurt as badly. Caya sat up in bed and listened for sounds that would indicate Thea's presence but could hear only the familiar, distant hum that always emanated throughout *Pathfinder*. After such a long time aboard the vessel, she really had to listen hard to distinguish it.

Why had Thea left without waking her? Did she regret their night together? Or perhaps Thea was trying to be considerate and letting her sleep? Still, how could she not realize that waking up alone was difficult after the first time she'd ever made love to someone, and not just someone, to *Thea*, the woman she had dreamed about, fretted over, and generally been so torn up about, she'd gone half-crazy while being locked up.

Caya got up and went through her usual morning routine while debating if she should page Thea, but she opted not to. She refused to start their future, no matter what it might be, by being clingy, needy, and even worse, demanding of Thea's attention. The woman was the damn president. She had more than two million individuals to attend to and a ship to deliver to Gemocon. Caya finished her breakfast and recycled the dishes. She couldn't help but smile at how awkward her sister still was using the recycler and dispensers on a daily basis. As traditionalists, they'd been used to cooking food, doing dishes by hand and laundry in an old-fashioned laundry machine. Briar usually stood well away from the recycler when pushing the dishes through the slot. Caya felt like that sometimes, as if the apparatus would demolecularize her fingertips.

Caya checked the time, as she expected Briar to arrive around ten and realized she had an hour before they needed to head to their clinic. She was excited about who they might see today and if they would get some feedback from Ameeli about the outcome of their first session. As she wondered about Ameeli's relationship with her husband, Caya's thoughts returned to Thea. Their night had been all about increasing passion. Each time they'd made love was more intense than the previous, even if they were growing more fatigued. They had eagerly turned toward each other twice more during the night, hungry for the closeness and connection. The last time, Caya had mapped Thea's entire body with her lips. A small voice in the back of her mind asked if it was as a precaution. Perhaps Thea thought this might be the last time—perhaps she had woken up to reality and changed her mind.

The door chime rang out, making Caya jump. Briar was early. Maybe she wanted to grab some herbal tea before they were off to the clinic. Pressing the door sensor, Caya lost her smile when she saw Lieutenant Diobring.

"Good morning, Lieutenant."

"Good morning. The president wants you to join her by the jumper gate."

Caya's heart fluttered, and she couldn't stop a broad smile from returning. "All right. I'll just page my sister and let her know."

"No need, Ms. Lindemay. She is informed." Diobring spoke fast.

What was up? For Thea to haul Caya out of her quarters with only one guard and take it upon herself to inform Briar—a new emergency must be occurring that needed both her and her sister present. "Where are we going?" Caya asked as she pulled on a long, thinly spun cardigan and stepped out into the corridor.

"Need-to-know basis." Diobring pressed his lips into a fine line as he strode next to her toward the jumper-gate area.

"I would imagine I need to know as I'm actually going there." Annoyed at Diobring's somewhat overbearing tone, Caya slowed down. "What's going on? Another terrorist attempt?"

"I said, need-to-know basis." Diobring sent her a sideways glance, and Caya suspected his impatience was mounting.

She remained quiet as they walked quickly along the corridor. No matter if Thea saw this as yet another demand on Caya's part, she would insist Diobring be taken off the roster as part of her guards. She wasn't comfortable with him being the only one in charge right now, as she normally had at least two, more often four, guards securing her safety.

The jumper gate was not very crowded, as most commuters had already gone to or from their workplace. Caya stopped by the gate that the president and the cabinet members used and which Thea always insisted Caya use when in transit.

"No. Come on. Farther down." Diobring took her by the arm and pulled her along. "We're getting into the tunnel to use an official government jumper car."

"What?" Caya had ridden in one of those several times, and as far as she knew, they weren't located in the far end of the gate. All the military and government jumper cars sat parked in the tunnel bulkhead at the president's gate. "I'm not going into the tunnel over there. That's crazy." She stopped and yanked her arm free. "And just so you know, don't ever lay your hands on me again."

His eyes narrow slits as his anger radiated away from him in waves, Diobring reached for her again. "You're not in a position to make a judgement call on what's safe for you or not. You have to come with me."

"I don't, actually. I may be in the president's protective custody, but I'm not a prisoner of the military or law enforcement. This is not a comfortable situation. I want to return to my quarters. Now." Caya turned around and began walking back. She realized her mistake when two large hands slammed down on her shoulders and pulled her toward the tunnel.

"No. No! Let me go!" Caya called out, hoping some of the people at the jumper gate would react. They did cast glances her way, but naturally, Diobring's uniform assured them he was in command and all was as it should. "I said, let go!" She slapped her communicator over and over, but it only gave a ticking sound and seemed broken. Thinking of Adina's self-defense classes where she had taught Caya how to free herself from an assailer, Caya raised her leg, bent it at the knee, and slammed it backward, trying to aim for the soft cartilage below Diobring's kneecap. She had to have managed a decent hit as he cursed and staggered backward, momentarily letting her go.

Caya didn't wait to check out his condition. She took off down the corridor, about to pass the regular jumper gate when she saw a jumper had come in and, judging from the blinking orange-colored light, was close to leaving. Knowing she took a risk of Diobring catching up with her, she changed her mind and jumped through the gate. She barely squeezed through the closing doors of the closest car. Sliding onto a seat, she looked frantically out the window. To her relief, Diobring stood on the other side of it, slamming his fist against the jumper car. He had to be trying to open the doors, but as the jumper cars had already started moving, the fail-safes would not allow that. Caya stared at the furious man, wondering how she could have trusted him. Suddenly he pulled out his side arm and pointed it at her through the window. Falling back onto the seat, Caya saw the window shatter.

❖

Thea walked along the corridor from the Assembly to her office, listening to her first assistant, Palinda, rattle off messages. She had to force herself to focus, as her mind, if unchecked, would immediately return to Caya as she slept next to her, undulated beneath her, or looked at her with her amazing eyes and said things like "I'm yours," and "Nothing has ever felt this right."

"Madame President? You have a message from Briar Lindemay." Thea's third assistant handed over the special communicator that Thea used for the handful of people she wanted to have access to her at all times.

"Thank you." Thea stepped aside and tapped the device. "Thea here, Briar."

"Now, where have you whisked my sister off to? She and I have clients to attend to in less than fifteen minutes."

"Excuse me?" Thea had been glancing at a tablet, but now she snapped her head up and frowned. "What's that about Caya?"

"I came to get her and she's not home. She has to be out somewhere, because the guards are with her." Briar spoke faster. "The thing is, she was well aware of our sessions at the clinic today. She was excited and wouldn't just forget."

"And I have no idea where she may have gone." Cold dread ran along every bone in Thea's body. "Have you asked Adina?"

"Yes. First of all, she has no idea. Nor do Korrian or Meija."

"No one else has the authority to escort her anywhere. Let me check with the master guardsman. I'll page you right back." Thea handed her tablet over to her first assistant. "Thank you, Palinda."

Paging the master guardsman didn't reveal anything at first. Then he paged Thea back within half a minute, which made her tremble.

"Madam President. The guards at Ms. Lindemay's quarters aren't responding. I've deployed a team to investigate. I double-checked the guest quarters. Nobody is there."

Thea's stomach clenched so hard, she could barely breathe. "Put out an all-ship alert to law enforcement and fleet security officers. Ms. Lindemay is of great importance, not only to her family and loved ones, but to *Pathfinder*'s safety as well. I will page Commander KahSandra to head up the search from here."

"Aye, sir." The master guardsman spoke rapidly. "I'll also put a special unit to locate the team of guards that were on duty last night, as well as the ones that took over this morning."

"There was only one guard last night when I—when I paid a visit to Ms. Lindemay." Thea paced back and forth now, opening and closing her hands to try to get some feeling back in her numb fingers. "Lieutenant Diobring had taken over the guard duty. As I was there, I thought it was quite enough, as my own guards stayed while I was present."

"I see. I'm not sure why Lieutenant Diobring would be on guard duty at all, but I'll look into it, sir."

"Do that, and get back to me as soon as you have something new to share."

"Yes, sir."

Thea stopped in the middle of her pacing and regarded her staff that was patiently waiting for her. She began walking toward them, and her steps suddenly felt heavy. A bad feeling erupted in her chest, and Thea was now sure that no matter what the master guardsman found out, it wouldn't be good. She motioned for her staff to keep walking with her as she paged Commander KahSandra. She briefed the commander on the current situation and gave her a presidential order to take charge. The woman's calm, assertive tone helped instill some calm, but Thea had to confess to herself she was frantic about Caya. Where was she? Was she in trouble, or had she for some unfathomable reason finally escaped her incarceration? After all, she had loathed being cooped up in the luxurious guest quarters for so long.

No. She had to reel herself in. Caya wouldn't have made love to Thea, allowed her to be the first, and told her how much she cared only to disappear without a word. And even if Caya hadn't cared like this for Thea, she wouldn't hurt her sister and her friends. She wouldn't betray the people she had vowed to help. Caya was so ready to help, even when she had been furious at Thea, she had faithfully shared her visions and done her part for the good of *Pathfinder*.

Again, Thea used her communicator, this time to update Briar. It was hard, as Briar was frantic and close to panicking. Luckily, Adina showed up at the corridor outside Caya's quarters to join Briar in the search.

Thea wanted to do something practical to locate Caya but knew others were better equipped. She would have to sit by and wait, carry out her daily routine, until her people reported back to her.

Her communicator beeped as she stepped inside her office. She closed the door behind her, wanting privacy as she hoped this would be Caya and everything would turn out to be a misunderstanding. Instead, it was the master guardsman again, and this time he sounded so somber, Thea's knees gave in and she had to sit down in one of her visitors' chairs before she fell.

"Report." Thea pressed her fingertips against her trembling lips.

"We have found the four presidential guardsmen that were unaccounted for, sir. They were all stacked like cattle in a small storage room six doors down from Ms. Lindemay's quarters."

"Stacked?" Thea tipped her head back. "Are they alive?"

"No, sir. All of them had syringes sticking out of their necks, sir. Madam President. It was done execution style. I've never seen something so callous. Crimes of passion, yes, horrific sights. But this...Someone got rid of them like garbage."

"Did I know any of them, Master Guardsman?" Thea hoped not. She wasn't sure if she could remain calm.

"One. A young woman, Guardsman Vimini. She was usually on your night shift, sir."

"Yes. I know who you mean." This was worse than anything she could have imagined. "Guardsman Vimini was a dutiful and conscientious woman who never took a chance on anything, always double-checking. Triple-checking, most often."

"Yes. She was one of the best of the new ones." His voice stark, the master guardsman spoke quietly. "I've turned the crime scene over to the law-enforcement agents. They are aware of Caya Lindemay's disappearance. They're looking at it from several angles."

Thea's communicator beeped again, signaling another page. "I'm being paged, Master Guardsman. I have to let you go."

"As am I. It might be a joint message, sir."

"All right. We'll talk more later, Master Guardsman."

Thea changed frequency and answered the page. "Commander KahSandra here, sir. I have new information from witnesses at the jumper gate. Some who stayed behind just to report what they witnessed have disturbing new information. I wanted to relay it to you, the law-enforcement agents, and the master guardsman simultaneously to save time. The witnesses all describe a similar scenario, individually. A man fitting Lieutenant Diobring's description came to the jumper gate with a young, blond woman. Most of the witnesses identified the woman as Caya Lindemay right away as they recognized her from the reports of the terrorist attack at the hospital on cube eleven. Diobring apparently hurried Ms. Lindemay along and then started pulling her in the opposite direction, onto the tracks. Ms. Lindemay began to resist and managed to get away from him. She entered one of the jumper cars just as it was closing the door and began to leave. Lieutenant Diobring then pulled out a sidearm and began firing through the walls of the jumper car."

"Oh, Creator of all things cherished," Thea whispered. She wrapped her arms around her waist and bent over, certain she was going to be sick. Her stomach burned as if she'd swallowed an entire bottle of pure white garnet.

"And Caya?" she managed to whisper huskily.

"No sign of Ms. Lindemay. The jumper cars in question are on their way back for the next full route, and we'll hold them here until forensic agents have gone over them. If—if Ms. Lindemay has been injured, there'll be traces of blood."

Only by pressing her hands so hard against her mouth she was likely to bruise herself could Thea prevent a whimper from passing her lips. She pulled herself together after drawing a few breaths. The others listening in came with advice and questions, giving her time.

"Someone aboard the jumper had to have seen her. What about the surveillance at the jumper gates? There are cameras aboard the cars, right? I want to see every single piece of footage of Caya when she's on the jumper cars." She knew her stark voice didn't leave any room for objections.

"Yes, Madam President," Commander KahSandra said rapidly. "I will page you once my unit has rerouted all the different camera angles to your office. It won't take long, sir."

"Good. And keep at it. You all know why it's imperative that we find her. We can surmise the terrorists are behind this, but we need confirmation. How did Diobring pass all the screening and become part of my inner circle among the military? Was he coerced, paid, what?"

"Senior Agent Tarason here, Madam President," a gruff male voice said. Thea vaguely remembered a short, stocky man with white hair. "Both our agency and the military overseers will scrutinize Lieutenant Diobring's motives."

"Good. Report back to me every fifteen minutes, or more often than that, if something of importance occurs. Anything, *anything* regarding Caya Lindemay is of importance. Do I make myself clear?"

Affirmative answers echoed over the communication system.

"Madam President, before we go, there's one more thing," Senior Agent Tarason said. "Before we even learned about Ms. Lindemay's attempted abduction, we received intel about a locale where individuals have been gathering regularly. I've deployed agents to investigate. It's our first major break since the last attack at the hospital."

"I will await your report on that matter as well, Agent Tarason."

They closed the communication conference, and Thea remained seated for another full minute before she rose and rounded her desk. She didn't want to remain in her office while everyone else searched for Caya. Thea wished she could just leave and be part of the search, walk along the corridors, streets, and squares, look through shops, libraries, and every hospital bed aboard *Pathfinder*. She turned her chair away from the door, since doing so made her feel a little more private.

Thinking of Caya made her vulnerable. It took her away from being the president and allowed her to just be Thea, a woman in love with another woman. She only had to close her eyes to see the image of Caya in the early morning, asleep while lying on her stomach, her amazing hair covering most of her face and half her back. Thea had carefully nudged the hair away, pressed a gentle, lingering kiss on her temple. She had never seen anything or anyone more beautiful in all her life than Caya Lindemay sleeping, entirely spent after a night of making love.

Forcing herself back to the present and its grim reality, Thea turned her chair back to face the desk and the door. Her people had their work to do, and she had hers. She was just pulling up her list of messages on her computer tablet when her communicator beeped again. Her heart began to race as she answered.

"Madam President, Admiral Heigel here." Korrian's tone, official and stern, made Thea square her shoulders and stand up. There was no chance of this being good news.

"Go ahead, Admiral," Thea said.

"We haven't received proper telemetry from our next buoy, but we assumed it was a malfunction, nothing else. Now we have good reason to believe it has been sabotaged. This means we cannot communicate with Gemocon until we're in range of the next subspace buoy."

"What else will go wrong today?" Thea rubbed her temples, as a tension headache was spreading like fire through her mind.

"I know, Thea." Korrian's voice grew milder. "Any luck finding out where Caya is?"

"None so far. I'm hoping surveillance will pick up on her or her sister will manage to pinpoint her location via her abilities. She's completely unprotected out there."

"Perhaps Red Angel needs to make a public appeal?" Korrian asked.

"It might come to that if I don't hear anything within the very near future. As for the buoy problem, is it possible to deploy a team to retrieve it?"

"No. It takes far too long for the ship to break out of magnetar drive. We're collecting what data we can from it, as parts of it are still functioning. I'll have more for you shortly."

"Good." Thea thought about the ramifications regarding their domestic issues as well as the intergalactic ones. "Korrian, we also need to ask ourselves why it was sabotaged, and by whom."

Chapter Sixteen

Caya stood at the far end of a public restroom, washing her hands. When someone opened the door, she pulled up the hood of the coat she had changed into. It was a rather threadbare, mid-calf-length coat, and the young woman who had owned it previously had not thought twice about switching it for Caya's light-blue caftan. Caya knew people were looking for her, some of them benevolent, but some of them with harmful intent. She was afraid she wouldn't be able to tell the difference in time if they spotted her.

Caya wore her trademark long, blond hair in an austere updo. She didn't look anyone in the eye but kept moving, trying to find a place to induce a vision. If that happened where anyone in the general public, or worse, any of Diobring's associates, found her while she was in the throes of one—she'd be vulnerable and unable to defend herself. She had thought she might be able to do it here, in the bathroom, but too many people came and went in here. Caya simply wouldn't be able to focus.

Stepping outside, she kept her hood up. The coat touched the back of her calves, and Caya was grateful it covered almost her entire body, more or less. She could still feel the stinging sensation when the window had shattered just above her when Diobring fired. Caya had glimpsed his face before he shot at her, and the blank stare in his eyes gave her cold shivers just thinking about it. Who could have gotten to Diobring, such a high-ranking officer in the fleet, and turned him into a traitor?

Caya wanted to page her sister more than anything, but the first thing she did after the jumper car left the gate was to destroy her communicator. If Diobring had culprits among his subordinates, they could use it to track her. Caya hardly dared think about Thea. She could only imagine how this might affect her. If only Thea had woken her up before she left. Perhaps Caya would have opted to go with her into work and wait for Briar there? It was a fruitless thought, but Caya was trying not to end up in the middle of a full-blown panic attack, and wishful thinking was one-way if not very practical.

She walked along the streets of cube fifteen, where she was positive she didn't know a single person. Nobody paid attention to her as everyone went about their day and had little time to notice one lonely young woman roaming the streets and alleys. Caya was getting hungry and looked for a public food dispenser, available to everyone. All the cubes boasted restaurants, mainly in the squares, where you had to barter or use credits to eat, but the simple food dispensers ensured that nobody went hungry aboard *Pathfinder*.

Two blocks farther down the street, Caya saw a line to a food dispenser and tried to look inconspicuous. She adjusted the hood and kept her eyes turned down, well aware of their unique coloring.

"Hello there," a woman said from behind her, making Caya jump. "Just stay calm. I wish you no harm. You're in danger of being discovered, but I can help." The woman spoke so quietly, Caya could barely make out what she was saying.

"I think you mistake me for someone else," Caya said and tried to sound indifferent.

"Shh. We don't have time to go back and forth trying to convince each other. I know who you are, and if you don't want to end up in the hands of the people you've kept us safe from, Caya, you need to come with me. Wait until you get your food and then follow me."

Caya wondered how far she'd get if she began running. The woman behind her had a nice, reassuring voice, but that meant nothing.

"Who are you?" Caya didn't even attempt to protest. It seemed futile.

"I will tell you everything, but we need to hurry once we have our food. We can't let the military find you. I'm sure you realize the lieutenant must have had help."

Caya's heart thundered, and she wanted badly to find a place to hide. More than that, she wished she were back with Thea, or Briar, and not alone in a cube where she had nobody to turn to.

The man in front of Caya nodded politely at her as he stepped away with his food. Caya looked at the machine but couldn't even raise her hand to press the sensors.

"Let me help you." The woman spoke again and stepped up to stand by her side. "Vegetables and dolzi-rice sound good?"

"Sure." Caya glanced sideways and gasped. A thin, red-haired woman dressed in white trousers and a blue tunic stood next to her, and she wasn't the stranger Caya had thought she was. As she accepted the food boxes, Caya could only remain as if frozen in time while the woman she had seen dead by the terrorists' hands in her vision received her food.

"I can tell you recognize me," the woman murmured. "It's all right. I knew you would. Just walk with me, please. She smiled casually and nudged at Caya to start walking. "Please."

It was Caya's best option all day. She walked next to the woman, unwilling to speak and prepared to bolt if she had to, trying to memorize which streets the woman used to reach her destination. Eventually, they stopped by a row of smaller quarters. The woman pressed her hand against a sensor and let it scan her retina. It opened, and she nodded for Caya to step inside.

Cautiously, Caya stopped on the threshold and glanced around the room. Two young men sat on a couch, both holding some game cards. They looked up at her and flinched, both of them frowning at the red-haired woman next to her.

"Tomita? Who's this?" the man to the left asked.

"It's her. Finally." The woman called Tomita put her boxes on the table between the men.

"What?" The man to the left sat up straight. "You mean *her* her? Caya Lindemay?"

"Yes. I couldn't believe my own senses when I felt her on my way to the dispenser. I mean, what are the odds?"

"Who the hell is talking about odds? I've been burning my potion ever since the hospital incident," the man to the right said.

Caya couldn't fathom how they knew her name or that it was her, and what were they talking about? Potions? Senses? What was going on? Just as she was about to head for the door, make her escape, and hopefully disappear into the narrow alleyways, an unavoidable vision hit her. She fell to her knees, dropping her boxes of food, but she was too far gone into her vision to hear them hit the floor.

The man on the left and Tomita were running through a jumper car, calling out to Caya to follow. She ran after them, calling out warnings, asking them to stop, but they merely waved her on, telling her it wasn't too late. They could still save the people, but she needed to stay back. Caya knew they couldn't, knew it in her heart, but she kept running after them, hoping against every sign hinting at the opposite that it wasn't. Then everything went black, and she was in limbo for several moments.

Hands held her, pulled her up into an embrace. The vision changed, moved backward like a reversed video. Tomita, although much younger, stood outside what looked like a learning facility, her face pressed to the bars in the fence.

"Come on, my girl. No need to wish for what we cannot have." A woman pulled at Tomita. "You too, Aldan. Neither of you will ever be accepted into a school like that, and you have to accept it. You will know so much more about life than these privileged children. Once you learn to make the most of your gifts, you will do more for the Oconodians than they ever did for you. It's not fair, but it's reality."

Tomita looked longingly at the children playing in the schoolyard. "But…"

"Tomita. You're going to help save them one day." The woman, perhaps their mother, began walking, holding one child by each hand. "My predictions are never wrong, and that's why we must start preparing how to get you aboard one of the Exodus cubes someday. If we don't, hundreds of thousands of Oconodians will die."

The vision ended so abruptly, Caya cried out and held her head.

"Caya? Caya? Are you all right?" Tomita called from a distance, and this time Caya knew she was back in the quarters.

Gentle hands lifted her and placed her on a soft surface, perhaps a bed or the couch. Caya opened her eyes slowly, afraid she might have a migraine coming on, as that sometimes happened when a vision was this violent.

Tomita sat on the side of the bed where they had placed Caya, placing a cold washcloth on her forehead. "There, Caya. You'll be fine. That vision was massive, wasn't it?"

"You're changers." Caya sat up and the washcloth fell away. Tomita took it and placed it against the back of Caya's neck.

"Yes, of course."

"But...but how?" Caya wasn't afraid. Somehow as soon as she'd figured out they were indeed changers, her fear of being assassinated or otherwise hurt went away.

"I would imagine in a similar manner as you and Red Angel. A well-placed bribe and a genetic resequencer and there you go—changed records. I'm Tomita Gochia." She pointed to the man on the right. "This is my brother Aldan," she said, then indicated the man on the left. "And this is Foy, his husband. I'm a tracker."

"What's a tracker?" Caya's brain still felt thick and slow.

"Interesting that you don't know." Tomita tilted her head. "You have been quite sheltered, or so we hear. Anyway, a tracker is just that. I can pick up scents, traces, and literally any sign available that most others would miss. I tracked you for an hour to establish your identity. Your hooded coat fooled most people, I'm sure, but for someone like me, you're easy to find."

"I see. And you move around outside, completely unprotected? How does that work?" Caya asked. "Aren't you worried you will be found out?"

"Every day," Foy said grimly, but we have a mission and a strong conviction that we're nearing the moment when our services will save the Oconodian and Gemosian people."

Foy, a tall, gangly young man, moved with economic, measured movements. Caya was reluctantly intrigued. "What's your gift?"

"I'm a master telekinetic. That means I'm not just a telekinetic, but I attended underground changer education back on Oconodos, which helped me perfect my abilities. So did Aldan, and that's where we met. He's a potion master and charmer. He would be the first one to claim he's a charmer in every sense of the word, but that's his ego talking. We got married right after school, and when Aldan and Tomita's mother died in one of the riots, we stuck together to be able to carry out her plan."

"We had no idea at first how to proceed without Mother." Tomita bit into her lower lip. "She was our seer. Without her to guide us we've been flying blind. Then we learned of you and your sister. It was such a revelation as you're a seer as well."

This was almost too much to process. Caya sat there on the bed, looking back and forth among the people in the room. They were slightly older than she was, but not by much. The two men both had open and honest faces, not that this in itself meant very much when it came to someone's reliability. Caya had learned to trust her vision and the knowledge and intuition that came from them. These three were fighting the good fight. Unlike the terrorists who didn't think twice about hurting anyone to reach their objective, Tomita, Aldan, and Foy were ready to do anything to keep the people aboard *Pathfinder* safe. Then there was the fact that Tomita was indeed the dying woman Caya had seen in her vision, but here she was, alive and well. "I saw you dying." Caya didn't bother with niceties. "When the hospital was attacked, I saw you dying."

"I almost did. Aldan and Foy found me, and they have connections as they work at one of the smaller hospitals. They managed to get a friend who is a doctor to help me. That white-garnet solution…It nearly killed me, and if I never have to live through that pain again, that's fine with me." Tomita pulled up her shirt and showed two scars that looked like they had been stitched up rather than fused. "We had to use a bit of a mix of traditionalist medicine and new technology, but at least it's proof of what I went through."

"I'm glad you're alive." Caya rubbed her forehead. She had a headache, but not a migraine, which was a blessing. "I was attacked today. I barely got away."

"We know. Our contact at the governmental building was actually at the gate when the guy with you started firing. Our friend tried to get on the same jumper as you to help you, but he couldn't get to it fast enough." Tomita poured a glass of water. "Here. Drink some. If you're like us, you get thirsty after your vision."

"Yes, I do." Caya drank some water. "And this friend of yours, is he a changer also?"

"Yes. He's a receiver."

"A what?" Caya put the glass down on a small shelf by the bed. "A receiver of what?"

"Of any transmission. He has learned to filter out irrelevant conversations, and he's very accurate these days. This has made it possible for our group to keep tabs on you."

"Not to mention the other group you're such a proud member of," Aldan said acerbically and sat down at the foot of the bed. "I wish you'd never done that. If they find out you're alive, you won't just be a target again. You'll draw attention to the rest of us."

"I know. Good thing nobody knows you're my brother." Tomita had paled.

"What are you talking about?" Caya looked back and forth between the siblings. "What group?"

"I managed to track and infiltrate a group that turned out to be one of four sleeper cells. And yes, before you ask, they sure aren't sleeping now. They were not aware of their purpose when they boarded the ship with their families, but now they are. One of their tasks is to recruit enough members to double their numbers. After I did some major playacting, they bought into my story and made me a member." Tomita sighed and ruffled her red bangs.

"Wait. What sleeper cells?" Her stomach in cold knots now, Caya pulled her knees close and wrapped her arms around them.

"Sleeper cells consisting of ultra-powerful changers and their sponsors. I'm sure you must have seen something about them in your visions?"

"I have seen groups of people, shadowy, like through a haze. I never know who they are, nor do I see any faces or where they're located."

"That's because of the shelter-minds." Foy sat down next to his husband and looked kindly at Caya. "They can block other changers, like you, who possess amazing perceptiveness, and Tomita, who can track like nobody I've ever seen. The fact that you have seen them at all shows the level of your power."

"Then what happened? After you became a member?"

"I learned a lot about them, but then I got too cocky. When I had to attempt to alert the authorities, I blew my cover...and they caught me. As punishment, and a means of eradicating me, they injected me with white-garnet-infused TPN." Tomita shuddered.

"Do the authorities know of them, these sleeper cells?" Caya swallowed, wondering how many of these people were out there, merely waiting to prey on the innocent passengers aboard *Pathfinder*.

"They are aware of the threat. They call them terrorists, which fits well, but I don't think they know just how organized they are—and definitely not that one in each cell is a particularly powerful changer. We call them super-changers. We have debated how to alert the authorities to the sleeper-cell situation, but we're torn." Aldan looked gravely at Caya. "That's where you come in."

"What do you mean?" Caya wasn't sure she liked where this was going. She needed to find a safe way to get back to Thea and to work with Briar.

"Like we told you, we lost our seer. We need you to take her place, or we won't be able to fulfill our destiny. We have to keep *Pathfinder* safe and help her reach her destination. Time is running out, and for you to appear here is an amazing sign. Your visions will be enhanced by Aldan's potions—which are safe to ingest, I assure you—and together we can get to work." Tomita took Caya's hand. "You can probe my past as much as you like to learn the truth. Aldan and Foy as well."

"I already did. Some." Caya looked into Tomita's bright-green eyes. "I just can't understand how many changers can exist aboard right under the noses of the authorities. I was sure Briar and I were the only ones. Kind of arrogant, I suppose."

"Not really. We all live in our respective realities. You were sheltered and homeschooled. We were sent to underground changer schools by a mother who was a peace activist. We all have our perspective, and our prejudices, I suppose." Tomita shrugged.

Caya knew Tomita was right. This was one of the reasons Thea and she had fought their feelings for so long, or part of it at least. Now when Caya saw Thea as an equal, instead of an iconic president on a pedestal, she also understood the toll being the president took on her—and why she had to make unpopular and hard decisions when she really didn't want to. Caya rested her chin against her knees as she hugged her bent knees even harder. "These super-changers… do you know the identity of any of them?" The repercussions of what they were telling her made Caya nauseous, but if she didn't get a handle on what they knew, she'd be of no use to Thea and *Pathfinder*.

"I was only allowed into one meeting, and by then they had donned their masks. I had ingested one of Aldan's subduing potions so they wouldn't peg me as another changer. That meant I couldn't put any trackers on them." Tomita looked apologetically at Caya. "From what I saw, they consisted of ten women and ten men—one leader from each cube—and they referred to each other by that number. I also heard rumors about a woman, a changer with mythical powers called Grand Superior. This topic was forbidden, but people are people, no matter their background. Gossip is popular. The fact that nobody on our levels ever saw her, or heard anything that might hint at her identity, showed what a grip the leaders have on their members."

"Yet you feel quite safe telling me all this?" How could these three be so sure they could trust her?

"You're Caya Lindemay. You're the one the super-changers refer to as the Seer, the changer they want to get their hands on to use against the president."

"I would never allow that to happen." Caya stood, too jittery to sit still on the bed. "I would rather die than betray the president or the people aboard *Pathfinder*."

"I think they know this, which is why they hoped to spring this surprise attack on you and take you in before you could self-terminate out of sheer loyalty." Aldan rested his chin on his palm. "We have to find a way for you to return safely to President Tylio's side. As we don't know if more guards than the one that attacked you are compromised, you need to take an obscurity potion."

Caya was ready to do just about anything to get back to Thea and her sister. She wanted to talk to Briar about what she'd just learned. More than that, she needed to inform Thea and help devise a plan to take down the super-changers and their…what did Tomita call them? Their sponsors?

Foy looked pointedly at Tomita. "She needs to learn about the orb before we do anything. It belongs to her now, as only a seer can harness its power."

"I know." Tomita sighed. "It's just that it's been a part of my mother for so long. When I hold it, I can feel her even if I can't make the orb enhance my gift."

"What orb?" Nonplussed, Caya watched as Aldan pulled out a drawer hidden in the bulkhead beneath the bed. He removed a large box and placed it between them.

"This is yours now, Caya." He opened the lid and pulled back a silky golden fabric. Something that looked like a stone orb, its diameter approximately twenty-five centimeters and its surface rough and crackled, lay among the fabric. "Pick it up. It's the only way to find out if we're right."

Nervous now, Caya placed her hands on the orb, only to yank them back when the stone object began to hum. "It—it moved."

"Excellent," Tomita said, her eyes welling with tears.

Caya gathered her courage and picked up the orb. It hummed faintly and felt oddly warm and smooth against her palms. As she turned it in her hands, it emanated a low tone and began to glow. First it was barely visible, and then the sound increased and the glow became a bright light.

"Hold it over your head," Tomita said and stood.

Caya did as Tomita suggested and held it up on straight, slightly unstable arms as she sat on the bed again. The tone turned into a piercing whistle, and yet another vision hit out of nowhere. She froze, and the last thing of the present she saw was how the orb rose to hover above her palms. Gentle hands guided Caya to lie down. The orb spun faster as her mind went to that place where the future waited.

Smoke was everywhere. Caya coughed at the acrid taste it forced into her mouth and down her airways. Alarm klaxons blared, people ran in panic, some carrying people with burns or broken limbs. Pressing her back to a bulkhead to stay out of the way, Caya felt how Pathfinder *shook and stomped beneath her feet.*

Tearing herself out of the vision, Caya gripped the orb between her hands. "We're going to be too late. We need to make our way to cube one. I have to talk to the president, and the three of you have to be there as well. I need to borrow one of your communicators while we're in transit." Caya turned to Aldan, handing him the orb. "Put this away for now. You can tell me more about it later, but we don't have time for more experiments right now. Do you have any of your obscurity potion on hand?"

"I always do." Aldan opened a cabinet by the far wall, pulling out four bottles. "These hold four doses. One dose lasts about an hour, and then you must replenish."

Caya nodded and drank a fourth of the bottle. "Creator," she said, wheezing. "That's strong." It tasted similar to the moonshine brandy her young friends among the Vantressa clan had once offered her.

"It sure is," Tomita said, coughing a few times. "Now, tell us what you saw?"

"The destruction of *Pathfinder*, or at least part of it. Does that match what your mother saw?"

"I'll say." Aldan pulled on a jacket and hung a bag over his shoulder. "The potion works into our system fast. Let's go."

Caya's head still hurt from the cascade of visions, but she pulled her hood up and followed. She trusted her new friends, the first ones she'd had of her own kind except her sister, to know the fastest way to cube one.

CHAPTER SEVENTEEN

Thea hadn't received any word regarding Caya's current status, and nobody had been able to locate her. Her stomach trembled, and she wanted to magically find room for a few moments to just *breathe*. Instead, she was in one communication conference after another and read written reports on her computer tablet.

"Time to head for the bridge, Madam President," Thea's first assistant said from the open door. "Fleet Admiral Vayand, cube one's captain, and three of your cabinet members are already there."

"Fine." Grabbing her coat, Thea hung it over her shoulders as she strode to the jumper gate. "I hate to repeat myself, Palinda…"

"I was just getting to that, sir. No reports from the search party. No messages from Ms. Lindemay. Briar Lindemay checks in every fifteen minutes, precisely. I'm sorry, sir. I know every single person who is not on duty elsewhere is looking for Caya." Palinda shook her head. "I wish I had better news."

"So do I." For the first time during her presidency, Thea wondered if she was going to be able to hold it together. Her mind strayed to Caya, to the image of how she looked when they spoke quietly about their feelings. No, they hadn't confessed to love in so many words, but they had both spoken of belonging together, to each other. More than anything else, Thea regretted not waking Caya this morning. So much could have been different…and Thea might have found the time, and the courage, to tell Caya that she loved her more than anything or anyone else in her life.

As they reached the bridge, Korrian glanced up and acknowledged Thea's presence with a nod. She worked at her console with a deep frown marring her forehead. Behind her, Meija stood by her smaller console, no doubt interpreting what they could find out about the sabotaged buoy.

"Madam President." Fleet Admiral Vayand came up to her, his face serious. "We have interpreted the telemetry from the buoy. Not only is it clear and obvious sabotage, but the next buoy's faint signal shows it's been tampered with also. Perhaps fired at."

"Fired at while in subspace?" Thea thought that was impossible. "How, and who?"

"The individuals behind this have managed to coax the buoys out of subspace. They didn't even have to get them all the way back into regular space to cause damage to them. You have been briefed about how fragile they are when handled. Only the fact that they were supposed to sit sheltered in subspace made it possible for us to use such sensitive technology."

"Admiral Heigel?" Thea motioned for Korrian to join them. "An update, please."

"The closest buoy has indeed been fired upon. The blast shows traces of alien alloys and chemical compounds. I never suspected the buoy situation to be part of the domestic issues with terrorism, and now we know. This is an alien presence. I recommend we go to level-one alert. There's a reason whoever is behind this doesn't want us to gain access to the information collected by the buoy." Korrian rapped her nails against the console next to them. "From what I've read of the advance team's logs while enroute to Gemocon, this makes me think of the—"

"Alachleves." Thea had read Admiral Caydoc's log entries at least ten times—everything from the ordeal on the planet with poisonous rodents, where the admiral had almost lost her life, to the battle with the Alachleves. Caydoc had placed these buoys to show *Pathfinder* safe passage, which meant that either the Alachleves had expanded their territory, or some rogue ships had happened upon the signals and figured out how to retrieve the technology. Either way it was bad news.

"Any way to boost sensors, Commander Vantressa?" Vayand asked, and only now did Thea spot a very pale Adina over by the engineering console. She had thought Adina would have remained with Briar, but of course at this level of emergency, *Pathfinder*'s chief engineer had to be at her post.

"I'm reconfiguring them to give us another couple of parsecs for our long-range sensors. I'm having some trouble fine-tuning them, though. Some form of blocker or scrambler seems to be deployed in this sector."

"I want to know the second anyone here notices so much as a grain of space dust in the wrong place." Vayand turned in a circle, meeting the eyes of everyone on the bridge. "We are closing in on our future home. Let's keep *Pathfinder* in one piece till we get there."

"Sir," Meija came up to them. "If the Alachleves have expanded their space—there's a risk their border is now perilously close to Gemocon."

"We're not going to allow anyone to violate our borders or a peaceful vessel like *Pathfinder*." Vayand stood rigid, and he made for an impressive sight with his long, gray hair and well-maintained body—especially for a man in his seventies. His steely grey eyes kept vigil over everything that took place on the bridge. "Admiral Heigel, we need to put a few more safety measures in place—"

The alarm klaxons went off all at the same time. Moving over to the president's seat, Thea sat down and felt the automatic harness sling around her body and tighten it in place.

"Report," Vayand barked, not sitting down, which was against protocol. "Lieutenant?" He motioned toward a woman at the operations station.

"All of our long-range sensors are showing approaching vessels. They're matching our course and speed."

"On the main screen. I want to see where these devils are coming from. Change course and reduce to magnetar two. I'm not about to take a volley at maximum magnetar."

Thea studied the sensor readings on the main screen. She had learned quickly how to interpret the colorful lines and dots, and now she could tell that at least twenty vessels of different sizes were on their way to intercept. "Can't we outrun them, Admiral?" she asked Vayand.

"I don't think so. Had we been traveling with any of the Advance ships—yes, perhaps. But this big chunk of metal? No." Vayand came over to her. "Sir. I think you should give the order for everyone to go to their designated secure station. At this time, the people need to know their president is at the center of things."

"All right." Thea pressed the sequence on her communicator that would allow her to do so. "Passengers and crew of *Pathfinder*. This is Gassinthea Mila Tylio, your president. I urge everyone to follow protocol and proceed to your safe station, quarters, or any public facility deemed an appropriate safety area. Strap in your children and the elderly. Don't forget your pets. We are currently under attack, and until you hear from a member of the bridge crew telling you it is all right to walk freely again, remain in your seats. This is not a drill, my fellow Gemoconians. This is reality. Be safe in heavenly splendor. Tylio out."

It was as if the aliens approaching them had just waited for her to end the alert. She barely had time to lower her hand from the communicator before the barrage of missiles began drumming against *Pathfinder*.

"Drop out of magnetar drive," Vayand barked. "Deploy assault craft units two, eight, and eleven. Standby units one, three, and twelve."

An ensign at the first row of computers smartly repeated the order and punched in commands.

"Shields at eighty percent!" The lieutenant at the ops station called out the numbers. "Seventy-five!"

"Return fire. Target their weapons' arrays, their propulsion systems, and if they don't back off, their life-support systems." Vayand spoke distinctly, making sure everyone heard him over the bustling activity on the bridge.

Thea gripped the armrests but knew she was secure in her harness for now.

"Unknown missile type incoming. Aiming for *Pathfinder*'s belly. Evasive maneuver patterns." The ops lieutenant was sweating visibly now, but she kept her calm behind her console.

"Brace for impact," the security officer said from his end. "We can't outmaneuver this thing."

"What about the assault craft?" Vayand asked.

"They're engaging the enemy, but if they get in the way of this explosive device, they'll be vaporized." The security officer spoke curtly as she simultaneously kept focusing on her screen. "Our birds have taken out two of theirs."

"Any losses among ours?" Vayand looked steadily at the screen that had shifted to the external cameras. The smaller screens around it showed all the different data, but Thea knew Vayand was of the old-fashioned type when it came to how he handled the bridge.

"One bird is down, sir. Pilot is alive, and I've marked it for retrieval later. We won't lose her, sir."

"I'll hold you to it, Commander."

"Impact in, five, four, three, two, one." The ops lieutenant countdown was drowned when the alien missile hit. *Pathfinder* shook and stomped so violently Thea had to press the back of her head against the headrest, engaging the cranium harness that wrapped around her forehead so fast it felt like being lashed by a whip. She watched the screen, mesmerized and sickened by the violence aimed at her people. She wasn't surprised when, half an hour later, Vayand finally gave the order she had been expecting.

"All cube captains, this is Fleet Admiral Vayand. Commence full separation. Once it is completed, scatter according to pattern eight-zero-milo-quippo. Once the scatter-sequence is completed, deploy safety crafts on all six sides and set shields to maximum."

A chorus of affirmative answers was heard via the communication system, and on the left of the big screen, Thea saw the different symbols for the cubes began to turn red. Unlike the careful procedure of shifting cubes among each other, the emergency separation sequence was done at impulse speed.

It took less than fifteen minutes for all the cubes to scatter and thus divide the enemy. As the alien assault vessels moved among the cubes and fired at will, but in a decidedly less efficient manner, cube one moved away from the worst of the fire to lead the *Pathfinder* forces. Vayand conferred with his counterparts in the other military branches, and eventually, the fight began to turn to their favor.

Thea was hurting all over from being tossed against her harness for more than two hours. She knew she wasn't alone in this discomfort, as she could well picture entire families strapped together in their quarters, wondering if they were going to make it.

"Enemy is withdrawing, sir. The larger vessels have already gone to magnetar drive. The smaller assault craft are guarding the perimeter half a parsec away. Do we pursue, sir?" the security officer asked Vayand.

"No, we don't, Commander. Set up a perimeter of our own. Once we're sure this is not a tactical ploy on their part, we'll start bringing our family back together, one cube at a time. Damage report?"

"Nothing major on the cubes so far, sir," the ops lieutenant answered. "We have twenty-eight assault craft dead in the water. Eighteen wounded pilots. Ten fatalities."

"And on the cubes?" Thea asked as she freed herself from the harnesses and stood.

"We have no conclusive reports from the cubes yet, Madam President," the lieutenant said. "Once we begin reattaching them, I'll start receiving more accurate numbers."

"I want to know as soon as you do." Thea stood behind her chair, holding on to the headrest.

"Are you all right, Madam President?" Vayand asked and walked up to her. "That was a grueling two hours, sir."

"I'm fine. Thank you. And you, Orien? You've been on your feet, and tossed around because of it, for the same two hours."

"You think I'm getting too old for this, Thea?" Vayand smiled wryly as she shook her head at his silly joke.

"On days like today, we're all too old." Thea tapped her communicator and assembled her team to wait for her outside the bridge. She had a lot to do, but now she could step off the bridge and do her duty from her office. It was too early to expect any news about Caya, but soon Thea would be able to continue that investigation as well. All the cubes were safe and accounted for, which was somewhat reassuring.

Thea operated under the assumption that Caya was hiding to stay away from potentially corrupt presidential guards. If only she knew which cube Caya was in, but the young woman she loved clearly had a knack for vanishing. If it kept her safe, Thea was all for it, but she also wanted her found and returned to Thea's care, where nothing would harm her. She didn't want to listen to the small voice reminding her that it was while in protective custody that Caya had definitely not been safe.

Thea yanked at her communicator. It was time to put the stalwart commander back on track. "President Tylio to Commander KahSandra. Report."

Chapter Eighteen

Is he all right?" Caya bent over Foy, who lay in an alleyway, his scalp bleeding from a laceration he had sustained when cube seventeen had lurched under their feet. The alien attack had hit before Caya had been able to warn anyone in the governmental building. Before the fleet admiral ordered the ship-wide separation, they had managed to get to cube seventeen, which after the previous shuffle had bordered on cube eight from underneath. Now she had no idea if the authorities would piece *Pathfinder* back together the same way as earlier.

"I think he'll live," Aldan said, smiling tenderly at his husband. "He has a wooden head, this one."

"Thanks a lot," Foy muttered, but cupped Aldan's cheek. "Thanks for catching me, love. I thought I'd go headlong into the life-support unit. They're not meant to be jumped into headfirst."

"I'll say." Aldan kissed the back of Foy's hand. "Ready to get up? We need to find a place where Caya can page the president without being easily spotted. Perhaps the main square. It's bound to be bustling now that it seems the attack is over."

"Wait." Tomita placed a hand on her brother's arm. "Just give me a sec." She looked around them, walked cautiously up to the end of the alleyway, and peered around the corner. Caya watched her new friend intently. She saw her body language change as Tomita glanced in the opposite direction, grew rigid, and then hurried back to them.

"Let's go back toward the previous square. It's not as big, but we can't continue this way. I saw several individuals that created goose bumps all over my body. We're all in danger if we head that way."

"She's hardly ever wrong. I take that back," Aldan said wryly. "She's actually never wrong."

"Let's go. Give me a hand." Foy stood, if a bit unsteady, and they began to make their way back in the same direction they'd come from. As they entered the main road, they saw several people in need of medical attention. Caya couldn't pass them by. She was the sister of a nurse, after all. When Tomita objected, looking over her shoulder, Caya looked pointedly at the wounded and took half a dose of her obscurity potion. She had half a bottle left, and she counted on it being enough to reach cube one later.

Tirelessly, Caya bandaged sprained and broken limbs, showing the other three how to do it. She taped wounds that needed stitching or fusing later and put cold or hot packs on bumps and bruises.

"Please. Can you help her?" a young voice said from behind. A boy around ten years old stood with a small child in his arms. Caya estimated the little girl to be about a year old.

"What happened to her? Is she your sister?"

"Her name is Rhosee," the young boy said. "She's fourteen months old. She was asleep in her crib when the attack started. Mom was passed out on the floor. She hadn't strapped Rhosee in because… because she was drunk again. I found Rhosee just now when I got home. They kept us in school. Strapped us in even though I begged them not to." He started crying soundlessly. "I told them I needed to check on Mom and Rhosee, but they had locked our harnesses."

"Where's your mother now?" Caya asked as she examined the child, trying to remember the basic things Briar had taught her. She had spent many shifts with Briar at the hospital, both on Oconodos and on *Pathfinder*. Being a neonatal intensive-care-unit nurse, Briar was an expert on babies.

"She's dead," the boy whispered.

"What?" Caya snapped her attention back on the boy. "Are you sure?"

"I…I think so." He was trembling.

"What's your name?" Caya took his chin gently between her thumb and index finger.

"Miron."

"My name is Caya." She didn't care that she used her real name at this point. "I'll call my friend Aldan over, and I want you to take him to your quarters. I want to make sure we do everything we can for your mother...just in case." Caya waved Aldan over and explained the situation.

"Don't worry. You deal with the little sweetheart, and I'll take care of Miron and his mother." Aldan saluted and took the boy by the hand.

"You're a natural," Tomita said where she stood next to Caya, wrapping a bandage around the head of a concussed old man.

"A natural what?" Caya blinked the threatening tears from her eyelashes and refocused on the little girl.

"A natural leader. You don't even think or stop to consider. You just *do*." Tomita bumped her hip against Caya. "I'll be saying I used to know you way back when you were just a young brat with a gift."

"Brat, huh?" Caya stuck her tongue out before she began to unclasp the small cardigan the girl wore over her little jumpsuit. "I can't find any bumps or bruises. No cuts." She pinched the pale skin on the back of her hand gently. When it didn't resettle immediately, Caya knew what part of the problem was. "She's dehydrated. If she took a tumble from her crib and hit her head...She needs a hospital. We can't care for her enough here. Where's the nearest local clinic?"

Tomita pulled out a small tablet and punched in a search command. "Two blocks to the left from here. I'll take her. You can't just walk in there without us knowing it's safe for you."

"You forget that I replenished the potion," Caya whispered. "I'll take her. I can ask for more bandages, blankets, and so on. Trust me, they're going to be so busy, and so grateful for any assistance, they won't look at me twice."

"I'm not sure—oh, look. Here's Aldan and Miron now." Caya saw the bad news written across Aldan's features. The young boy was pale and rigid where he walked next to him. "Oh, no. I'm so sorry, Miron." She took the boy by his shoulders. "No, listen. You have to be strong for Rhosee. She has only you, and she's going to need you. I'm going to carry her to the clinic a few blocks from here, and I need you to help keep people from running into us. All right?"

"A-all right." Miron looked dazed but nodded. "Before it was just Mom, me, and Rhosee…"

"And now it is you and Rhosee." Caya tried to sound as reassuring as possible as she made her way through the street full of wounded and traumatized people. The little warm weight in her arms tugged at her heart, and she prayed to the Creator she wouldn't be too late. Glancing down at the small child, she thought she was paler, and her lips were faintly blue tinted. "Come, Miron. We need to run. Can you help get people out of the way?"

"Yes!" Miron ran ahead of Caya, yelling at people to move, nudging the ones that didn't shift fast enough from their path. "We have an emergency. A wounded baby. Move, move!" Miron's high-pitched voice rang out between the bulkheads, and more people heeded it, making it easier for Caya to run.

She almost sobbed with relief when she saw the sign indicating the clinic at the other end of the street. Caya kept glancing at Rhosee, and when they were almost at the door, she could tell the little girl had stopped breathing. "No!" She didn't dare continue without administering the heart-lung stimulation. Briar had taught Caya the resuscitation technique when she was a few years younger than Miron. Not hesitating, she placed the one-year-old on the deck and began performing compression across her sternum. Mindful that this was a small, frail child, she used her fingertips rather than the heels of her palms. "Miron. Get help. Tell them to bring a portable ventilator." Caya bent to ventilate the little girl by using the air in her own lungs. These were traditionalist methods and usually not taught in modern medical universities.

"Here, she's here," Miron said from behind.

"Good. Someone who knows what they're doing," a stern female voice said. "Move a little to the side, but keep the compressions going." A woman with steel-grey short hair knelt by Caya's side while running a scanner across the small body. "She's in distress, but you've kept her circulation going. Good job."

Caya was too winded to answer. Merely nodding, she kept the compressions up until the doctor had attached the little girl's body to a small machine that breathed for her and an external heart stimulator. Caya could see color return to little Rhosee's face. Her lips were pink rather than blue, as were her tiny fingernails.

"Rhosee?" Miron fell to his knees next to the little girl. "Look at me. It's Miron. It's me." He wept now, wiping his nose against his sleeve, and Caya could barely contain her emotions at the sight of the two children.

"Miron," she said and took him by the shoulders. "Listen to me. I have to go, because I need to see someone and it's very important. But if all goes well, I promise you, I'll come back and see how you and Rhosee are doing. I give you my word." She ruffled his messy hair. "All right?"

Miron hiccupped and looked up at her with huge, wet eyes. "You promise, Ms. Caya?"

"I do. Unless I'm prevented somehow, I'll come looking for you. And if I can't, I'll do my best to tell my si—a really good friend of mine." She bent to whisper in Miron's ear. "This is a secret just between you and me. If I can't make it, I'll try to send Red Angel."

The boy gasped and covered her mouth with his hand. "Creator of all things."

"Exactly. So be brave. Stay close to Rhosee. I'll see you soon." Caya kissed his forehead, and just as the doctor turned to her, looking like she was about to interview her about the little girl, Caya smiled apologetically and disappeared into the crowd.

Thea stood in the foyer of the governmental building. Around her were the members of her cabinet that had been present on cube one when *Pathfinder* separated. The ones who resided in other cubes, who had their family members still there, were naturally concerned for their wellbeing, but as communications were reestablished, more and more were put at ease.

Thea wasn't one of them. Every time a message was put through, it emphasized the fact she had no news of Caya. If she had been concerned before the attack, when it was a matter of Caya keeping herself safe and out of sight of everyone, now when casualty reports showed horrific injuries and even fatalities, it was an entirely different heartache. Behind each anonymous statistic, someone had lost a loved one. The idea one of them might be Caya burned through Thea's midsection like wildfire.

"Madam President. Fleet Admiral Vayand is pleased to report that ten cubes are now locked into position around cube one. We are once again protected—"

"What?" Thea snapped her head up, narrowing her eyes at the minister of defense. "What did you just say?"

"We, um, cube one is once again protected with ten cubes locked into place around us." The man, tall and bulky, shuffled his feet. "This is of outmost importance as the government and the main bridge—"

"That's what I thought you said, though I didn't want to believe it." Thea spat the words. "That implies that the surrounding cubes are nothing but a humanoid wall to keep the elite in cube one safe. That implies that somehow you regard the people in those cubes, the Gemoconians who have risked everything to find a new and safer home, as expendable. As long as we in here are safe, then to hell with everything else—is that how you regard your fellow passengers aboard *Pathfinder*?" Furious enough to tremble, Thea growled the last sentence.

"No, no. Not at all, sir. I would never dream of reasoning like that. I—I'm grateful for the fact all the cubes are accounted for. My wife and children have yet to dock with us. I actually think they're last in line to do so." The man ran a handkerchief under his chin. "I'm sorry if—"

"No." She held up a hand, effectively silencing the minister of defense. "I am the one who is sorry. I spoke out of turn, and I apologize. We're all rattled for having been attacked without any justifiable cause. I pray to the Creator your family is docked safely and that you're reunited within a few hours like planned, Minister."

"Thank you, Madam President. No need for you to apologize to me either. We are all aware what burden of responsibility can do when there is no reprieve from it." The minister looked relieved to be out of her line of fire, and though Thea didn't think she deserved his understanding and kind approach, she was grateful for it.

"Madam President?" A voice so like Caya's, but with a little more timbre, spoke next to her.

Thea turned and saw Briar and Adina, the latter holding a protective arm around Briar, who was pale and looked fatigued. "How are the two of you holding up?" Thea took Briar by her shoulders and kissed her cheek. "Have you heard anything?" It was unlikely they would hear anything before Thea did, but there was the off chance Caya would get in touch with her sister by her own volition.

"Nothing. Nothing at all. Ever since my shift ended, I've been sitting by the screen in our quarters, scanning the crowds from the new reports, hoping to catch a glimpse of her. At any other time, I would've kept working after my shift was over, to help out, but all I can think about is finding her." Briar's copper-blond curls fell in disarray around her pale face. Her turquoise eyes, so like her sister, but not quite as hypnotic, glistened with tears.

"I'm so sorry for not having any news for you." Thea caressed Briar's cheek. "If you want to remain in the building you can either stay here or use my quarters. Briar, I would like for you to have personal guards if you do decide to leave."

"That's not necessary," Briar protested, but she put no strength behind her words. "Honestly?"

"Humor me." Thea exchanged a glance with Adina. The tall commander looked so worried and worn; Thea realized Briar must be in a worse emotional state than she let on. Perhaps it was because the sisters' special connection had been severed. If Thea was so profoundly affected by Caya's absence, her sister, who in many ways had been like a mother for Caya, had to feel shattered. "And let Adina take care of you. I know firsthand how easy it is to shut someone out—you think you're being strong, that you're protecting them from your own emotions. Don't make that mistake. Adina needs to be there for you, and you certainly need her and the rest of us, to see you through this until Caya returns."

"And who will you turn to, Thea?" Briar asked softly. She took Thea's hand and made no secret of how she'd entered Thea's mind, which Thea surmised was only fair after the personal pep talk she had just given Briar. "You—you love her," she whispered, her eyes huge in her freckled face. "You truly do. I always thought you did, somehow, but now…Oh, Thea. She will come back to us. She will. She has to." Briar threw her arms around Thea, crying quietly against her shoulder. "I'm so sorry," she whispered after a while as Adina slowly pulled her back.

"No need, dear. No need at all. We're in the same place, in a sense." Thea had not shed a tear while holding Briar and rocking her. Now, however, she found it difficult to contain her emotions, but people were waiting for her to address the people of *Pathfinder* as soon as it was completely attached. She would give a good, well-thought-out speech, and she would make sure that it entailed words only Caya would be able to interpret and understand.

CHAPTER NINETEEN

It happened again as they rushed along the corridor leading to the closest jumper station. Caya was right behind Tomita, holding Foy's communicator pressed against her ear to try to hear what the person responding said. So many people were shouting and talking around them, she could barely make out what she said herself.

"I need to convey a message to the president, sir," Caya yelled.

"Don't...we all. Leave a...message at the official line for grievances. Thank you."

"Ah!" Caya pressed the sensor again. If she hadn't tossed her own communicator she would have reached Thea instantly. Now she had to deal with the president's minions, who clearly couldn't hear what Caya said or simply hadn't been told to let her message through. She tried Briar again but only got her message service again. Same went for Adina. Of course so many systems had to be down now when it truly mattered.

Nausea struck her and she wobbled to the side. Caya slapped her hand over her mouth to keep from throwing up in the middle of the crowd. "Tomita," she whimpered as the light around her became hazy. "Foy..."

"Hey, guys!" She's going down." It was Foy's voice. Strong arms carried her to the side, where she fell into a vortex of scattered images, voices, and nothing that made a lot of sense at first.

"Run, Caya. Now! Run!" The voice was Tomita's and Caya ran. She was on a moving object and then she was airborne. She saw the number eighteen pass before her eyes, and then pieces of metal singed her skin, layers upon layers of destroyed bulkheads fell around her, and bodies were tossed into space.

Gasping for air, Caya fell, and as she opened her eyes, she was startled to find she was back with her friends. They sat right outside the gate to the jumper that would take them to cube one. Caya followed the chart above her that showed the route of this particular jumper. They were in cube four, and to get to cube one, they had to pass cube eighteen.

"We have to warn them." Caya stood, staggering to the side before she found her balance.

"That's what we're trying to do, yes." Aldan frowned as he tried to look into her eyes. "You seem a bit out of it, Caya."

"I'm fine. But you don't understand. We have to stop at cube eighteen and alert them. They've just reattached and something... not quite sure what, is going to cause an explosion. Maybe white garnet. Maybe a malfunction after the attack. People will die."

"Then hurry," Tomita called and rushed toward the jumper sitting on the magnetic tracks. "This leaves in a few seconds."

It was such a wondrous feeling to never be doubted. These three very new friends took her visions at face value, which saved so much time. They barely jumped through the doors before the jumper sped down the track into the tunnel system.

Around them, a few people sat hollow eyed with evident shock. The jumper was surprisingly empty. Perhaps people stayed away from it due to fear of new attacks, alien or domestic. That was probably quite smart, as you would be seriously trapped if a new attack happened and they were right at a cube junction. Caya stood quickly. Tomita rose as well, taking Caya's hand. "What's wrong?"

"In my vision, people got tossed into space. The explosion occurred at the junction between cube eighteen and another one. So, which cubes border on cube eighteen apart from four right now? Is the ship's configuration the same as before the separation?"

"Not sure. But earlier, only three cubes bordered against it, as it was located at the belly of *Pathfinder*. Four, six, and one."

"And we're in four." Foy regarded the screen above them. "Though only for a few moments longer. Then we will move into eighteen. We'll stop at a gate just inside. We need to stay on for two more gates before we're even remotely close to a law-enforcement facility."

"They're going to toss us in the—"

A screeching sound made them flinch, and the entire car began to shake. Sparks erupted from the walls.

"It's in here," Caya cried out and began dragging at her friends and the people around them. "The white garnet. It's in the jumper walls. Or on the outside. We need to move back through the train. Come on! Run!" She didn't care that she was being rough with the dazed people, who looked confused at the now-running material that permeated the walls. It didn't look like what Adina and Briar had once showed her. Perhaps it was something else, or something mixed with white garnet?

She ran back through the jumper cars, forcing as many as she could to come with her, and eventually the aisle between the seats were crowded with panicked people.

"It's too crowded here. We need to move back one car at least, or two." Foy pointed at the one they'd just passed. "I can't see any of that sparkly, gooey stuff in there. Perhaps we can detach the affected car from the rest of the jumper?"

"It's worth a shot. These people won't stand a chance if that stuff explodes." Aldan looked grimly at Caya and Tomita. "Caya is too valuable for her to risk her life—"

"Don't even try." Caya gently shook Tomita's shoulder. "We're going to be all hands on deck here. Come on before it's too late."

They hurried back, and the closer they came to the car they'd left only minutes ago, the stronger the acrid scent of the foreign agent became.

"Enough. This is as far as we can go without inhaling the damn stuff." Tomita stopped them. "How do we separate this car from the next? Is there some emergency lever? Or a way to connect with the staff overseeing the jumpers?"

"No idea." Caya wished she had paid more attention when Korrian spoke of how she came up with the idea for the jumper system. "I know they're magnetically connected, like they are with the track. We're going to have to try to break the magnetism between them—or better yet, change the polarity."

"Make them repel each other," Aldan said and nodded. "It's just that we have only seconds to do it."

Caya looked at the line that showed where one jumper car ended and the next began. She knelt and felt along the black, rubbery border. Peeling it back, she tried to see if there was anywhere she might flip a switch.

"It's too late." Tomita stood now and pulled Caya to her feet. Tomita and the two men stood on one side of the border and Caya on the other. The jumper began shaking more violently, and Caya tried to move farther toward the front, to pull the others back with her, away from the disintegrating car, but Tomita shook her head. "No. Listen to me. It's too late!"

A loud rumble just behind her friends made Caya scream in panic. "No. No! Jump." She leaned forward, clawing for them, screaming their names. She managed to grip Foy's sleeve, but he shocked her by shoving her hard across her chest without actually touching her. *Telekinetic.* The word struck her as she flew through the air backward. She thought she heard a loud whooshing sound before pain exploded throughout her and everything went black.

CHAPTER TWENTY

I don't want any of your bloody excuses. I want her found!" Thea growled and slammed both palms against her desk, making them sting.

"Madam President, we have intel that she was on a jumper heading for cube eighteen when it—" Commander KahSandra went rigid as Thea rounded the desk.

"I don't give a damn about your intel. I want you to search every part of *Pathfinder* and find Caya. She may well have had time to get off that jumper—or perhaps she was never on it. She would have foreseen what was going to happen. She was alive to have visions of the attack—and she tried to warn us about something. If that incompetent idiot hadn't prevented her from reaching me, she could have been back here. Alive. And I have to believe she still is. She might have had a vision of the attack against the jumper system as well." Shaking hard, but ignoring her reaction, Thea motioned for the commander and her ensigns to leave.

Alone in her office, she fell to her knees on the floor, every last remnant of strength leaving her in a gush. She bent forward with her arms around her waist, trying to hold herself together as violent sobs threatened to tear her apart. Nothing before in her life had brought her such torturous agony. Not Hadler's abuse or her father's dismissal, and not even the loss of her mother. Caya was part of her soul. She would lose the biggest and best part of herself if Caya were gone. How could she face Briar again if she had to tell her that her little sister was dead? As the one in charge of Caya's incarceration, ultimately Thea was responsible.

"Please," she whispered to the empty room. She rarely prayed, but now the words poured from her cold lips in a husky, broken whisper. "For the love of Thee, my Creator, I pledge my soul to Thee, I give my days and nights to Thy realm. I vow to carry Thy light. I promise honor to Thy children, and my eternal love and gratitude will be Thine." Thea remained still, staring at the screens that showed the realignment of twenty cubes…and a kilometer away from *Pathfinder*, what was left of cube eighteen.

Fury began as a small flame just below her sternum and then grew steadily until an inferno tore through her at the sight of the destroyed cube. It looked like a large space-dwelling predator had dug its claws into it and ripped off almost an entire side, then buried its fangs into it and shredded the decks like they were made of paper. If she squinted, she could make out small dots around the cube, and it sickened her to realize some of them were her people, floating frozen in space—men, women, and children that she was elected to serve and protect, to bring with her to a new, safer world.

Thea knew she should be grateful that not all of cube eighteen's passengers were sucked out. Emergency bulkheads had slid into place. Yet, some survivors had sustained severe damage, and the casualty toll would be steep. The mere thought that one of the floating dots on the screen might be the woman she loved was unbearable.

Thea stood slowly and began reading the information, one screen at a time. When the jumper car had exploded right at the junction between cubes four and eighteen, it had triggered a chain reaction that tore it away from the rest of *Pathfinder*. Whereas the emergency bulkhead seals had worked on cube four's side, several of them did not on cube eighteen. So far, her subordinates estimated that more than ten thousand passengers had lost their lives from being sucked into space. The rest were being ferried over from what was left intact of cube eighteen right now. Thea had given orders that as many as possible of the dead floating in space were to be retrieved if possible. Had this happened earlier during their journey, they would have been jettisoned in body covers, or cremated, depending on their families' wishes. Now, the surviving family members would have the additional option of burying their dead on Gemocon, as they were not far away from their destination.

Thea smoothed down her hair, making sure the chignon was in place, before walking over to the closet by the door. With jerky movements, she yanked her long black jacket off its hanger. She put it on and examined her reflection in the mirror. Straightening the seams of her dress, she then adjusted the ten rows of pearls around her neck. A quick touchup of her makeup made her look impeccable and strong. She needed every bit of her strength now to make it through the day. She would not allow herself to crumble. As the president, she was not allowed humanoid frailty.

Thea opened the door, and her presidential guards lined up without a word. They walked around her, backs straight, eyes calm and vigilant.

"We're going to the hospital in cube eleven," Thea said to her assistant, who had showed up like a ghost next to her. "I'll meet the chief there and visit some of the patients from cube eighteen."

"Yes, Madam President." Her assistant tapped furiously at her tablet.

"I also want to visit engineering and the bridge."

"Yes, Madam President."

As they strode toward her private jumper, Thea allowed the sound of their marching feet to calm her. She needed the steady cadence to get her through this.

Caya coughed and tried to open her eyes. Every time she did, fine dust settled on her corneas and she closed them quickly again. She felt around her. Metal. Coarse metal on the floor and on the walls. She dared to crawl a bit farther and came across another type of alloy, like a rod. But the rod was stuck to the floor and emanated some sort of heat. She couldn't figure out what it was, but it seemed to be quite long. She kept crawling, eyes closed hard.

"Hello?" Caya called out and coughed again. "Anyone there? Tomita! Foy!" Where were they? Were they all right? "Aldan!"

The last thing she remembered was how they'd stood at the line bordering between two jumper cars as they neared cube eighteen. What had happened after that was a blur. Surely the memory of someone pushing her backward couldn't be right? Her last clear memory was how they had told everyone to go to the back of the jumper...Yes. That was it. They had looked for a way to separate the cars because of the corrosive agent they'd seen. She tried to remember, but after she was pushed back, it all went black.

"Tomita? Aldan? Foy? Please, anyone?" She was weeping now, because Caya knew deep inside that there was a lot to mourn. She could feel it. "Answer me!"

"Hello?" She heard another weak voice, far away. It sounded like a man. Was it Foy or Aldan? She didn't think so. He sounded different.

"I'm here." Caya crawled toward the sound on some cold metal floor. Are you all right?" Caya called out back.

"I'm stuck. Can you reach me?" It had to be a man. His voice was low.

"I'll try. Where are we, sir?"

"In one of the jumper tunnels in cube four."

Caya pushed herself along the rod, which she now realized had to be one of the magnetic tracks. So, they never made it to cube eighteen? Then where were Tomita, Foy, and Aldan?

Caya closed her eyes and listened into her mind, trying to conjure up a minivision of her friends while she crawled toward the trapped man. Oddly, she saw nothing. Nothing! Just blank space. Yes, that was it. *Space.* Caya shivered. She saw outer space with distant stars and other celestial bodies when she focused on Tomita, Foy, and Aldan. What did that even mean?

Dust filled her mouth and nose, and she sneezed several times as she pulled herself along the track. Other than her groaning efforts to reach the injured man, silence surrounded her. Had there been an explosion? Was cube four dead in the water? Perhaps she and the man were the only survivors caught in a closed-off part of the ship. Dread trickled down her spine. Thea. What if the rest of *Pathfinder* was destroyed? She'd never reached Thea and hadn't had a chance to tell her…anything. Perhaps Thea had been lost with the rest of the ship, not knowing how loved she was or how Caya regretted not letting her know when it still mattered, when it might have actually changed something for the better between them. Now, Thea might never know how all-important she was to Caya, how empty and hollow her life was without her.

Caya sobbed and then drew in deep gulps of air, not sure it helped. She tried to determine if the oxygen level was normal. All her gasping for air made her even more light-headed, but she didn't think there was a leak. Pushing her fear of having lost Thea and everyone else she cared about to the back of her mind, she kept crawling. At least she might be able to do something for the man up ahead.

"Are you still there, miss?" the man asked, his voice weaker now.

"I'm getting closer. What's your name?"

"Olion." The man coughed, probably affected by the fine dust as well.

"You're Gemosian?"

"Yes." He sounded cautious.

"I'm Caya." She pulled with both hands at the same time now. Using one hand at a time helped her move faster, but her arms ached from overexertion.

"What's trapping you? Can you tell?" Caya wanted Olion to continue talking. His voice, as weak as it was, helped her not panic.

"One of the magnetic beams from the ceiling must've fallen on top of my legs. I can feel the humming. I'm not on the track though. That's a good thing, or the ceiling beam might have pressed down hard enough to sever my legs. The magnetism in these tracks is powerful."

"I'll do my best to help you." Caya didn't want to think about having to leave him to get help. And if they were lost in some piece of wreckage, they were on their own. Perhaps people thought they were dead and had left them to float inside a debris field until they perished. Hating how she conjured up horrible images, Caya focused on Olion. "You sound like you know a lot about the jumpers, Olion. You an engineer?"

"Yes. Well, almost. I still have a year left at the university. I'm hoping to get my degree once we arrive at Gemocon. I think I can be of use, and it will make it possible for me to help my family to a better future."

Olion sounded so much like Briar that tears rose in Caya's eyes. She blinked them away and they ran down her cheeks. "We'll make sure you get that chance. How old are you?" He couldn't be as old as his husky voice suggested. It must be the dust that made it sound rough.

"Twenty."

"Oh, me too. I had a birthday two months ago. You must be very smart to already have gone to university and have only one year until you graduate." Caya was impressed.

"I skipped ahead a few years when I was fifteen." Olion coughed again and moaned louder.

"What's wrong?" Caya tried to go faster.

"My knee. I think it's fractured. The beam has started to shift toward the tracks, and it's pulling at my leg.

On a positive note, Olion sounded much closer, but if the magnetic beam was tugging at him, he might be crushed against the track. Caya had no way of knowing how long the beam was, and if it slid into place along the tracks it could injure her as well. She shook off the sudden dread. "Talk to me, Olion. I don't have far to go now."

"You should stay clear. I think the beam will go at any moment now. It might tear my leg right off and—"

"Shut up. Don't you dare surrender to such thoughts. I'll be with you in just a few moments."

"All right." Olion sounded weaker but kept talking. "That was a brave thing your friends did. "

"What?" Caya nearly forgot to haul herself along the track.

"Your friends. The two men and the woman you were sitting next to?"

"Did you see what happened? I can't remember."

"We were close to the junction between cube four and eighteen. You were all running toward the jumper car that was emitting the... was it smoke, by the way?"

"A kind of smoke, yes. Go on."

"They passed over to the car just before the damaged one. You yelled something like 'There's not enough time but we have to try,' and that's when they stopped. You were all on the floor, pulling at something." Olion coughed again, his breathing more labored than before. "You were about to move over to their side when the explosion came. Then that tearing sound..." He drew a trembling breath. "It was awful."

"What happened then?" Caya wiped at the dust mixed with tears on her cheeks. She could easily picture what he described for her.

"One of the men shoved you really hard and sent you flying back into the car. I was in the one after yours, and I clung to a seat when, for a moment, I saw you fly straight into space. Damn. We nearly decompressed, but then the walls closed. The emergency seal I read about, no doubt."

"Oh, sweet Creator." Caya was crying again now." Her friends. Had they been sucked out into space? Had Foy known what he was doing when he pushed her back? Probably. No. Most likely. They had sacrificed themselves. After knowing her for such a brief amount of time, they gave their lives to try to save hers...why? "And then?"

"I don't remember anything after that. Where did our jumper cars go? I mean, we're here, right on the track. Our jumper had seven cars. Three of them were lost behind the bulkhead. Four were left behind here. There might be something left of them behind me. I think I hear faint voices back there."

Olion sounded so close now that Caya reached out in front of her and felt for him. Her right hand touched something warm. A shoulder. "That you?" she whispered, her throat hoarse from crying.

"Yes. I'm glad you're here, but I wish you weren't. The beam is sliding along my body now." Olion spoke with dread flooding his voice. "Get past me on my other side. You might stand a—"

"Stop it. Remember what I said? I'm going to get you out of here. Preferably with your leg attached." Caya felt along the young man's body and found the vibrating beam just above his knees. His lower body was turned sideways under the beam, and his upper body was positioned flat onto his back. What if he had broken his back? She might paralyze him or, worse, kill him, if she miscalculated while trying to move him. "Listen, all right? I think we can use the momentum of the moving beam to our advantage. Correct me if I'm wrong, but the closer it gets to the track, the faster it's going to move, isn't it? Like a stronger pull?"

"Yes," Olion whispered.

"And when it moves faster, it won't pin you down as hard, not until it's close to the track, at least." Caya was thinking fast and trying to engage her physical abilities at the same time. If she could at least have a vision of being successful in saving Olion, she wouldn't hesitate. "All right. You tell me when it reaches just below your hip. I'm going to scoot over to your other side. Once it goes over your hip, which is the highest point of its trajectory toward the track, it will pick up speed and swoosh along the flat area of your stomach and chest. We can't let that happen. It will eventually hit your chin." And take his head off.

Caya didn't say that out loud. She didn't have to. Quickly, she crawled on her belly around Olion and felt for his arm on the other side. "Tuck your free arm as close to your body as you can. Stick it into your trouser pockets if you can. That way you're less likely to get stuck." Caya refused to tremble as she gripped Olion's arm and waited for him to tell her where the beam was. If he passed out or she miscalculated, it was all over. She felt with her foot behind her and found plenty of space behind her. The tunnel floor was smoother here than it had been where she woke up earlier.

"Caya. It's almost there. It's shaking much harder."

"When it hits your highest point, your hip, remember, yell at me."

"I will." His teeth were clattering.

Caya gripped his arm harder and braced herself.

"Now!" Olion's voice broke as he screamed the word.

Caya didn't hesitate. Digging her naked heels against the debris on the tunnel floor, she pulled.

CHAPTER TWENTY-ONE

"Madam President. Your presence is required in the Assembly." Thea's first assistant stood by her elbow, handing her a computer tablet.

"Required, Palinda?" Caya raised a sardonic eyebrow at the word choice.

"Yes, sir. The Assembly is ready to vote on the new minister of treasury." Her assistant had stood her ground since Thea's first day as the Oconodian president, and Thea would expect nothing less of the firm woman. "As you know, Minister Salvat resided on cube eighteen, and her death has been verified."

"And this was only moments ago!" Thea winced at how she had just yelled at her assistant. "Or that's how it feels anyway. Doesn't Sinthia Salvat get even a hint of mourning or official respect before we give her title to someone else?" Thea knew the rules but still resented the perceived callousness.

"Madam…" Palinda placed a careful hand on Thea's arm. "It needs to be done. We cannot afford to leave such a vital position in your administration empty. Here are the three names brought to the Assembly by the EPT, the Election Preparation Team." She reached passed Thea and tapped the tablet she had just handed her. "There."

Glancing at the short list of names, Thea did her best to muster some energy and interest, but she couldn't think of anything but Caya. "Well then," she muttered. "Hand me my coat, please. We might as well get this over with, as no life is sacred aboard *Pathfinder* anymore."

Palinda frowned but handed Thea her long coat. As Thea strode toward the part of the government wing of cube one with the black coat billowing behind her, she tapped her private communicator on her right shoulder. "Tylio to Briar Lindemay."

A crackling, static noise made Thea fear the communication system was down, but then a breathless voice replied, "Briar here, sir."

"Where are you? I hear voices." The last time Thea had talked to Briar and Adina, they had been on their way to catch their breath in her private quarters. She checked her timepiece. That was more than seven hours ago.

"I'm back on duty, temporarily transferred to the hospital in cube four, Madam President."

Cube four. Thea nearly stumbled but righted herself before it became obvious to her entourage. "I realize you're sorely needed there and I won't keep you, Briar. I merely wanted to check in on you and Adina. I have no news of Caya…yet."

"Neither have I, and I insist on taking that as a good thing." Briar spoke curtly. "I would *know* if my sister was dead. I'm inundated with so many emotions right now, I can't pinpoint her, but trust me when I say she is alive, Thea."

Thea clung to Briar's words as if they were the only thing keeping her sane at the moment, and most likely that was true. "Thank you," she murmured. "Tell Adina I checked in, please, when you hear from her."

"I will. She gave me Commander Dodgmer and his team to help keep the emergency unit safe, as we're the first checkpoint near the…the jumper tunnel. Adina figured we needed engineers with security experience." Briar's voice caught and she coughed, no doubt to hide her lapse.

"Good to know. I'll let you return to your patients. As soon as I learn something, I'll page you, Briar."

"Thank you, sir. Remember. Wherever she is aboard *Pathfinder*, or even in some obscure part of cube eighteen, she is alive. Briar out."

When Thea reached the large doors to the assembly, Palinda pressed the sensor and they walked inside. Forty-eight Oconodians and twelve Gemosians stood and bowed in respect as she took her seat in the chair that eerily resembled a throne, something Thea had always disliked. Now she could barely focus on the matter at hand, her thoughts teetering on the precipice of a hope that might be entirely futile. She had to learn to trust Briar's gift as much as she depended on Caya's.

The EPT gave their reasons why the Assembly would choose between their list of candidates. Thea listened, but very few words actually registered. As soon as she saw the short list, she knew which candidate would get her vote. Akka Tuvier was a capable national-finance expert who always appeared levelheaded and thoughtful. She was eighty-one but more youthful that most of her younger colleagues in the Assembly. If her health remained stable, she would have ample time to train a younger successor.

The voting began, and the members of the Assembly all used their tablets and their fingerprint and retina scanners to choose their respective candidate. The results displayed on the main screen above her as soon as the last vote was cast, and Thea was pleased to find that Mrs. Tuvier won with a vast majority.

Now Thea could focus on the matters at hand that needed her attention. She would soon address the traumatized Gemoconian people—and she had a young woman to find. Before the members of the Assembly returned to their respective cubes, she needed to speak to them as well. It never hurt to lay down the law before the men and women who represented her.

Caya opened her eyes carefully, as she could still taste the dust in the air. "Olion?"

"Here," a husky voice said to her left. "Are you all right?"

"I am. I think. You?" Caya squinted and managed to make out a sharp profile against the faint light behind Olion.

"You pulled me away just in time. I can't believe it." Olion sounded younger, relieved and on the verge of crying. "My knee hurts like hell though."

"No wonder. Let me find something we can use to stabilize it before we start moving."

"Moving?"

"We can't very well stay here. You need medical attention and I—I want to get ahold of my sister." Caya stopped herself before she spoke the truth. She had two important things to do when they got out of there, if the rest of *Pathfinder* was intact. First, she needed to make sure Thea and Briar and her friends were all right. Second, she had to tell Thea how much she loved her. Even if it meant going back into protective custody, being at Thea's mercy, she needed to tell Thea how she felt before it was too late.

As she felt for something to use for Olion's knee, her fears resurfaced, and she once again dreaded that everyone she loved was dead. She beat the thought back by opening her mind to her clairvoyant gift. Nothing appeared, which made Caya wonder if her potential concussions had affected her changer abilities adversely. Not that anyone aboard *Pathfinder* would believe her if that was the case. Once a changer with the mutated gene, always a changer.

She felt some debris that had to have fallen off the walls or the ceiling, then lifted the thin beams and ran her fingers along the edges. They were about half a meter long and without sharp edges. "Hey, Olion. I have something here. I can fixate your knee with these using my jacket."

"That'll be great. I'm going to start crying for real if the pain doesn't ease up soon. I really don't want that." His trembling voice made the gallows humor limp a little, but she gave him points for trying.

"You'll be fine and so will I." Caya dragged the thin rods back to Olion. "These are of some other alloy. Not magnetized." She felt along his leg. "I'm not as good as my sister with this, but she's a nurse and I'm just a student."

"I'm sure you're a hundred times better than me." Olion whimpered as she moved his leg a little. "Don't mind me. I'm not good with pain, but I truly want to get out of here. My mother is bound to go insane with worry. After surviving the Loghian refugee camp, she's not going to take it well if I mess up when we're so close to Gemocon."

"Can't say I blame her. I'll do my best not to get on your mother's wrong side." Shaking from sheer fatigue now, Caya placed the beams on either side of Olion's fractured knee. She tore off her jacket and bit into the hem while yanking at the fabric. The jacket was rather thin, and eventually she was able to tear off four long strips. "Here we go. This may hurt some." She pushed the first strip under Olion's knee and pulled it out halfway on the other side. Making a knot, she stabilized the fracture before she repeated the process in three more places. Olion moaned, but she worked as quickly as she could. When she tied the last strip around his thigh, she sat back down on her heels, tore one more strip from her destroyed shirt, and wrapped it around her hair to keep it in a tight bun. This would make crawling and pulling Olion along with her easier.

Tugging at Olion turned out to be easier than she'd feared. His arms were all right, and he was able to push himself backward toward the source of the light. Soon they both gasped for air and coughed against the dust. Caya lost track of time, and her entire world seemed to consist of crawl-grasp-drag, over and over.

"Wait, wait. I need to rest," Olion gasped after what felt like an eternity. "It hurts too much. I can't afford to faint."

"All right. Let's rest a few moments." Caya sat down and examined Olion's impromptu knee orthosis. It seemed to be stable.

"I think the air feels less dusty." Olion sniffed it carefully. "Or am I grasping at straws?"

"No. I think it actually tastes less dusty as well. That can mean one of two things. Either we're close to a jumper gate, or enough time has gone by for the dust to begin to settle."

"I hope for the first." Olion shifted next to her. "Seems like the tracks aren't as filled with debris here either."

"We're farther from the explosion, or whatever caused this."

"You realize that we're incredibly lucky, don't you?" Olion spoke gently, patting her arm. "We're alive even if the jumper was destroyed to a degree where we couldn't even detect it at all in the dark."

Caya didn't want to talk about the devastation that took the life of her friends. "I know. It's painful to even contemplate."

"Sure is." Olion lay down next to the track. "I have to rest some, but don't let me fall asleep—" He sat up again. "What's that noise?"

Caya had already heard it. A low, buzzing noise that approached from where the faint light originated. "I don't know. I hope it's not a jumper because I doubt it will fare very well among the debris and broken rail back there."

"That's not what it sounds like," Olion called out as the sound closed in on them. "The jumpers make this special whistling sound as soon as they leave the gates. This is different."

He was right. As Caya stood on her knees, she saw the light grow stronger. "Something's coming. Not very fast, but it might still hit us. We need to move to the side now!" She pulled at Olion, not caring about his knee at this point, but set on saving his life. He seemed heavier than before, and Caya sobbed in frustration as she gripped him under his arms to maneuver him to lie along the tunnel wall.

The whirring sound was now so close, the light was blinding them. "Creator of all things, don't hit him. Please!" Caya called and tossed herself on top of Olion, hearing him cry out as her right leg pressed against the makeshift bandage. She was going to save him as her friends had saved her. Perhaps this was why she had survived the destruction of the jumper cars.

The whirring noise stopped, and the momentary silence was deafening in a weird way. Caya was still sobbing her words over and over, shaking all over. "Don't hit him. Save him. Please. Please…"

"You were right, sir. There was movement up ahead. Actually, whoever it is, they're still moving." A male voice broke through Caya's frantic prayer. "And from where I'm standing, there are at least two of them."

"Are they wounded?" Another voice, this one female, called out.

"I don't know, sir. I'll check." The first voice came closer, and gentle hands touched Caya's back. "Hello there. We're here to help. Can you tell me if you're hurt?"

Caya turned her head sideways and tried to look up at the man. "You have to help him. My friend. Olion. Please. He's hurt."

"That's what we're here to do." The man spoke calmly. "What's your name, ma'am?"

"Caya. But take care of Olion first. I'm fine. I'm—" She caught herself before her speech was reduced to hysterical babble. "Is *Pathfinder* still intact?"

"For the most part," the man said, sounding a bit evasive. "And we'll help you first so we can get to your friend. He's name's Olion, you said?"

"Yes." Caya fell against the man when he helped her get to her feet. Her ankle hurt so badly, she wondered if she had fractured it.

"Oh, hell." The man caught her and lifted her easily up in his arms. "Nissandra? Here's the first of the two. A young girl."

"I'm ready for her, Mino." The woman, Nissandra, was as strong as her male counterpart and placed Caya on what felt like a gurney. The fine dust, even if it was less dense here, still played havoc with her eyesight. "There we go, sweetheart," the woman said and put a blanket over Caya and strapped her down. "I'm not going to mess with you. I'll leave that to the people at the emergency clinic."

Caya heard Olion cry out, and then he was placed on the other side of what had to be an EVAC jumper.

"This one has a busted knee," Mino said. "It's been stabilized though. Did you do that, Caya?"

"Yes." So tired now, she could barely speak, Caya tried to reach Olion to pat him reassuringly. "Where are you taking us?"

"The local emergency clinic in cube four for you, but I think your friend will need more advanced care. He'll go to the university hospital in cube eleven."

Caya slumped back onto the gurney. She wanted to go to Briar's hospital, but she could get word to her from cube four. It wasn't fair to take up an EVAC transport just so she could see her sister.

Briar would come to cube four soon enough, and Caya could ask her about Thea. She also needed to know about Miron and Rhosee.

Once her foot was treated and bandaged, she would catch a jumper to cube one and go to Thea. Caya rubbed her wet cheeks against the pillow. She debated asking Nissandra if she had heard about the status of the president but didn't want to attract that type of attention. She would have to believe that Thea was all right. She just had to be.

CHAPTER TWENTY-TWO

"Caya?" Impossibly, as Caya was still in the cube-four emergency unit, Briar stood in the doorway to the miniscule cubicle. Caya sat with her foot bandaged and elevated on a gurney after having had her bad sprain treated. The pain was down to a buzz, which was a nice change. The nurse had also cleaned some minor scrapes and cuts, and Caya was about to be released. And here was Briar. Caya blinked at the flood of tears streaming down her cheeks.

"Briar? But how did you—oh, thank the Creator." She held out her arms, and Briar threw herself across the small space and hugged her hard.

"Caya, sweetheart. I'm working from here today."

"Oh." It hurt to be hugged, but Caya didn't care. Her sister was here. She was all right. "Adina? And Thea?"

"Adina's fine. So is Thea. Adina's in engineering, and you can imagine they have a lot to go over. I don't expect to see her very much in the next few days." Briar pulled back. "Thea is busy doing her thing. And she's absolutely frantic over you. I could hardly believe it when I saw your first name on the list of patients being treated out by the nurses' station. What are your injuries?" Sniffling, Briar kept caressing Caya's right arm.

Caya hugged her again, so relieved to finally have word of Thea, even if she had already surmised that the president was alive and well from the staff's demeanor. "Practically no injuries. A sprained ankle and some superficial cuts and bruises." And a broken heart because of her new friends who had saved her life, but she would share that explanation with Briar later. Her heart would survive as long as Thea remained safe.

"And a minor concussion," a female voice said as the nurse returned. "You need to remain in bed for a few days and stay off that foot even if we healed the sprain. You don't want to re-injure it." She glanced at Briar and blinked. "Red Angel? Oh. This your... sister?" She regarded Caya with new respect. "You're that Caya. Caya Lindemay."

"I am and she sure is." Briar slid an arm around Caya's shoulders. "I'm in the middle of a shift, but is there anywhere she can rest until I'm ready to take her to my quarters—" She stopped speaking as Caya patted her arm.

"I'm not ready for that yet. I need to do something first." She stood and carefully tried her ankle. Wiping at the tears, she smiled at Briar, who looked concerned. "Don't worry. I'm not going to disappear again. I'll come by your quarters, once I've talked to... someone." She nodded discreetly toward the nurse, who was still in the cubicle, entering notes into the computer by the wall.

"Before I go, I want to ask you to help me keep a promise. I got to know a young boy, Miron, and his baby sister, Rhosee. I promised them I'd come back—and if I couldn't right away, that you would. Their mother died in the initial attack." Caya knew she was asking a lot. "You know I wouldn't ask unless it was for a good reason. As soon as I held them, I knew they were...well, somehow connected to us." She looked into Briar's eyes and tried to convey her feelings. To her surprise, Briar merely nodded.

"I'll find them. The names Miron and Rhosee aren't all that common. Don't worry. I'm on it." She kissed Caya on the cheek. "I have Dodgmer and his team outside. Why don't you borrow him and get to where you're going?" She winked at Caya and kept combing through her hair with her fingers and stroking her arms. "And before you leave, you can't go anywhere looking like that. "She motioned at the torn clothes next to Caya, who still wore a thin paper-like bed-jacket. "Let me pop out to the clothes dispenser. I'll be quick."

It took less than five minutes for Briar to return. "Here you go, sweetheart. I used a few credits and pulled out some clothes and sandals from your saved pattern buffer." She handed Caya a dark-blue shirt, tan trousers, and black sandals. She leaned close as the nurse looked away and whispered, "My badge is in your left pocket. With that, you can get out of here without alerting anyone. Dodgmer is Adina's guy and I trust him with all our lives, but over at headquarters...who knows?"

"What about you?"

"I'll sneak out when one of my colleagues uses their badge. If anyone asks, I'll just say I lost it in the mayhem today."

Hugging Briar hard despite the pain, Caya murmured, "I love you, sis. You're the best. The very best."

"I'll hold you to that. Now, move with caution. We're bordering on cube one now, so you just have to cross the park," Briar said, just as quietly.

"Thank you. Be safe until I see you next time. Hug the little ones for me." Caya pulled off the flimsy hospital shirt belonging to the emergency clinic and donned the other set of clothes. They felt a little big on her. She must have lost some weight.

Briar escorted her to one of the minor exits, where Lieutenant Dodgmer waited, smiling broadly at Caya. She didn't care about protocol and clearly neither did he as he wrapped her up in a firm hug.

"You're too thin, girl," Dodgmer said, grumbling.

"That can be fixed," Caya said lightly. Turning to Briar, she hugged her again. "No. Please." Caya stopped and took her sister's hand.

"I'll see you soon."

"Yes, you will." Briar frowned. "Are you sure I shouldn't page Thea?"

"If you tell her I'm alive and well over the communication system, others will find out. I'll tell you exactly how, but later. Until a short while ago, I didn't know if any of my loved ones were safe. I even dreaded being lost in the debris field myself. I hate that she's worrying, but promise not to page her. Not yet. I'll make my way to her as fast as I can."

Briar scanned her closely. "All right. You better be fast. She's close to panicking about you, sis. Creator only knows what she might do to coax you out."

Caya squeezed her hand. "I promise." With Dodgmer, she made her way to the hospital jumper gate, which was thankfully intact. Checking the map of its route, she saw it would take her only about fifteen minutes to reach the Caydoc Park jumper gate, as they had altered *Pathfinder*'s configuration, no doubt to make up for cube eighteen's absence. Caya stayed close to Dodgmer, and the burly, tall man kept his arm protectively around her in a way that probably made them look like father and daughter, which suited Caya just fine.

She thought of the governmental building, where she had lived her life ever since she announced her changer status at the presidential ball.

There was where her new future would begin—or her past catch up with her.

❖

Thea stood before the Assembly for the second time

Her heart thundered. This promised to be the hardest thing she had ever done, but also the most important. She was being selfish, as her people had lost so much and so many during the initial attack by, presumably, the Alachleves, and in cube eighteen, but she couldn't wait a single moment longer. If Caya was alive and staying away because she was unaware how Thea truly felt about her, she had to do this.

She was certain her advisors would balk at her current plan, but she'd had enough of sitting idly by and doing nothing while Caya was still unaccounted for. She needed to find the woman she loved, whom Briar claimed was alive, before it was too late. If Caya thought coming back would mean being thrown into protective custody once again, Thea had to convince her this wouldn't happen. Caya would need a security detail when she left her quarters, but she would be free to come and go as she pleased. Thea had learned from her mistakes and prayed she wasn't too late. If telling *Pathfinder*'s passengers everything would make Caya trust her, Thea would bare her heart and soul to them all.

"Honored members of the Assembly." She gripped the edges of the podium firmly. "I'm sure you are eager to get back to your respective cubes and the people who rely on you for information and guidance. I will try to keep this announcement short, but it is important to me that nobody in my administration be blindsided by this news, so please bear with me. I'm also going to transmit what I have to say via ship-wide video transmission." Thea nodded tersely at the woman in charge of the communication equipment. Out of the corner of her eyes she saw her own image take form on a small screen and knew she was live on all screens not broken in the attack throughout the ship, including the massive ones on every square or park area.

Looking into the lens of the camera, she couldn't swallow because of her dry throat. She also couldn't stop tears from glazing her eyes but prayed this wouldn't be readily visible. That was probably too much to hope for. She managed to gently clear her throat before she began to speak.

"Members of the Assembly, passengers and crew of *Pathfinder*, I stand before you now not only as your elected president, but also as a private individual."

❖

Caya stopped in the center of the Caydoc Park as the main screen lowered at the center by the stage where she had been a guest at the naming ceremony for Gemocon not very long ago. Around her, other people stopped as well. Unlike on regular days in the famous park, nobody sat on the grass with picnic cases or blankets. Instead they came to a fast halt now after hurrying along the paths earlier, just like she had.

Caya's knees nearly gave way when Thea's beautiful face came into view. She stood there, magnified and hovering above them at some podium, looking every bit the states-woman as her ice-blue gaze seemed to drill into each spectator. Thea's voice sounded as strong and decisive as always when she greeted her Assembly and her people via the screen. Caya stopped breathing when she realized from Thea's choice of words that this would not be one of her usual ship-wide transmissions.

"When I became president of Oconodos, I knew I had the most difficult of presidencies ahead of me since our esteemed former President Ardono and his cabinet had made the final decision regarding the Exodus mission more than seventy years prior to my term. I've worked tirelessly with my administration, the Assembly, law enforcement, and the military to make this happen. My sacrifices have been great, but really nothing compared to the people of Oconodos and, later, the people of Gemosis." Thea squared her shoulders and placed a hand on her chest. "Since last year, I have gone against my own heart in several ways, and though it is my job as your elected leader to put everyone else first, I have reached a point in my life where I must make an exception."

Caya took a few steps closer to the screen. What was Thea doing? Alarm klaxons went off inside her mind, and she frowned as she noticed how the people around her began to murmur and gesture, as if they too were concerned about their president's frame of mind.

"I'd like to think I've been a good president so far. I've chosen outstanding advisors and ministers, which is more than half the battle. My collaboration with the military and law enforcement has been, if not seamless, then at least fruitful and rewarding. So, why am I addressing the Assembly and the public in this manner?" The camera zoomed in on Thea's face, and now Caya knew the woman she loved was about to do or say something she could never take back.

"No. No, no, no." Caya began running, not caring that she was hurting her newly treated ankle. She flew across the grass, pushing people aside with gasped apologies while aiming for the main entrance to the government block. Dodgmer was right next to her, and to his credit, he didn't object or try to stop her.

Caya heard Thea's voice as she ran but didn't stop to look at any of the smaller screens on the walls as she reached the governmental building.

"Many of you may know that I divorced my former husband last year. I won't go into any private details regarding that step. The thing is, I have found the person I want to spend the rest of my life with—"

"No, Thea. Please stop talking. Just stop. Don't do it," Caya muttered as she ran. A man in front of her heard her, but she ran past him and didn't even stop to let the guard check her subcutaneous ID-chip. Instead she ignored Dodgmer's warnings and passed him by jumping over the waist-high gate and didn't stop even as the guards' stun-rays singed the air around her.

"I have never loved any other person like I love her, and I realize telling her this way is controversial," Thea said, "but I need her to know. She's somewhere aboard *Pathfinder*. At least I hope she is. She has to be." Tears in Thea's voice made Caya pick up speed. She flew up the half-staircase and then rushed past some of the ministers' assistants that pressed themselves flat against the wall. Caya could hear Dodgmer's booming voice order the guards to cease firing.

Glad she knew her way around the government building, Caya disregarded her burning lungs as she approached the two guards on sentry duty outside the Assembly doors.

"This young woman holds my heart. Darling, please." Thea's voice nearly broke. "If you hear this, make yourself known. Nothing bad will happen to you or anyone else you might associate with. You have my word. Please come back so we can talk…"

"Damn it, Thea. Shut up. Stop talking." Sobbing now from sheer frustration, Caya reached the door only for the guards to raise their weapons and aim at her. A direct hit by a heavy stun, point blank at her chest would most likely be lethal. She didn't care. "I need to get in there. I'm the one she's talking about."

"Of course you are. Naturally, President Tylio is talking about some kid." One of the guards sneered at her. "I think you have company coming, young lady." He motioned with his chin for her to look behind her.

"I know they're there. Guess you couldn't stop them, Lieutenant Dodgmer." Caya glanced behind her where Dodgmer, now disarmed, stood surrounded by presidential guards. "Listen to me. If you don't let me in to see the president, it will be on your head later. Can you afford to take the chance?" Caya's heart pounded so hard now, she could barely speak.

"She's right. Don't you fools recognize her?" Dodgmer spat. "Open the fucking door!"

"I suggest you do as Ms. Lindemay and Lieutenant Dodgmer say." A voice so sweet, and so welcome, spoke with soft authority, making Caya pivot.

"Meija!"

"Ms. Solimar, sir!" The guards saluted, hand to chin. "We… um. We…"

"You are going to open the door before it is indeed too late." Meija motioned for them to obey. "I vouch for this young woman." Meija glanced over her shoulder. "And you guys, give the lieutenant back his side arm and rifle and return to your posts. For the sake of our Creator, does it take six of you to chase one single young woman?" She shook her head.

In the meantime, the guards had opened the door in time for Caya to hear Thea say, "We owe the woman I love so much. In fact, those of us alive and well aboard *Pathfinder* owe her our lives in more ways than one. Her name is—"

"Stop! I'm here. Thea, please." Caya ran down the center aisle. "You don't have to do this. You don't have to." She came to a halt just below the dais, looking up at Thea with new tears running freely.

"Caya," Thea whispered, but she had stepped away from the microphone, which meant only the Assembly delegates could hear her. "Caya…"

"I'm here. I was already on my way to you—I mean, before the attacks and before your public declaration of…well, of something." Caya wanted to throw her arms around Thea, but the delegates were watching, not to mention *Pathfinder*'s passengers and crew, shipwide.

"Ladies and gentlemen of the Assembly, people of *Pathfinder*. I take the liberty of closing this session as it has fulfilled its purpose." Meija surprised them all from the podium. "Everything is quite all right. Go in heavenly splendor, everyone." Meija signaled to the person in charge of the transmission to close it. She turned to the members of the Assembly. "As for the delegates before me, I suggest you return to your cubes, where you are sorely needed. Report back to the ministers once you have established what your people need to make it through these upcoming weeks. We will all do our best to render support to each other. Thank you."

"She's that clairvoyant changer!" An outraged voice showed that Meija had acted just in time. Caya's identity was revealed, but none of it had gone out via the comm system or video link. "Madam President, are you letting one of them into your chambers? That's an outrage."

"No, it's not," Meija said as she ushered Caya and Thea out the back door. "It is, however, none of your business at this point. The president will address the people of *Pathfinder* when she has had time to confer with the ones closest to her. I suggest you do the same. Also, the president relies on your discretion. It is vital she knows whom she can trust for future reference. Go in heavenly splendor."

Chapter Twenty-three

Thea used every ounce of her strength to remain on her feet. The walk to her office was short, but her legs felt as if someone had filled them with lead. Next to her, Caya kept looking at her as they walked behind Meija, who with a mere glance kept the presidential guards a few more steps behind than usual.

She had so many questions for Caya. Thea wasn't sure if she wanted all the answers as she recognized her own mistakes along the way and how she had imprisoned Caya, when all she wanted was basic freedom. As they reached her offices, Meija ushered them in and closed the door behind them without a word. Thea knew nobody would get past the formidable woman.

"Thea…" Caya came up to her and took both her hands in hers. "There was a moment in the tunnel when I thought I might have lost you."

"The tunnel?" Thea gripped Caya's hands tighter. Then she realized and nearly lost cohesion in her knees. "*That* tunnel. From cube four to eighteen."

"Yes. I was on a jumper with friends when what I think was some strange white garnet mix began eating away at the metal in the cars. I survived, along with one other person. Olion. We managed to pull ourselves halfway out by the tracks, and then the EVAC team came to get us."

Thea could hardly believe her ears. "You—you were that close to cube eighteen?" she whispered, horrified. "Why?"

"Because I had a vision of it happening. I just didn't know when." Caya yanked Thea forward and wrapped her arms around her, holding her close. "I tried to get through to you, or anyone among your staff, but they didn't let me. I tried Adina's and Briar's communicators, but I just kept getting their message service. Sometimes not even that. I didn't get to eighteen in time. I'm so sorry." Caya trembled and began to cry against Thea's shoulder.

"Shh. Nothing of this was your fault. I heard about your attempts to reach me. We will all carry the guilt for not listening." Thea buried her face in Caya's rich, blond hair. "I'm the one who is sorry."

Caya raised her head slightly to look at her. "What do you mean?"

"I didn't listen to you long before the Alachleves attacked. You begged me to free you, to let you be in charge of your own destiny, but I was so certain I knew how to best keep you safe. I know now that my actions stemmed from fear. The more you pulled back, needing your space, the more I tried to tug you toward me. There's no excuse for it." Thea didn't sugarcoat anything. This might be the last time she was allowed to hold Caya this way. Once Caya realized Thea had bestowed presidential pardon and protection upon her, she would be gone. Why would Caya stay with her jailer?

"My turn to hush you. You're being too hard on yourself. Nobody aboard *Pathfinder* is under more stress and strain than you. Yes, I would have wished for you to give me my freedom a lot sooner, but perhaps it was meant to happen the way it did. I acted like a bratty child half the time, which of course didn't make you have much confidence in me.

"As for the Alachleves—they would have attacked either way. What was so strange about my vision, which I couldn't quite interpret, was the attack against the jumper system. In my vision, I knew it wasn't over after the initial attack, but I didn't understand until it was too late that it wasn't the Alachleves that attacked cube eighteen. You couldn't have foreseen or prevented either attack."

"No, perhaps not, but if I had let you do your job and trusted you much earlier—"

"But you did. You did trust me. You trusted in my visions more than I did sometimes."

"Yet I couldn't save cube eighteen." Thea knew this would haunt her for the rest of her life, but holding Caya close made it at least bearable. Or it would become bearable with time.

"We might just have to accept we weren't meant to." Caya drew a deep, trembling breath.

Thea sat down on a small settee by the far wall and pulled Caya with her. She kept her arms firmly around her lover, thankful to the Creator she was allowed to do so. "Can you explain what you mean?" Thea caressed Caya's damp cheeks, smoothing the remnants of tears away.

Caya took one of Thea's hands and kissed her palm. "Some things that happen in our lives are meant to be. I may see them in my visions, but they're fixed—immovable. Then there are a million things that aren't static like that, those things that can be manipulated and have varied outcomes. We have to learn from what happened to eighteen. I found new friends who ended up sacrificing their lives for me, but I can't keep myself from learning from this awful, horrible experience just because it tears me to pieces. If I turn away from it, they will have died for nothing."

"New friends?" Thea caressed Caya's hair. "They sound exceptional. Who were they?"

Caya hesitated only for a second, and then she told Thea about Tomita, Aldan, and Foy and their powers. She spoke of the sleeper cells, the super-changers, and the grand superior changer.

Thea pulled back to look into Caya's eyes. "They were changers? And there are more? We…There were always rumors of more changers, but no evidence and no intel from our security officers indicated the terrorists were part of a network—let alone any sleeper cells." She hugged Caya closer again. "Darling, you're going to have to work with law enforcement and the military security officers regarding this. If we don't stop further attacks, we may never reach Gemocon."

"As long as I'm with people I trust. Diobring showed me I can trust very few people, but I'm ready to do everything in my power to get us there—and when we do arrive, to help keep the population safe." Caya tipped her head back. "And to me, keeping you safe is most important of all. I heard everything you said, not just to me, I might add, but to the entire ship."

Thea's cheeks went warm. She didn't regret her desperate measure, not at all, but she was glad Caya had interrupted her just before she revealed her identity. "I should say I'm sorry, but I'm not." Thea ran her thumb along Caya's lower lip. "It was all true."

"Well, that makes it easier." Caya framed Thea's face with her hands. "I love you too, Gassinthea. I have loved you since the day I met you."

Thea could hardly breathe. If she didn't know better, she would have suspected an oxygen leak. "You brave girl." Thea took one of the hands Caya held against her cheeks and kissed it over and over. "You amazingly brave girl." She didn't mind the tears that now fell freely down her face. "I will love you till the day I die."

Caya's mouth fell open. "Oh."

Unable to resist, Thea pressed her lips to Caya's and kissed her.

❖

Caya clung to Thea, arms around her neck. Her mouth feverishly invited Thea's tongue to join hers, and it was as arousing as it was poignant. Her still-rather-sore body ached when Thea ran her hands up and down her back, but she didn't care. She was back in Thea's arms, and she had told Caya she loved her several times.

"I can't get enough of you," Thea murmured as she kissed her way down Caya's neck. "You're here. You're safe. As long as you're safe, I won't ask for anything else."

"That's exactly how I feel. When I crawled through that tunnel, praying for you to be all right, I hated myself for never telling you how I feel. I've loved you for so long."

Thea raised her head and stared at her, motionless and with dilated pupils darkening her eyes. "Caya…"

"I love you." Caya took Thea's left hand and pressed it between her breasts. "Here. Can you feel my heart racing? Every single beat is for you. The way you hold me, kiss me…and look at me now. I don't ever want to leave you ever again. You told me you will love me till the day you die." She leaned close for a soft kiss. "That's exactly how I feel. I will always love you. But can you endure spending your life with a—"

"A changer? Yes. Without a doubt. We belong together, darling." Thea held her tighter and kissed her again, hungry, devouring, and so full of passion that Caya whimpered into her mouth. "We can't do this here," Thea said and pulled back enough to look into Caya's eyes. "I want you so much, all of you, but I'll be damned if I'm going to take you on top of my desk."

Caya had to laugh through some residual tears. "Something about that sounds very sexy, but not very presidential."

"I'm glad you agree." Thea sighed and smoothed down Caya's hair. "I think."

"Will I go with you to your quarters later? Or…do I go home with Briar? I'd rather not live in the guest quarters anymore." Caya prayed Thea would understand.

Thea kept stroking Caya's hair. "I would love for you to stay with me in my quarters. If you can see yourself living with me from now on, you'll make me very happy." As calm and brave as Thea sounded, Caya could tell she was nervous.

"I want to be with you," Caya said. "But it may not go down so well with some of your Assembly delegates and the more reactionary passengers."

"I'm not about to run for reelection, but even if I were, I wouldn't care. I need you in my life, and you are what matters. Besides, it's about time everyone aboard *Pathfinder* knows about you and your gift—and how you've saved us so many times. I wish I could have met your new friends." Thea rested her head against Caya's shoulder.

"There are more of us out there, and by us I mean benevolent changers that can be of great use and of service to the Gemoconians if we're not tossed in the brig or air-locked." Caya was joking, but she could easily spot the signs that Thea didn't find her comment funny as she pressed her lips together and shook her shoulders gently.

"Nobody will touch you. You have a presidential pardon and protection logged into your official record. You will not fault me for doing that. You'll have your freedom, but that means I have to find alternative ways to try to keep you safe."

"As you did it in such a great way, which doesn't infringe on my privacy or personal freedom, far be it for me to protest." Caya had bent close for another kiss when Thea's communicator beeped.

"Tylio here. Go ahead."

"Madam President, Fleet Admiral Vayand here. I think I have given you enough time to sort, hmm, the matter that needed sorting, judging from your shipwide transmission earlier. I have arranged for a briefing in fifteen minutes with the generals, admirals, and your cabinet. I want to reassure you that you have my and Admiral Heigel's full support in regard to your personal happiness, but some ruffled feathers need smoothing among some of the others."

"I understand very well, Orien. I'm on my way. After the briefing, we need to bring a smaller group of leaders together. It's important."

"Yes, Madam President."

"Very well. See you shortly. Tylio out."

Caya could hardly bear to watch Thea walk out of her office and had to remind herself that it wasn't a good start to their relationship to appear clingy. Then she felt strong arms around her neck, pulling her in for a tight embrace.

"I loathe leaving you here." Thea kissed her with such passion they both whimpered. "Promise me you'll be safe."

Tilting her head and scanning Thea's immediate future, Caya detected nothing to cause concern. She nodded and smiled. "Trust me, Madam President. I'm going to be very, very safe."

"That's so good to know." Thea kissed her softly on the lips. "I won't be long."

"And I'll still miss you."

Caya would never forget Thea's expression of utter love as she stopped and turned in the doorway. "And I you."

Caya wanted to tell Thea about the orb, but it was too soon to share its existence. Shortly she would venture out to Tomita, Aldan, and Foy's quarters and retrieve the orb and what was left of Aldan's potions. These things would be her secrets for now. Later, once she'd mastered them, she would use them to become the true oracle Gemocon required to flourish. She had seen enough to know the attacks from the sleeper cells and terrorists were only the beginning. *Pathfinder* was bringing a storm with it to Gemocon. Caya wiped at a single quivering tear among her eyelashes. "Dear Tomita, Aldan, and Foy," she whispered. "The Creator will bless you and remain by your side on your journey to the far beyond, my dear friends. I will miss you."

Caya had to let her friends go. She was blessed in so many ways, and now that she knew Thea loved her—she had one more reason to remain strong.

EPILOGUE

Twenty minutes to reaching high orbit. Escorting assault craft establishing trajectory. Pathfinder *is aligned to initiate separation phase in two minutes. Prepare cubes eight, four, and six for separation."*

The computer droned the information from the bridge over ship-wide communicators. The tall woman stood among the crowd in Caydoc Park and watched the view from the external cameras on the major screen. Above them the faux sky gave the impression of a beautiful summer's day. Down on the planet they were about to orbit, Gemocon, it was early fall on the northern hemisphere. The advance team had worked tirelessly in preparation for *Pathfinder*'s arrival. The woman had eagerly followed every report from Gemocon regarding their progress. They had gone through their fair share of setbacks but somehow managed to use the last two years to draw up plans for infrastructure and housing.

Every time the woman had seen her daughter's name in any of the reports, her heart had ached. It had been so long. Too long. Every time she looked at herself in the mirror, she knew nobody would recognize her. Her black curls were now gunmetal black and her once-flawless complexion weathered and scarred. That, combined with an eyepatch covering her empty right eye socket, made her into a whole other person. Considering how the last twenty years had been, she wasn't the same when it came to her soul either. Gone were the doting mother, the fleet-officer career woman, and the once-loving wife.

Her son was aboard *Pathfinder* with his wife and little boy. She hadn't seen them in person, but the passenger manifest was easy enough to hack into, as was the surveillance system where she could watch them go about their daily routine. Her daughter, successful in her chosen profession despite her mother's absence, waited for the young family on Gemocon.

"Eleven minutes to high orbit around Gemocon. Commencing chain separation sequence. Separating cubes eight, four, and six. Prepare cubes twelve, nine, and two."

The computer interrupted the woman's thoughts, and she gazed transfixed at the cubes as they appeared on the screen. The last time they had separated it was an emergency action while being under attack and nobody had an outside view of that happening. Now *Pathfinder* dislodged the cubes one by one, placing them like a string of pearls in orbit around Gemocon. Each cube had its own bridge to control it independently. Around them, freighters joined the assault craft, helping the bridge crews estimate the trajectory.

"Excuse me?" A man just behind her tried to pass, and she stepped aside. He glanced at her and did a double take at the sight of her eyepatch. No doubt he was astonished, wondering why she hadn't simply had her eye replaced. She fully intended to have it done eventually. There simply hadn't been time before *Pathfinder* departed.

"High orbit achieved for all cubes. One hour until departure of the first 16,800 passengers. Estimated time of arrival planet-side at the shuttle landing sites in ninety minutes."

The computer kept delivering messages to each cube, making sure the passengers knew when to report to their respective shuttle bays. The tall woman knew it would about fifty days until the cubes were empty of civilians. Some, like the president and her cabinet, would disembark first in order to assume the offices prepared for them on the planet. The twenty-seven shuttles that had been attached to the outside of the shuttle bays could ferry six hundred passengers at a time. The schedule estimated three runs per day until it was time for the remaining crewmembers to land the cubes. Each cube would become the hub of a new city, except for cubes one, eleven, and eight. Cube one held the governmental structures, cube eleven the university hospital with all the best specialists, and cube eight harbored all the main universities and agricultural research facilities. Together they would form the embryo of the new Gemoconian capital, which had yet to receive a name.

The woman had to remain aboard cube one for another three weeks until it was her time to disembark, if the schedule held up. She didn't mind. This would give her time to make a final decision regarding her future. She watched how people around her cheered as the first shuttles left their respective cubes and headed for the planet's surface. So far, the woman took comfort in being a face among many, but eventually she would decide if she would remain incognito or once again become Lieutenant Commander Pamas Seclan, long-lost mother of Commander Aniwyn "Spinner" Seclan, CAG of the Advance Team and her younger brother Pherry.

Pamas watched the Gemoconian scenery come toward them on the big screen. The cube-one shuttle camera showed the web of landing sites and gates as it landed. The roaring shouts spread throughout the crowd in Caydoc Park, echoed by the cheers from the ground crew on Gemocon. Pamas wiped at a tear running down her cheek.

Pathfinder had made it. They had actually arrived at Gemocon.

About the Author

Gun Brooke resides in the countryside in Sweden with her very patient family. A retired neonatal intensive care nurse, she now writes full time, only rarely taking a break to create web sites for herself or others and to do computer graphics. Gun writes both romances and sci-fi.

Gun can be contacted at fiction@gbrooke-fiction.com
Web site   http://www.gbrooke-fiction.com
Facebook   http://www.facebook.com/gunbach
Twitter   http://twitter.com/redheadgrrl1960
Tumblr   http://gunbrooke.tumblr.com/

Books Available from Bold Strokes Books

A Quiet Death by Cari Hunter. When the body of a young Pakistani girl is found out on the moors, the investigation leaves Detective Sanne Jensen facing an ordeal she may not survive. (978-1-62639-815-3)

Buried Heart by Laydin Michaels. When Drew Chambliss meets Cicely Jones, her buried past finds its way to the surface—will they survive its discovery or will their chance at love turn to dust? (978-1-62639-801-6)

Escape: Exodus Book Three by Gun Brooke. Aboard the Exodus ship *Pathfinder*, President Thea Tylio still holds Caya Lindemay, a clairvoyant changer, in protective custody, which has devastating consequences endangering their relationship and the entire Exodus mission. (978-1-62639-635-7)

Genuine Gold by Ann Aptaker. New York, 1952. Outlaw Cantor Gold is thrown back into her honky-tonk Coney Island past, where crime and passion simmer in a neon glare. (978-1-62639-730-9)

Into Thin Air by Jeannie Levig. When her girlfriend disappears, Hannah Lewis discovers her world isn't as orderly as she thought it was. (978-1-62639-722-4)

Night Voice by CF Frizzell. When talk show host Sable finally acknowledges her risqué radio relationship with a mysterious caller, she welcomes a *real* relationship with local tradeswoman Riley Burke. (978-1-62639-813-9)

Raging at the Stars by Lesley Davis. When the unbelievable theories start revealing themselves as truths, can you trust in the ones who have conspired against you from the start? (978-1-62639-720-0)

She Wolf by Sheri Lewis Wohl. When the hunter becomes the hunted, more than love might be lost. (978-1-62639-741-5)

Smothered and Covered by Missouri Vaun. The last person Nash Wiley expects to bump into over a two a.m. breakfast at Waffle House is her college crush, decked out in a curve-hugging law enforcement uniform. (978-1-62639-704-0)

The Butterfly Whisperer by Lisa Moreau. Reunited after ten years, can Jordan and Sophie heal the past and rediscover love or will differing desires keep them apart? (978-1-62639-791-0)

The Devil's Due by Ali Vali. Cain and Emma Casey are awaiting the birth of their third child, but as always in Cain's world, there are new and old enemies to face in post Katrina-ravaged New Orleans. (978-1-62639-591-6)

Widows of the Sun-Moon by Barbara Ann Wright. With immortality now out of their grasp, the gods of Calamity fight amongst themselves, egged on by the mad goddess they thought they'd left behind. (978-1-62639-777-4)

18 Months by Samantha Boyette. Alissa Reeves has only had two girlfriends and they've both gone missing. Now it's up to her to find out why. (978-1-62639-804-7)

Arrested Hearts by Holly Stratimore. A reckless cop with a secret death wish and a health nut who is afraid to die might be a perfect combination for love. (978-1-62639-809-2)

Capturing Jessica by Jane Hardee. Hyperrealist sculptor Michael tries desperately to conceal the love she holds for best friend, Jess, unaware Jess's feelings for her are changing. (978-1-62639-836-8)

Counting to Zero by AJ Quinn. NSA agent Emma Thorpe and computer hacker Paxton James must learn to trust each other as they work to stop a threat clock that's rapidly counting down to zero. (978-1-62639-783-5)

Courageous Love by KC Richardson. Two women fight a devastating disease, and their own demons, while trying to fall in love. (978-1-62639-797-2)

One More Reason to Leave Orlando by Missouri Vaun. Nash Wiley thought a threesome sounded exotic and exciting, but as it turns out the reality of sleeping with two women at the same time is just really complicated. (978-1-62639-703-3E)

Pathogen by Jessica L. Webb. Can Dr. Kate Morrison navigate a deadly virus and the threat of bioterrorism, as well as her new relationship with Sergeant Andy Wyles and her own troubled past? (978-1-62639-833-7)

Rainbow Gap by Lee Lynch. Jaudon Vickers and Berry Garland, polar opposites, dream and love in this tale of lesbian lives set in Central Florida against the tapestry of societal change and the Vietnam War. (978-1-62639-799-6)

Steel and Promise by Alexa Black. Lady Nivrai's cruel desires and modified body make most of the galaxy fear her, but courtesan Cailyn Derys soon discovers the real monsters are the ones without the claws. (978-1-62639-805-4)

Swelter by D. Jackson Leigh. Teal Giovanni's mistake shines an unwanted spotlight on a small Texas ranch where August Reese is secluded until she can testify against a powerful drug kingpin. (978-1-62639-795-8)

Without Justice by Carsen Taite. Cade Kelly and Emily Sinclair must battle each other in the pursuit of justice, but can they fight their undeniable attraction outside the walls of the courtroom? (978-1-62639-560-2)

21 Questions by Mason Dixon. To find love, start by asking the right questions. (978-1-62639-724-8)

A Palette for Love by Charlotte Greene. When newly minted Ph.D. Chloé Devereaux returns to New Orleans, she doesn't expect her new job, and her powerful employer—Amelia Winters—to be so appealing. (978-1-62639-758-3)

By the Dark of Her Eyes by Cameron MacElvee. When Brenna Taylor inherits a decrepit property haunted by tormented ghosts, Alejandra Santana must not only restore Brenna's house and property but also save her soul. (978-1-62639-834-4)

Cash Braddock by Ashley Bartlett. Cash Braddock just wants to hang with her cat, fall in love, and deal drugs. What's the problem with that? (978-1-62639-706-4)

Death by Cocktail Straw by Missouri Vaun. She just wanted to meet girls, but an outing at the local lesbian bar goes comically off the rails, landing Nash Wiley and her best pal in the ER. (978-1-62639-702-6)

Gravity by Juliann Rich. How can Ellie Engebretsen, Olympic ski jumping hopeful with her eye on the gold, soar through the air when all she feels like doing is falling hard for Kate Moreau, her greatest competitor and the girl of her dreams? (978-1-62639-483-4)

Lone Ranger by VK Powell. Reporter Emma Ferguson stirs up a thirty-year-old mystery that threatens Park Ranger Carter West's family and jeopardizes any hope for a relationship between the two women. (978-1-62639-767-5)